His Vampire Harem
By Lily Harlem

Gay Romance Books By Lily Harlem

Caught on Camera
His Vampire Harem
His Vampire Harem 2
Dark Warrior
High-Sticked
The Chase
Who Dares Wins
Bad Idea
Mile High Kink Club
Kangorilla

His Vampire Harem: text copyright © Lily Harlem 2018

All Rights Reserved

With the exception of quotes used in reviews, this book may not be reproduced or used in whole or in part by any means existing without written permission from Lily Harlem.

Warning: The unauthorized reproduction or distribution of this copyrighted work is illegal. No part of this book may be scanned, uploaded or distributed via the Internet or any other means, electronic or print, without the author's written permission.

This book is a work of fiction and any resemblance to persons, living or dead is purely coincidental. The characters are productions of the author's imagination and used fictitiously.

Please note this book is intended for mature readers.

Artwork by Studioenp.

Edited by Writer Marketing Services

Prologue

London

Thunder rumbled around the small living room, seeming to shake the ceiling, floor, and walls. A streak of lightning glowed at the window, flashing and burning bright as if trying to set light to the curtains. On the mantel, the flame atop a candle quivered as another gust of wind tumbled down the chimney.

Marie Linnet tugged her dark green robe around herself. Storms gave her the creeps. It was past midnight but she didn't think she could sleep through it. With the rain pounding at the window—or was it hail?—there would be little rest until the ferocious weather passed.

The fire in the grate had long since gone out, but despite being cold she didn't want to light it again.

I should go to bed and pray I get some rest.

She cupped her hand behind the candle and blew it out. She then flicked off the small table lamp beside the sofa, and left the room as another roar of thunder ripped from the sky.

Once upstairs, she brushed her teeth, cleansed and moisturized and hung up her dressing gown on the back of the bathroom door.

She kneeled beside her single bed, clasped her hands together and thanked God for everything in her life she was grateful for.

Climbing beneath the covers, she shivered. Most of the time she didn't mind living alone, or that she'd never found a man to share her life with, but on chilly nights, and with a storm which sounded as if the devil himself had created it, she wouldn't have been opposed to having a man's warm body to snuggle up to.

She didn't bother to turn the bedside lamp on as she'd left her current read at work. It was a paperback she'd found in the charity shop, a soppy romance, but it passed the time while she was waiting for her boss to find her something to do. She often wondered why he bothered having a personal assistant. He was such a control freak he barely allowed her to do anything. But that suited her, it meant she could read to her heart's content and get paid for it. She wouldn't complain about the situation if he didn't.

Pulling the covers up around her neck, she stared at the ceiling. It was doused in shadows but when another flash of lightning attacked the room, it was as bright as day, highlighting a dust mote which stretched from the pink tasseled lampshade to the Artex.

Another shiver attacked her belly, winding its way up to her shoulders. There were houses either side of hers, homes full of people, nice people, her neighbors. But still, with the storm so violent, so malevolent, her small terraced house could have been alone at the top of a hill, being shaken by the wind, and a target for an electrical strike.

She closed her eyes, putting the image of the lone house from her mind.

You're safe, Marie. Go to sleep.

Lying flat on her back, she stretched her legs out straight and rested her hands over her abdomen, her usual sleeping position. The sheets were cool and smelled of fabric conditioner, her one pillow was slim and meant her neck didn't ache when she woke.

She closed her eyes, then immediately had to contend with another white-hot flash searing over her lids. She swallowed, determined not to let her dislike of storms spark an adrenaline surge because that really would be detrimental to her chances of getting any rest.

Many years ago a friend had taught her some meditation techniques. Breathing in slowly through the nose, then out through the mouth. She did that now, filling her chest with air, and then pursing her lips as she blew out. She tried to clear her mind as she repeated the action by counting to three on the inhale and again on the exhale.

It wasn't as though her thoughts were frantic, they were just too focused on the war in the sky raging above her.

Another roll of thunder clattered overhead, shaking the windowpane not five feet away.

She breathed in, then slowly out.

An image of a man appeared in her mind. It wasn't anyone she knew, nor a famous movie star or singer. He was tall with broad shoulders, a trim waist and long, lean legs. He wore a smart black tuxedo complete with bow tie—one of her favorite things to see a man dressed in—it even had the silky black stripes on the legs of the pants, and was obviously an exquisite cut.

She continued her deep breaths in, her throat filling with air, her ribs expanding, then out, deflating, resting.

His face was clear in her mind's eye. Clean-shaven, not bearded as so many men were keen on now, which wasn't to her taste. Sharp, angular features; no bump in his nose, and neither too big jawed nor too narrow. His mouth was full and sensual, and his eyes so dark it was impossible to tell the difference between pupil and iris. His eyebrows and his hair matched his eyes, jet-black, not a hint of gray, and despite being neatly trimmed and brushed she could see it was thick and soft.

Her fingers tingled. She wanted to touch his hair, see if it felt as silky as she imagined.

A particularly loud clap of thunder interrupted her breathing rhythm, and as the accompanying lightning invaded her eyelids again, the man she'd created smiled.

For a moment she held her breath, stunned by his beauty and how real he felt before her, then she remembered to breathe.

The smile was mesmerizing, as if a light was glowing from him, a light that could rival any bolt of lightning the devil's storm produced.

A warmth attacked her; it started in her belly and fanned up to her chest, over her slight breasts and into her nipples. They tightened beneath her cotton nightgown and the pleasant sensation produced a smile on her own lips.

This seemed to please the man in her imagination and his smile widened, showing perfect white teeth and balling his cheeks a little.

She realized she was falling asleep, despite the storm. The meditation technique was working. Relaxing further, she allowed herself to fall into what promised to be a very nice dream. The sooner she left reality, and the weather, the better.

"That's it," he said, his voice a low murmur. "Drift away, my love."

"I am…" Her languid state deepened, her body heavy and sinking into the mattress. But she stayed with her dream, her concentration firmly on the man.

"Good, that's it," he said, coming closer. "There is nothing to fear."

"I know." Her nipples were still tingling, and a tickling sensation was fluttering between her legs.

"Do you like what you see?" he asked.

"Yes."

"It's all for you." He reached for the button on his jacket and undid it, then the next and the next. With graceful movements he shrugged it off and let it slip from his fingers to the floor.

A little piece of her wanted to tell him not to do that with such an expensive, likely Savile Row jacket, but the sight of his white shirt, stretching over his chest and shoulders stole her words. She could even make out his small dark nipples beneath the material.

"I like what I see too," he said, his gaze drifting over her and his eyelids becoming a little heavy.

His gaze made her feel naked, but also beautiful and feminine. He was looking at her the way she'd only ever dreamed of a man looking at her.

"You're everything I've ever wanted, Marie."

"What's your name?"

"Mammon."

He came closer and his delicious cologne besieged her senses. It was all her favorite scents; pine, sandalwood, geranium, and it made her mouth water to taste him.

"Mammon," she repeated. The syllables were like honey on her tongue. "It's unusual...but I like it."

He tugged at his bow tie and in one long smooth move it unraveled. He held it forward, then, like his jacket, let it fall. "I guess you want to see what's beneath here." He ran his palms down his front, pressing the cotton to his torso.

She swallowed. "Yes."

How had she ever managed to create such an incredible specimen of a man? Even for a dream he was something else. Special. Intense. Perfect.

He smoothed his fingers over the buttons on his shirt, and when he reached his waistband, they were all undone. He pulled the shirt free and it gaped, exposing an abdomen rigid with muscle and a dark fan of hair leading from his navel to his pants.

She pressed her legs together. The tickle between her legs was turning to heat...and need.

"That's it, look at me, Marie, look at me, you can. I give you permission." He slowly removed his shirt, giving her time to see each inch of flesh as it was revealed. A small scribble of chest hair sat on his sternum, the ideal amount, enough to be masculine but not bear-like. When his shoulders were naked, she saw that his muscles were in perfect proportion, and beneath his tanned flesh they danced and flexed with his movements.

She held in a small moan, wanting to touch him, trace her fingertips over his body and explore all the small rises and dips.

"All in good time."

But her body had other ideas. The muscles in her virginal pussy had clenched, and the heat had turned to hot dampness. There was an ache deep inside her and she longed for it to be soothed.

"Do not be scared, for I will be gentle," he said. "I know this is your first time."

"Thank you."

He released his belt, freeing the silver buckle. He undid the button on his pants. Slowly, he pushed them down. He didn't wear undergarments.

Her heart thudded, and her abdomen tensed.

His cock was big, much bigger than she'd ever expected. Not only was it long, it was wide too.

That will never fit inside me, not even in a dream.

"I can make it happen," he said, taking a step closer and then seeming to hover above her. He was completely naked now. His skin flawless, every muscle honed to perfection.

But it was his cock her concentration was on. Veins stood proud on his shaft, and the domed head was glossy. Beneath it his balls hung heavy.

"Look into my eyes," he said, hooking his finger beneath her chin and raising her face to his.

This first touch was electrifying, as if a finger of electricity from the storm outside had stroked her. She gasped as pleasurable heat journeyed over her skin. The want in her pussy increased, she needed him to touch her there.

"We will not rush this, we have all night. And I have been searching for you for many moons."

"You've found me."

"Yes, I have, my love." He lowered his head with his lips parted.

She parted hers, waiting for his kiss.

It came, and was deep and delicious. His tongue stroked hers and she lost herself to him. It was the kiss of an angel, the other half of her soul. Her life was complete in that moment.

She trembled as he moved his attention across her cheek, down her neck, then his lips trailed over her skin to her breasts.

Her nightgown was gone. She didn't question how—this was a dream. She was glad he had access to her nipples and arched her back, curled her toes and tried to steady her heartbeat as he began to suck on each one in turn.

"Oh, please," she said, sinking her fingers into his lustrous hair. "More of that."

He chuckled, as though amused by her want.

"I need you. I want you to take my virginity."

"Oh I will, don't you worry, Marie." He was hovering above her again, barely seeming to touch the bed, his perfect body almost floating. "Open your legs."

"Yes. Yes." She did as instructed, and cool air washed over her damp pussy. "Take me."

"I knew you were going to be the sweetest of humans," he said, sliding his hand across her belly, then tickling through her pubic hair. He sought her entrance and pushed in.

"Oh," she gasped, reaching to cup his jawline. "Mammon."

"This will not be easy. You have a long road ahead, but I will make it pleasurable. Now, at this moment, you will only know bliss."

"I believe you."

He added another finger, stretching her and spreading her arousal.

"Kiss me," she gasped.

He smiled again, that beautiful, heart-stopping smile of his. Then his lips were over hers, his fingers were gone and in their place the thick head of his cock—it was cool, she hadn't expected that.

She raised her legs and clamped them to his hips.

"You are mine," he said softly. "Now and forever." He eased forward, entering her.

She tensed. A stitch of pain accompanied his invasion. She'd never had anything thicker than her finger there. "Oh…"

"Trust me, surrender to me." He'd spoken against her lips, his breath warm as he stared into her eyes.

She allowed herself to get lost in his gaze as he drove deeper, filling her, stretching her to what she was sure were impossible limits.

She held her breath, refusing to cry out, and closed her eyes.

"No, look at me, Marie. Open your eyes. Now."

His voice was stern and she was quick to obey. His cock was still riding in, the cool shaft pressing against the walls of her pussy.

"You have nearly taken your master," he said. "This one sweet time of perfect connection and creation."

"I don't…know what…you mean."

"Oh, but you will." He gritted his teeth, closed his eyes and tipped his head back. One final thrust brought him to full depth.

Marie cried out. It hurt, in a strangely good way, and his hard body had rubbed up against her special place.

"Find pleasure with me, my love," he said. "Let's make this even more powerful by submitting the will of the human spirit, *your* human spirit, to me."

He ground his hips over her, then, appearing to glide effortlessly as his cock came almost out, he pushed back in.

Again her sweet spot was stimulated along with her insides. She was intoxicated with lust, and with him. He'd filled her body and her senses. Within minutes she was aware of the pressure building, the need to give into her release growing.

"You are nearly there, succumb to the desires of the flesh." His eyes flashed as he stared down at her. "I need to witness this moment that will change everything."

"Ah, ah, Mammon don't stop." She held her breath, the orgasm she'd been waiting for all her life was there. It balanced on a precipice for a heartbeat then toppled her into bliss.

She spasmed around his cock and clung to his shoulders, digging her nails into his flesh.

"For the power of the devil," he groaned then pounded in, higher than before, and froze. "All power to me."

A wild roll of thunder crashed around them, burning flashes of lightning filled the room.

And then he was gone.

The weight of his body, his heat, his taste, his scent...his cock. Gone.

Marie could hardly catch her breath, and she feared for the survival of her heart it was beating so fast. "Mammon!"

She flailed her arms and jerked her body, looking for his.

That couldn't be it, that couldn't be the end of her dream.

The end of Mammon.

Her pussy was still clenching and releasing around nothing, her clit still engorged, and delicious aftershocks were ravaging her belly and sending pleasure down her legs and up to her breasts.

She dared not open her eyes, because then it would definitely be the end of the dream. Instead she squeezed her eyelids closed tighter, stilled and prayed he'd come back to her. Mammon had been so vivid, so real, there had to be more.

As she lay there, the storm raging, her heart rate calmed and so did her breathing. She ran her hands over her breasts. Her long night gown was back in place, covering her breasts and down to her waist. But from there it was dragged up, bunched so her nakedness was exposed.

She swallowed, wishing evidence of his kiss was on her tongue, but it wasn't, all she could do was try to remember his taste. Delving between her legs, she found her clit was still sensitive. The orgasm had been real, even if created within a dream. A wet dream; she was sopping, her pussy thick with liquid, more than if she'd masturbated, much more.

She drew her fingers up from the sheets, then with her other hand flicked on the bedside lamp.

Spread on her fingers was thick, pearly-white liquid. It sparkled in the light and was warm.

"What just happened to me?"

Chapter One

Paris.
Twenty-Five Years Later
Darius

"Darius, this way, you're doing great. Amy, can you just...a bit to the right, yes, drape your whole arm over, no, more of a casual pose...try and look relaxed...yes like that."

I glanced at Amy as the photographer, Malik, barked his instructions. She was a pretty thing, not as tall as some of the other models but still long and willowy; they all were. Her cheekbones were high, her lips violent red, and right now, like me, she wore a flamboyant Venetian style eye-mask and very little else.

"To me, to me." The photographer had his camera held up again. "Benjamin, lighting. Come on, we haven't got all day."

His assistant, Ben, rushed to do Malik's bidding.

I maintained my sultry expression with my lips downturned and my chin tipped nonchalantly. We were supposed to look like Italian hipsters from the eighteenth century. Apparently that look matched the scent of Oui's latest designer fragrance, Phantom's Kiss.

Amy's slight weight tipped against me, and her hair tickled my chest as she swathed herself across my lap.

"Yes, that's better, more, like that," Malik said. "You're bored, bored but beautiful, and over-indulged too, in everything, get that look, good, good, fuck yeah, that's the look!"

The camera clicked and whirred as he took his shots.

My peripheral vision was hampered by the eye-mask, but I could see people watching—lighting assistants, make-up artists, wardrobe. Malik was a big deal when it came to the world of photography, and I guessed as the last three years had gone on, I'd also become a big deal in male modelling. I had more jobs than I could ever dream of, and my agency demanded higher and higher fees on my behalf.

"Good, that's it. Now, Darius, can you slide your hand over her hair, look possessive. She's yours and you'll fight anyone who comes near her, her scent has bewitched you. You're under her seductive spell."

I did as he'd asked, smoothing Amy's silky blonde hair against her scalp. The strands were warm from the spotlight above and they slipped over my palm and through my fingers. I summoned a glare for the camera, daring anyone who looked at the picture to mess with my woman.

My woman!

The truth was I'd never had a woman, despite being surrounded by some of the most beautiful females on the planet day after day. Not one had captured my attention in the capacity of anything other than friendship.

Oh, I could admire perfect bodies, pretty smiles and sweet natures but there was always something missing. None of them lived up to my dreams of what a soul mate should be.

"That's it. That's the money shot." Malik lowered his camera. He wore a wide grin and his cheeks were flushed. "It's a wrap, great work people."

I blew out a breath, relaxing my cheek muscles then closing my eyes and squeezing the lids. Hours under bright lights was drying, and holding still was surprisingly tiring.

"I need a smoke." Amy rested her hand on my thigh and pushed upright. "You coming for one?"

"No, I've quit."

"Wish I could, but if I don't smoke I'll eat, and I can't do that."

"You have to eat, Amy." I frowned at her. "It's important, you know that."

"I do eat. A bit…occasionally." She stood, her bare breasts just inches from my face. Her nipples were small and such a delicate shade of pink they were only just discernable from her flesh.

She plucked at her eye-mask and pulled it off. Like mine, it had long feathers pluming from the side. "This thing is hot, right."

"Yeah, it is." I stood.

A small smile crossed her face and she touched the tip of her finger to my collarbone. "So what are you doing later, Darius? Want to go get some dinner?"

"Yeah, sure, but my flight back to London is early so nothing late."

"Well that doesn't sound very exciting, does it?" She traced lower, to my chest, stopping at the base of my left pec. "And you don't sound very enthused either at the thought of a date with me."

The cogs of my mind clicked into gear. This was the third time I'd worked with Amy, and the third time she'd mentioned getting together. I'd said yes to be polite, as I'd been brought up to be, but now...now she thought our evening was a date—a date that might extend to something more.

I sighed and stepped back. "Actually, thinking about it, I might give it a miss, Amy. If you don't mind." I paused. "I've got a headache coming on. The lights, you know." I gestured upward.

"So take some drugs." She shrugged and allowed her hand to drop to her side. "Legal or illegal, I'm easy." She laughed, a high-pitched tinkling sound.

I smiled. "Tell you what, I'll lie down for an hour and give you a call if I feel better."

"Okay. You do that."

"But it's fifty-fifty. I might just get room service."

She placed her hands on her hips. A frown creased her usually perfectly smooth brow.

"What?"

"You're a funny one, you know that?"

"I am?" I tugged off my eye-mask, then rubbed at the mark it had left on my forehead.

"Sure. I mean look at you, you're like some kind of Adonis, so beautiful it's hard to believe you're even human—"

"Don't be ridiculous." I chuckled.

"I think your pay packets tell you I'm not the only one who thinks that."

She had a point.

"And," she went on, "you could have any woman you want, but you don't. Yet..."

"What?" I was curious as to where she was going with this conversation.

"But you're not gay either, are you?"

"That's a very personal question." I bristled.

"No it's not, not in this industry, everyone knows everyone's sexual persuasion. But we don't know yours, Darius."

"I'm a private person." And hardly about to shout to the world that I was a virgin—and, as she suspected, probably gay.

"I think..." She turned and scooped up a citrus yellow t-shirt, then tugged it on. Her nipples poked at the material. "That you need to lighten up. Have some fun, experiment." She stepped close, really close, and set her lips by my ear. "Find out what you *do* like," she said breathily, "then do it some more."

"I know exactly what I like, Amy, but for the record, I don't date colleagues."

"You don't date colleagues," she repeated, then sighed. "So how are you ever going to meet anyone? From what I see, all you do is work, work, work."

She was pushing me too far. Heat was growing in my tightening chest, never a good sign, and my vision was blurring slightly. "Maybe I don't want to meet someone. Perhaps I like my own company."

"No one likes being alone." She stepped away and held up her right hand. "Apart from anything else it makes your wrist ache." With a cackling laugh, she turned and walked from under the glaring lights. Being rejected wasn't something high-end models were used to, there was always going to be a sting in her tail.

And it had stung. I was beginning to wonder if I'd ever meet *the one*. But it was a thought I'd been suppressing. A worry I hadn't dared give much light to.

"*Puis-je avoir le masque s'il vous plait?*"

A middle-aged woman from the wardrobe department stood at my side. "Sure, here you go, thanks." I passed the mask to her, then strode to my dressing room.

I have to get out of here.

The dressing room was cool and quiet, and I quickly dragged on faded Levi's, sneakers and a tight black Diesel t-shirt. I couldn't shake the irritation Amy had created in me. It was as if she'd seen into the dark recesses of my mind. A place I hadn't even been allowing myself to visit.

Quickly I fastened my necklace, a chunky stone cross my mother had given me years ago. I hadn't worn it for the shoot.

The dressing room had a fire-escape door, and not wanting to face anyone, I grabbed my rucksack and went outside. I found myself in a small, bricked courtyard set against the Seine. It was steeped in shadows as twilight approached, the corners gloomy, the high windows unlit.

There was no one else there, though there could have been, the path along the river was right in front of me and made the courtyard accessible.

I gulped in air, wishing the heat from my conversation with Amy would leave me. But it wouldn't. Once the emotional power, the electrifying build had begun, there was only one thing for it.

I walked to a set of black wrought iron railings half shielding the courtyard from the path and gripped their cool speared tips. The river was moving with gusto, a plastic bag giving away its speed. On the opposite bank ornate street lamps had illuminated, spreading an amber glow over the ground.

Trying to concentrate on the light didn't help. The energy was churning inside me now, reeling from the very center of my chest up to my neck, my shoulders and down my arms.

I'd hoped the cold hard metal of the railings would hold it off.

It didn't.

"Fuck it!" I released them, turned and spotted a pile of litter—a newspaper, crumpled cigarette box, some fast food wrappers, and a glass bottle.

The burn in my right arm was intensifying. It was painful now. There was only one way to get rid of the pain. I'd have to do it. See this through.

I clenched my teeth, tensed my belly and squeezed my fingers together. The blistering pain was making me sweat. It had turned into a ball of flames in my guts.

I held my breath and directed my hand toward the litter.

Sparks glistened from my fingertips, frenzied and brilliant, then shot through the air. They took the agony with them, tearing it from my body.

The litter whooshed to life. Bright yellow and orange flames sprang upward then licked against the brickwork.

I repeated the action, sending more flashes of heat from my fingertips toward the fire and getting rid of the last bit of my frustration. It wouldn't do to keep it in. I knew from experience that didn't end well.

I blew out a breath and let my hand fall to my side. I sagged against the railing. Releasing sparks always left me exhausted. It drained not just the negative energy from my body, but also some of the good energy; the energy that meant I could function.

Watching the flames, I waited for my heart rate to settle. My pulse was loud in my ears and my fingertips still hot. But at least the frustration had gone from the pit of my stomach. My chest no longer felt tight with irritation.

The fast food wrappers quickly shrivelled to ash, the cigarette box lit bright for a few seconds then imploded, and the newspaper was creating pretty dancing flames, enjoying their moment in time.

I straightened, set back my shoulders and brushed a crease from my t-shirt. I needed to put Amy's comments from my mind and get to my hotel room. Tomorrow I'd be back in London. I'd visit my mother, tell her how the shoot had gone and that I'd created sparks. I always told her, only her. She was the only person who understood that I was different.

You were made different, Darius, you came to create light in my life, so much light it sometimes sets you on fire.

She often said that to me. I didn't know how she'd come to that conclusion but I couldn't think of any other explanation so I went along with it and was careful not to let anyone see my sparks.

A sudden movement to my right caught my attention.

I turned to the farthest corner of the courtyard which was in near blackness.

From it stepped a man wearing a dark hoody pulled up over his head and black jeans.

Surprise bombarded me, it quickly turned to anxiety.

Did he see?

He walked toward me. There was something a little sinister about him but I told myself it was just the way he had the hood pulled up and his hands shoved into his pockets.

Part of me wanted to move, get out of there, but equally I didn't want to be thought of as afraid. He was just a man, the same as me, after all.

"Do you have the time?" he asked, his voice deep and husky.

I'd been expecting him to speak French. "I...er, yes." I glanced at my Rolex. "It's just gone seven-thirty."

"I thought so." He stopped and pushed his hood back, revealing super-short blond hair and a diamond earring in his left ear. His nose was long and straight, his eyes pale and his lips plump.

"Have a nice night," I said, wondering why he'd asked if he'd had an idea of the time.

"You too." He paused, then when I stepped away, he said, "though the night is young."

I hesitated. There was something in his tone that made me curious. What did he mean, 'the night is young'? And why had he been standing in the shadows?

"I've had a long day," I said, keeping my back to him but not moving.

"I'm sure you have."

Maybe he recognizes me from a magazine or billboard.

"I've had many of them," he went on. "Long days, that is. Never prompted me to start a fire by shooting sparks from my fingertips though."

Shit!

A wave of panic fluttered in my chest and I had to push down a sense of nausea. I'd been so careful for years. Why had I let Amy push me to the point my caution had slipped?

"It's okay," he said, walking to the dying flames and crouching down to stare at them. "We all have different methods of stress relief."

"And what are yours?"

Change the subject, Darius.

He didn't look at me, instead he picked up a stick and poked the glass bottle. It rattled away from the pile of ash and clinked against the wall. "I suppose my 'thing' is drink."

"Ah, I see." That explained everything. He was a drunk who'd been sleeping in the corner of the courtyard, likely in a doorway.

Chances of him even remembering this conversation tomorrow were slim.

Thank goodness.

"I like to drink," he said. "But I go months without it." He tossed the stick to one side and stood. "Like now, not a drop."

He stepped closer to me, almost as if to prove he didn't smell of alcohol.

He didn't. If anything his scent was sweet and spiced, an expensive cologne I couldn't identify. There was a hint of tobacco too, a smell I liked but resisted.

"Not a drop has passed these lips." He smiled and ran the tip of his tongue over his top lip.

I watched him and my own lips parted slightly.

"For so long," he spoke quietly. "Not a drop."

"It sounds as though you're doing really well..."

"Lloyd, that's my name." He held out his hand. "Lloyd Oakley."

"Oh, I...I'm Darius Linnet." I placed my hand in his and shook. "Nice to meet you."

His flesh was cool, but at the same time a strange heat traveled up my arm. It wasn't like when I had the sparks, it was more like a fizz of excitement, a small shock-wave of interest.

"You're quite beautiful," Lloyd said, keeping my hand in his grip and studying me.

I laughed, a sudden burst of noise that was filled with relief he'd moved on from my flame throwing antics to my looks; my looks was something I was used to discussing.

"Why is that funny?" he asked.

"Well, you're a guy, I'm a guy, we've just met and you're telling me I'm beautiful."

"But you are, you must know that."

"I guess. It's how I make my living. I'm a model. That's why I've had a long day. I've been shooting an ad campaign for a new cologne, Phantom's Kiss."

"A model." He released my hand and took a step back. He folded his arms and allowed his gaze to roam from the top of my head to my sneakers then back up to my face.

For some reason his scrutiny made me shift from one foot to the other. I didn't know why, having people survey my physical attributes was an everyday occurrence.

"Mmm," he said. "I can see that you would make a very good model, it just wasn't what we were expecting."

"Expecting?" *What is he talking about?* "Who's *we*?"

"But we should have, though." He frowned as though talking to himself. "Why would it be any other way? Of course you're perfectly stunning, how could you *not* be?"

Chapter Two

Lloyd

I could hardly believe it, after all this time—years, decades, centuries of looking—I'd finally found him.

Or at least I hoped I had.

Darius Linnet.

The man who held the key to saving our souls.

He just didn't know it...yet.

I wanted to touch him again, then take him with me, to meet the others. There was so much to do. So much to explain, to discuss, but that couldn't happen.

Not yet.

Already I sensed his skittishness. He'd thought about bolting when I'd walked from the shadows. I could tell by the way he'd glanced at the river, then at the door he'd emerged from. He'd also been ready to leave after he'd told me the time. My usual ability to snare both men and women into wanting my company didn't seem to be working on him.

Which further confirmed my suspicions. There was only one reason for that, only one explanation, which could possibly be considered.

Darius wasn't altogether human.

"I really have to go." He rubbed his temples, though his attention stayed on me. "I've got an early flight."

"You have? Where?" I didn't like the thought of him leaving when I'd only just found him. Not that I had any intention of letting him go far from sight, he was too precious. He was also in danger—grave danger.

"London."

"Is that where you live?"

"Yeah."

I smiled. "Me too."

He raised his eyebrows a little. "You do? Are you in Paris on business or pleasure, Lloyd?"

Oh, I liked the way he'd said pleasure. His mouth was soft and sensual and his voice low, his vowels well rounded within his sexy English accent.

I smiled. "Pleasure…well, if you call visiting family pleasure."

"I'm sure it's very pleasurable." His smile dropped. "And if you have a big family you're lucky."

"There's a few of us. What about you?"

"There's only my mother. She brought me up alone."

Of course she did.

"And you're close?" I asked.

"Yeah, very. I'll see her tomorrow, she likes to know how my shoots have gone, and I always pick her up a small gift when I've been out of the country."

I was enjoying talking to him and wanted the conversation to extend. "What have you bought her from Paris?"

"There's these colorful macaroons she loves. Ridiculously expensive for what they are, but still…"

"She's worth it, right." I could barely remember my mother. It had been centuries since I'd seen her. "And you can afford it, what with modelling, it must pay well?"

He smiled. "Yeah, it sees me okay. In fact, I should get her something else, some perfume perhaps. She likes to smell nice."

"So are you like famous? Really famous?"

He shrugged. "In the industry, probably." He nodded at the path by the river. "I need to get going."

"Me too."

He stepped away and I followed. I had no option. "Where are you staying?"

"Four Seasons."

"Very nice."

"It is." He turned to me as I stepped into line with him. "Er...goodbye, Lloyd."

"Actually I'm heading your way, staying near The Four Seasons myself."

"You are?" he asked.

"Yes, and then going back to London. Important work to do."

"What business are you in?"

I shoved my hands into my pockets, trying to look casual and that his apparent agreement to allow me to walk with him was no big deal, even though it was. "I'm involved in looking for missing persons." I wasn't entirely sure how to explain that searching for the cambion of fables had been my job for as long as I could remember.

"Private investigation?"

"Something like that." I nodded ahead. The Eiffel Tower was lit with the colors of the French flag. There would be time to explain everything to Darius at a later stage. Right now, I needed to understand his lifestyle and movements around the globe, and most importantly let the others know he existed. "It's a nice view, huh."

"I never tire of Paris, it's charming, and dare I say it, romantic."

"I agree on both accounts." I paused as a woman with three huge white poodles walked past us, the dogs straining on their leads. "And you grew up in London, with your mother?"

"Yeah, same house she's always lived in. She inherited it from her parents a few years before I was born."

"There's something nice about being so settled."

"I guess. She'll never move. She's retired now and has everything she wants nearby. Her friends, the church, and she volunteers at a local homeless center."

"Sounds like a great woman."

"The best." He turned to me. "She has incredible faith in people. Almost to a fault."

"Go on."

He paused and tugged off his rucksack. As he rummaged in it he said, "She always sees the good in people, whatever their background, their past, their sins. She believes everyone's soul can be saved, every life can be turned around." He tugged out a navy blue sweater and started to put it on.

"Here, let me." I held out my hand and he passed me his rucksack.

I watched him drag on the sweater, pulling it over his neat shoulders, defined chest and down to the waistband of his jeans. His body was in perfect proportion, not skinny, not overly pumped up, and he was skimming six feet one.

"Thanks." He took his rucksack and slipped it onto his back, adjusting the straps and bouncing a little as if to make it comfortable.

"So she's a Christian?" I asked.

"Yeah, and it's how she raised me." He glanced downward and kicked a stone. It skittered along the path then plopped into a drain. "So what were you doing?" he asked as we came to a halt at a curbside.

"What do you mean?"

"Back there, in the shadows. You just appeared, I thought the courtyard was empty."

A bus zoomed past, its bright headlights flashing on the road, and its length buying me thinking time. I didn't want to bring up the sparks flying from his fingers again. I sensed that was a delicate subject. "I'd been for a smoke," I said, "Along the river. I had some things to mull over, about a case, you know." I could hardly tell him that some force, some unknown instinct had made me secret myself away in that random courtyard. "It was quiet, no distractions." I laughed. "It wasn't getting dark when I arrived. I guess I leaned against the back wall, my mind started whirring, trying to put pieces together like a jigsaw, and before I knew it darkness had crept over the place."

He glanced left and right, then stepped into the road.

I followed.

It wasn't until we reached the other side he spoke. "I get like that sometimes. Thoughts spinning around in my head. It's like they're storms, loud and bright." He huffed. "They won't go away."

"I have the same problem." I tapped the side of my head. "It's annoying, right?"

"Sure is."

We walked in silence for a few minutes, as if our stormy thoughts had taken over our minds.

"So when's your next shoot, Darius?" I asked. The more I knew, the better, and besides, the others would ask me.

"Day after tomorrow."

"In London?"

"Yeah. It's for Rolex." He pulled back his sleeve, revealing his watch again. "I've done a few for them, which is kinda cool. They give me gifts."

"It's a nice watch. If time is your thing."

"Isn't it everyone's?"

"No, I don't think it is." I smiled. "And is it just you, or will there be naked women draped all over you at this shoot?"

He tipped his head back and laughed, a lovely deep belly laugh that bounced off the wall of the building next to us.

A warm feeling filled my usually cold, empty chest and a fizz of longing curled up my back; a longing to hear him laugh again and again.

"Naked women draped over me," he repeated. "Yeah, most likely. That's how today has been."

"And you get paid for that, you lucky sod."

His laughter faded. "I guess lots of guys are envious of that side of my job."

"And is it worthy of their envy?"

"Not really. It's not as if I feel anything for them or have relationships with them. No matter what love-filled, passionate image the camera picks up, as soon as the money shot is in the bag, that's it, home time."

"But you must date them?" The Four Seasons Hotel came into view. "Drinks, dinners, glamorous rock and roll parties?"

"No."

"Really? With your looks, you must be able to take your pick of the girls and have invitations raining down on you."

"I had some fun to start with, parties and that, but nothing particularly wild and exciting, certainly nothing for the gossip columns."

"Why no wild and exciting?"

We'd nearly reached the hotel and he stopped beside a darkened doorway and turned to me.

"I guess..." he said. "None of it really turned me on."

For the love of Benedict. Give me strength. This man turns me *the Hell on.*

I swallowed, my mouth a little dry. "What didn't turn you on? The parties or the women?"

He ran his hand over his hair, brushing it back from his forehead. His palm slid downward over his crown, to his nape, then around his neck.

I followed his fingertips, watching them flutter over his carotid artery, stroking the tanned skin there as if inviting me to think of the blood beneath.

A wave of need rolled inside of me. Now my mouth was watering.

"Neither," he said, quietly. "Neither the parties nor the women turned me on."

I wanted to ask if he was gay. The words were on the tip of my tongue. Did his sexual persuasion match mine?

Ours?

"Are you...?" I started.

What if I scare him? What if that's a trigger question?

"Am I what?" he asked quietly, his concentration firmly on my face.

"Are you free later this week? In London? Perhaps we could meet for a drink."

"Why?"

I chuckled, hoping to lighten the situation. "Why not? We could be mates, Darius. Nothing wrong with having friends to hang out with, is there?"

He continued to study me. Shadows sliced over his features, catching on his angular cheekbones and the dip below his lower lip. "No, I guess there isn't anything wrong with that."

"Cool." I pulled out my phone. "Let's swap numbers so we can hook up."

"Sure." He dug into his front pocket and produced an iPhone.

After a quick switch of contact details, he shoved it away. "I hope you find your missing person."

"You know what." I rammed my hands into the pockets of my hoody and took a deep breath. "I think my musing in the courtyard has been of great benefit to the case."

"It has? You know where to look? A lead?" His perfectly shaped eyebrows shot up.

"Yeah, the pieces of the puzzle have come together. It's taken a while, but finally I'm there."

"That's great." He rested his warm hand on my shoulder and gave it a squeeze. "I'm pleased for you. And I'm sure the person's family will be very grateful."

Forty minutes later I was back at Montmartre. I raced up the stairs of the apartment we'd rented for the last month and burst through the door.

"I've found him!"

"What?" Rhys stood and took a step forward.

I panted for breath. I'd run faster than I should have through the city, risking drawing attention to myself. I was out of breath not from exertion but from excitement. "I've found him, the cambion."

"You have not." George looked up from the laptop resting on his knees. He was on the sofa and as usual he wore his peaked cap and tweed waistcoat.

"Why would I lie?" I shut the door. "He's here, in Paris. Why else did we all have that strange feeling, that longing to be here? I'm not the only one who's been out walking, searching, day after day, night after night." I glanced around. "Where's Oscar?"

"He went out on his bike," Rhys said. "Said something about a hunch. He wanted to go to the Louvre." Rhys stepped closer with his hands held out, palms upward. "So tell me, us, more."

"It was a good hunch." I paused. That hadn't been far from where I'd found Darius. "But we should wait for Oscar."

"No." George set his laptop aside but left it open. "Give us what you've got. We'll fill him in later."

The door opened. Oscar walked in. He was dressed as usual in black biker leathers and the scent of the evening air clung to him. He stopped, his dark eyebrows pulled low, and stared between the three of us. "What's going on, boss?" he directed gruffly at George.

"Lloyd reckons he's found him." George nodded at me.

"Him?" Oscar repeated, slamming the door with a flick of his wrist.

"Yeah." Rhys grinned. "Come on, mate, dish what you know."

I dragged off my hoody and tossed it onto the empty dividing counter between the living area and kitchen. I then reached for a cigarette and lit it. "I was down at the river, walking, you know." I blew out a stream of smoke and tapped my chest. "That craving we've all had, inside, to just search, check out every nook and cranny, every street and alley, leave no stone unturned. That's what I was doing."

Rhys sat down again but stayed perched on the edge of the seat as if ready to spring into action. Oscar leaned his butt on the back of a chair. George folded his arms and his eyes narrowed.

I had their undivided attention. Good.

"Twice I walked past this building, made of stone, some gothic features, you know. I wondered if it was just ancient and that's why it was calling to me."

"Get to it." George frowned.

"I am." I rocked back on my heels and drew on the cigarette again. "My head was buzzing, my chest a little tight, and I spotted this courtyard within the walls of this building. It was deserted, a bit unkempt, and had a few dark doorways. So I took to one, set myself back in the shadows, clear of the sun, and waited."

"You've been out all day."

"Yeah, I waited nearly all day. But it was worth it."

"So tell us," George's voice was a low growl. He was usually a very patient man, like me, but waiting for information was clearly pushing him.

"And then this guy emerges from what must have been a fire exit. He's tall, ripped, and so fucking beautiful you wouldn't believe it and—"

"He's beautiful?" Rhys asked.

"Yeah, no kidding. He's a model. You know for adverts, magazines and television."

"Fuck." Oscar rubbed his forehead. "Really? I thought we were..."

"Looking for a monster, yeah me too," I said. "But no, Darius Linnet is not a monster, he's the perfect specimen of a man. His features could have been chiselled from marble, his eyes are the color of the bluest sea, and I...I could stare at him all day and all night for all eternity."

"Darius Linnet," Rhys repeated.

I swallowed. Emotion bubbled up inside of me now I'd said the words out loud. He was *the one*.

"Stands to reason," George said with a shrug, "if you think about it."

"I agree now I've thought about it," I said, clearing my throat. "A human mother, and a demon father who can distort his own looks and gender to appeal to the person he's seducing. It's not surprising his son is designed to seduce the entire human race, male and female alike."

"Why had we never thought of that?" Oscar said.

"*I* had." George tutted. "Now go on, where is he now, Lloyd?"

"At The Four Seasons."

"One of us needs to be there." Oscar straightened. "I'll volunteer."

"I agree he needs constant surveillance." George stared at me. "If he really is the cambion we've been searching for."

"He is." I held up my hands and wiggled my fingers, remembering the sparks flying from Darius's fingertips. "He has lightning in him, I saw it with my own eyes. That proves it, right?"

"You did?" Rhys stood again. "How? I mean…what happened?"

"When he appeared, he was frustrated, angry. It was evident in his body language. I was only half watching him at this point, you know, admiring a hot bod and a cute face. But then he started shooting sparks from his fingertips at this pile of litter. It went up in flames. Like whoosh, on fire."

George stood and placed his hands on his hips. "Are you telling the truth?"

"Why the fuck would I lie?" I folded my arms. George's attitude was beginning to annoy me, as it sometimes did. Being the eldest out of the four of us—at three and a half centuries—he could get tiresome with his bossiness, lording-it-over-us was what I'd once accused him of. "It's him. I tell you. Darius Linnet is the demon's son we've been searching for all this time."

"In that case," George said, "he holds the key to everything." He nodded at Oscar. "Get your butt down to The Four Seasons. And keep your phone on. We'll be in touch."

Chapter Three

Darius

The hotel room at The Four Seasons was lavish. The pile carpet so deep my toes nearly got lost in it, and the bed so huge it would easily have fit four or maybe five people. It had a grand canopy over it too, reminding me of a historical set I'd been on the year before.

After showering, and pulling on sweats, I flicked on the TV, hoping to find an English channel. As I did so my stomach rumbled and I reached for the room service menu. Briefly it crossed my mind that I should call Amy and let her know I wouldn't be joining her, but I pushed that idea aside. I was sure she wouldn't be giving me another thought. Or if she was, she was moaning about me to one of her super-model mates.

Now dinner with Lloyd, if he'd suggested that, maybe I would have.

You only just met him.

He'd freaked me out a bit at first, emerging from the shadows with his hood pulled up. But I'd enjoyed his company. He was witty, sharp, and had something about him that made me want to get to know him better. He was intriguing, not like the people I met on the modelling circuit. I got the feeling he didn't have a vain bone in his body, and phew...from what I'd seen, he had a seriously nice body. As tall as me, a fraction broader perhaps, and with big hands. I liked big hands, hands that looked as if they worked, did something useful. Not like mine.

His face was interesting, not classically handsome, and not all out rugged. But when he spoke I was drawn to watching his mouth, and his pale eyes seemed to draw me in. He had depth, secrets, and I wanted to know more.

I spotted steak and chips on the menu and rang down my order, adding red wine to it. Flicking through the TV again, I came across an old episode of Friends and left it on.

As I watched the antics of Monica and Chandler, I found my mind wandering again. Would Lloyd call me? Or should I call him? Where would be a good place to meet in central London? Somewhere hip but not so hip the music was loud and we wouldn't be able to chat. I wanted to get to know him. Oh, but maybe not a bar—he'd said he wasn't drinking. A café, perhaps? We could have coffee or tea or hot chocolate, whatever he fancied.

Thirty minutes later, and getting restless for my food, I wandered to the window. I was on the fourth floor, and had a view of the main street. Cars were parked in neat rows and more moved past each other. It was dark now, the moon rising in a velvet-black sky, but in the city, the glow never dulled to anything less than warm amber.

Several pedestrians were out and about. The usual Parisian dog walkers, a couple with their arms linked, and a tall, broad man in a black leather jacket and pants, teamed with chunky biker boots. He was securing a crash helmet in the back-box of a large motorcycle. He finished what he was doing, put the key in his pocket, and then looked up at the hotel.

For a split second I thought he was staring straight at me. I felt his gaze land on mine, hot and intense. My heart did a strange flip and I stepped backward, pulling the drapes neat again. I flicked off the TV. The silence in the room was deafening so I put it back on.

"Damn it," I muttered, feeling jittery. I rubbed my fingertips together, remembering the release of sparks earlier. Lloyd saw me do it. He'd admitted he had. But why wasn't he more curious? Most people, surely, would have been fascinated at such a spectacle.

Is that why I like him?

Perhaps him knowing my dark secret and still wanting to talk to me, go for a drink with me, had made him all the more appealing. He hadn't run a mile, called me a weirdo, or rushed to the press.

He still might.

I could imagine the headline. *Top London Model is a Fire Starting Freak.*

I shuddered, hating the hurt and worry such a report would bring my mother. She was such a soft soul. I never wanted to cause her heartache, only help her and be there for her, the way she had me throughout my childhood. I touched the cross on my necklace, and then gave it a quick rub before removing it. I worried about sleeping with it on and breaking the chain.

Perhaps Lloyd would have to pluck up the courage to tell me his secrets—and I was sure there were some.

Knock. Knock.

Not bothering to add a t-shirt, I opened the hotel room door.

"Mr Linnet. Your meal, sir." A smartly dressed waiter pushed forward a trolley holding a large silver dome, cutlery and a small bottle of red wine, unopened next to a glass.

I handed him a few Euros. "Thank you, I'll take it from here." The delicious scent made my mouth water as I tugged the trolley closer.

"Very good, sir." He smiled, stepped away and turned.

As he did so, I spotted movement at the end of the corridor, near the elevator. I paused, realizing it was the man I'd seen on the street; the one in black leathers who'd looked my way. He appeared to be holding a small box and was walking toward me.

I hesitated, half in and half out of the hotel room, my hand resting on the handle of the trolley.

He walked with a confident swagger, his biker boots thudding on the red and gold checked carpet.

"Are you Darius Linnet?" he asked as he approached. His voice was low and rasping.

"Yes." Was he a fan? A crazed stalker?

"Good." His jaw line was peppered with dark stubble. "I have this for you."

"Thanks." I took the box he offered. It was purple and silver striped with a lid.

"It's from Oui! to say thank you for today."

"Oui!" I smiled. Ah, he was a delivery person. "That's kind of them." I nodded at the elevator. "You could have left it at Reception, save you coming up."

"It's no trouble."

He was staring at me, the way people who recognized me often did—though his stare was more intense, brooding, and heavy.

I wasn't looking my absolute best since there were no clever make-up artists tucked in my suite, but that didn't seem to bother him as his gaze drifted to my chest, my tight abs then lower still, hovering on what was likely a bulge in my sweats as I hadn't bothered with underwear after my shower.

He might be big and macho, but he's definitely gay.

His appreciation was obvious. His previously flattened lips curled into a smile and his eyelids became a fraction heavy as he blinked slowly.

"Thanks again," I said, retreating into my room, and trying to ignore the tingling in my cock his attention had elicited.

He didn't reply, instead he nodded once, then moved backward until his shoulders hit the wall opposite. He folded his arms and crossed one leg over the other, toe pointing into the floor, as if settling in to stand there for some time.

"What are you doing?" I asked.

"Waiting for someone."

"Oh...well I hope they don't keep you long."

"Doesn't matter if they do." His gaze was still on mine.

I shut the door, feeling a bit strange after the encounter, and placed down the box. After setting my meal on the dresser and pouring a glass of wine, I tugged off the lid of the box.

Within it sat two bottles of perfume. They were the 'his and hers' versions of Phantom's Kiss. I smiled and picked up the female one, removed the stopper and sniffed the top. My mother would like it. It was flowery and light, her kind of scent.

The male one was denser, as if to counterbalance the ladies'. It had a spicy tang, perhaps black pepper or aniseed, I wasn't sure which.

I set them back in their box beside my suitcase, took a sip of wine, and then went to the door. Looking through the peephole confirmed that my biker delivery guy was still in the corridor. He was staring straight ahead, unblinking, his jaw tense.

I quickly backed away, then felt foolish. He wouldn't have known I was looking at him.

My appetite had diminished, but I sat and ate what I could. I hadn't had lunch so knew I needed nourishment. I found my thoughts straying to Lloyd again, and wondering what he'd eaten for his evening meal. Would he have gone to a restaurant alone? Or perhaps out with friends, a girlfriend, colleagues?

Girlfriend? For some reason I hoped he didn't have a girlfriend.

With the steak and chips more or less eaten, I placed the plate back on the trolley and covered it with the dome. After draining the last of the wine, I used the bathroom then found myself hovering around the doorway again.

I had a desperate urge to look through the peephole. See if my biker delivery guy was still there.

"Oh, just do it," I muttered.

I placed my eye up at the glass.

I caught my breath.

Yes, he was still there. He hadn't appeared to have moved, and again he was staring straight at my door.

Fuck.

What was he doing? Was he going to stand there all night? Should I call Reception? Security maybe? Or should I pull open the door and ask him outright?

I decided on the latter, then hesitated. He was a big guy, bigger than me. If he was a crazed fan then I didn't want to aggravate the situation, but I did want to find out what he was up to.

I reached for the dinner trolley, then opened the door. I'd go with the pretence of wanting to remove it from the room.

"Oh, hi," I said, feigning surprise at seeing him as I lined the trolley up with the corridor wall.

He nodded, once. "Mr Linnet."

"What are you doing? I mean, how long are you going to be waiting here for?" I asked, trying to sound not particularly interested.

"Shouldn't be long now. My buddy is staying in this room." He jabbed his finger at the door to his left. "I'm waiting for him to get back so we can finish up a game of poker."

"Ah, okay. Well good luck...with the poker." I smiled and shut the door, but not before getting a good look at his legs. They were thick with muscle and the leather not only hugged them perfectly, it created some very interesting bulges and creases around his groin.

A rush of heat went over me as I slipped the chain, securing myself in. Damn it. Today I'd seen not one but two guys who'd made me flustered. Each different, and each equally alluring.

I flicked off the main light and flopped onto the bed, my head almost disappearing in the huge pile of pillows.

You're going to have to admit it, Darius.

I sighed. I knew my inner psyche was right. I was gay. It had taken a long time to admit men gave me a stirring in my cock women didn't. Men fascinated me. Men's bodies, intriguingly, were all the same yet very different, and their minds equally so.

My mother would hate it. She'd never understand. But I'd reached a point I knew I had to be true to myself, even if I kept that truth hidden from her.

And the rest of the world?

I could do that. Of course I could. I was hardly on the party scene and if I had a relationship with someone like Lloyd, someone who wasn't in the business, I should be able to keep it under wraps.

Assuming Lloyd is gay and fancies me.

Not Lloyd then. How about the big, hot biker outside the door right now? If I were to proposition him what would he say? If I let him explore my body while I found pleasure with his, that would be okay...wouldn't it?

I grabbed a pillow, then held it over my face and released a silent scream. It was that or allow the heat to grow in my chest, the burn to grow in my arms and then I'd have no choice but to release sparks into the bathtub.

But I'd released once today, and another build up of heat wasn't likely for forty-eight hours at least. Unless something really alarming or exhilarating happened, that was.

Frustrated as I was, I also felt a strange kind of relief. Admitting to myself where my sexual orientation lay wasn't as hard or as shocking as I'd thought it might be. Neither was deciding to act upon my desires should the chance arise. I guessed that was the way with an inner sanctum, it was somewhere already visited. A place which had grown with me since day one even if I'd kept it quiet and in darkness.

Eventually I set the alarm on my phone, turned off the light and closed my eyes, hoping for sleep. It stole across me quickly; my body melting into the bed, my heavy limbs stilling and my thoughts scattering.

My dream took over my half-wakeful thoughts and I found myself where I often did in sleep, at least for the last five years of my life: standing on Tower Bridge staring at the Thames and a small bricked-up archway in the wall lining the bank of the river. The archway had once led to Traitor's Gate, a watery entrance to the Tower of London and the cold, dark cells within its prison. Above me ravens circled, casting cool shadows over my body. An old-fashioned car, it's exhaust spluttering, limped past with a lone driver. A dirty beggar child held his hands forward, then his image evaporated. The scents were different to modern day London, pungent and foul. I was grateful for a slight breeze that lifted my long hair and caressed my cheek.

I ran my hands over my chest. My breasts were large and firm, the nipples sensitive. Slipping lower still, I smoothed over the deep dip of my waist then the flare of my hips. It was how I'd come to expect myself in a dream.

Female.

There was a small rowing boat on the river holding three men. One was clearly a prisoner. His arms and legs were bound and he was blindfolded. They were edging toward the area of Traitor's Gate. I felt I knew him, the prisoner, but of course I didn't.

But still something drew me to him. So I began to walk over the bridge, toward the turrets of the eastern side of the Tower, the way I always did. People stared at me as I hurried along, my dress swishing against my legs and my breasts jostling with each step.

I left the bridge with an urgency growing inside me. I had to get to this prisoner. He had a key for me. I didn't know what the key was for. The need for it was powerful, though, and growing with each step. It was like needing to breathe when underwater, or gasping for a drink when walking through a desert.

"Hey, pretty lady."

I slammed to a halt and pressed my hand to my chest, my flesh warm as my breasts heaved in the low neckline of the dress.

A stranger appeared before me. Except he wasn't a stranger, he was familiar somehow, and handsome, so handsome. Beautiful. Just my sort of guy.

"Here, for you." He offered forward a bunch of flowers, red roses, his biceps flexing against his white shirt.

I hesitated, searching the river for the prisoner. He'd gone.

"Take these, my love," the stranger said, crooking his finger beneath my chin and turning me to face him. "And know that I have found you, that I am coming for you...soon."

I woke and sat bolt upright, blinking in the darkness. That part of the dream had changed.

I'm coming for you...soon.

Usually he just said he was there, and that was it, the end of the dream. The prisoner, the stranger, my female body would be no more.

There'd been something sinister in his voice, too, a grim determination. His words were still echoing in my head, each syllable rattling against my eardrum as if they'd actually been spoken at my side.

My heart pounded. I pressed my hands to my chest, relieved to find the breasts from my dream had gone and as usual my pecs were hard and masculine. I'd become used to the imagined female body, it'd been there since my teens. I never dreamt as a male. For a while I wondered if everyone had that experience, but my mother said that wasn't the case. It was because I was special, like my sparks. She also said it wouldn't be wise to tell people about that either.

So I hadn't. And when I'd once orgasmed as a female then woke to a softening cock and a wet patch, I'd kept that to myself too.

I lay back down and turned over. The clock read two a.m. Briefly I wondered if the biker was still outside the hotel room or if his friend had come to play poker yet. Was he really playing poker, or was that a metaphor for something else entirely? Something naked, hot and sexy?

I reached down, slipped my fingers around my cock and began to rub root to tip. I needed to release the tension the dream had created. It was sexual tension combined with frustration. I didn't know what it meant, or who the prisoner was. All I understood was it took me back in time in the city I called home.

What is the key for?

Gritting my teeth, I sped up, working my cock to full hardness.

I arched my neck and moaned as my balls tightened. The friction of flesh on flesh created a pleasant heat which drove me on.

I thought of Lloyd, of him doing this to me. His hand around my cock and his breaths quickening as he went faster and faster. Then of the biker and what he might be doing with his friend...what if *I* was his friend? Bent over, taking him, allowing him to enter my body, pushing me to orgasm with his no doubt huge cock.

"Ah fuck." I gasped, then as the first shot of cum left me, I imagined Lloyd on his knees before me, taking me into his mouth, swallowing my pleasure.

I jerked my hips, shoving into my own hand. Another spurt of release dragged a groan from my chest, then another and another.

Eventually I emptied. After lying still for several minutes, allowing my breathing to settle, I reached for some tissues and cleaned up my mess.

Resting on the bed again, a nice sense of satisfaction came over me. It was different to usual. I was more fulfilled.

It's because I had someone—no, make that two people—to think of as I came.

Two real, living, flesh and blood men who were both drop dead gorgeous.

Chapter Four

Oscar

I stared at the door, then stared some more. The thing about being immortal is time has no meaning. If I stared at Darius Linnet's hotel room door for a century it wouldn't matter to me. I could do it. And I would happily.

For like Lloyd, I too, was certain he was the one.

His cambion energy came off him in waves. It was pouring from the room now, like a scent seeping from around the door and filling my nostrils. It was hot and powerful, it held so many tantalizing secrets.

When I'd first seen him I'd wanted to hold his face in my palms and study his eyes, the shape of his nose, his lips. Kiss him, explore his taste, the outline of the blood vessels beneath the surface of the skin on his neck.

But of course I couldn't.

That would send him running for the hills. I'm a big guy, surly too. People often cross the road to avoid me.

Most of the time they are right to. I could drain them dry in seconds.

But Darius…damn, I wanted to taste him, quench a thirst that had been growing for a few years now, but more than that I had the urge to protect him, to get to know him, to discover his secrets and show him some of mine.

A little after two a.m. a low muffled moan came from within his room. He was alone. I could guess what he was doing.

My cock hardened as I thought of the outline of flesh beneath his sweats earlier. It was easy for me to imagine his shaft solid and erect and with Darius's hand wrapped around it.

Within seconds the space issue in my leathers had me shifting from one foot to the other. If I hadn't been standing in a public corridor, albeit an empty one, I'd have joined Darius in a late night wank.

When he groaned again, I had to suppress the urge to break his door down and go to him. The man was too damn gorgeous to be sleeping alone and resorting to his own hand. If he wanted me to tip him over the bed and sink deep then I would, tonight and every night for all eternity.

Darius Linnet was the one.

For me.

For all of us.

At six a.m. there was movement within his room. It was only then I broke into the empty room opposite his and spied through the peephole, waiting for him to emerge.

Which he did ten minutes later; hair damp from the shower, wearing a denim jacket, Levi's and black sneakers. He had a rucksack on his back and was dragging a small roll-along case.

I counted to ten—long enough for him to reach the elevator and press the button, but not so long I'd lose him.

That wasn't an option.

I let myself out of the room and quickly followed him. The elevator doors were closing, trapping him inside. I pushed my hand through the gap, halting their progress.

When they opened and he saw me, surprise lit his handsome face.

"Sorry," I said. "In a rush. Got a plane to catch."

"Er, yeah, me too." He quickly pressed the door-open button.

"Thanks." I stepped in beside him, so we were standing shoulder to shoulder.

He was a fraction shorter than me and smelled of cologne, peppery and sexy, I wondered if it were the one I'd bought him.

I hoped so. To think he was wearing something I'd given him as a gift thrilled me.

"Where are you flying to?" I asked, even though I already knew.

"London. You?"

"London too." I resisted the urge to turn and stare at him. Instead I allowed my gaze to linger on his reflection in the smoky mirrored doors.

"Charles de Gaulle?" he asked.

"Yeah." I recalled the e-ticket George had emailed to my phone. George was a computer whizz with no aversion to hacking when necessary. It wouldn't have taken him long to find out which flight Darius was on. "Nine ten."

"Same flight as me." I saw Darius's reflection turn to me, linger for a moment, then look down at his feet.

I had a longing to ask him if he was okay. If he'd been sad or lonely when he'd masturbated the night before. If he'd wished I'd joined him, or if he had a man, or maybe a woman, back in London waiting for him.

No. Please. No one else.

The elevator doors opened and I gestured for him to step out first.

"Thanks."

I enjoyed the view of his butt as he walked ahead of me. He paused at Reception, handed in a keycard, then navigated past several huge urns of pale cream and pink flowers. When he reached the hotel shop he loitered by the window as if something had caught his eye.

I held back, wondering what he was doing.

I didn't wonder for long. He was studying the gift boxes containing the his and hers sets of Phantom's Kiss. After being tipped off by Lloyd, it was where I'd stopped on the way to his room the evening before. A gift was a good excuse to meet the man who was going to rule our world from this point on, so I'd purchased the box of aftershave and perfume.

Darius rubbed his forehead, as if smoothing away a frown.

Does he suspect me of buying it here? An excuse to see him?

I shook my head. No, surely he'd just think it a coincidence. I was sure he received gifts all the time from companies keen to associate their product with his looks and style, being that he was famous and all that.

Damn, he's going to be hugely famous in the vampire world if we're not careful. And it won't do him any favors. In fact, it might be the death of him.

I shuddered at the thought. Darius was so beautiful, so vibrant and alive. The very notion of him dead, or being turned, didn't sit well with me.

Once again, as I'd thought several times in the night, we were lucky to have found him first. Before his demon father, and before some of the more ruthless vampires at The Order; ones who fantasized about the elusive key and the salvation it was rumored to hold.

A wave of protectiveness came over me—not that I hadn't felt it from the moment I'd seen him, I had, but now, as he wandered out onto the street, it was a powerful force inside me. I couldn't ignore it. The urge to prevent him ever coming to harm was as instinctual as my need to feed on blood.

I hurried after him, ignoring the curious glance from the concierge. The hotel really needed to sharpen their security.

Once out on the street Darius paused, his suitcase held behind him. He appeared to be looking for a cab.

"Want to split the fare?" I asked, stepping up next to him and dropping my shades. The sun wasn't high yet, its rays not reaching the street, but still, I didn't like the burning sensation on my retinas. "As we're both going the same way."

He continued to scour the traffic. "I thought you had a bike?"

So he *had* seen me arrive. I'd suspected as much.

"Ahh, the leathers," I said quickly. "I see why you'd think that and yes, I have been using one for my courier work. But it's a friend's. I borrowed it. He'll collect it from here."

"Oh, I see." A line formed between Darius's eyebrows.

I hoped I hadn't pushed it too far with my reasons for being at his side.

"Well in that case, sure," he said with a shrug. "No point paying two fares."

I smiled, then spotted a cab and flagged it down.

We quickly alighted. My leg brushed his as we sat and a lovely warmth from his flesh radiated onto my cold skin, even through my leathers.

"You travel light." Darius adjusted his case and rucksack.

"Yeah, suits me." I leaned forward. "*Charles de Gaulle* please, mate."

"Not even a washbag?"

Rubbing my coarse stubble, I threw him a grin. "I'm not one for preening."

"That must be nice."

"What do you mean?"

"In my trade, preening, or rather grooming, has to be maintained."

"I like your clean shaven jaw." I swiped my tongue over my bottom lip, wondering what his cheek would feel like against my mouth. "It's cute."

"Cute." He chuckled. "Not sure how I feel about being called cute."

"It's a compliment. I like how you look, a lot."

He held my gaze.

I returned it solidly. He may as well know I found him attractive. Hell, he was the most handsome man I'd seen for decades. Everything about him drew me in for closer inspection.

He turned away and pointed out of the window. "You ever been to the Louvre?"

"Yeah, a few times."

"Got a favorite picture?"

"The Raft of the Medusa." I visualized it in my head; a huge canvas that instantly took the viewer to the stormy seas of the Atlantic.

"I haven't heard of that one," he said.

"It's by Théodore Géricault. It's a raft, adrift and crowded with desperate sailors."

"Does it have a story behind it?"

He appeared interested and that pleased me. "Yeah, a bit grizzly, though, because it's a true story. The *Méduse* was a French naval frigate which hit a sandbank on its way to Senegal. On the raft are the surviving seamen."

"Were they okay?"

"No." I shook my head and studied his eyes. "The sailors turned mad, chaos ensued. They killed each other, ate the dead." Still I stared at him.

His eyebrows pulled low but he held my gaze. "That's awful."

"It is. But within the painting there's one symbol of hope for the wretched souls."

"What's that?"

"At the front of the raft, a few men are pointing forward, as if they've seen a rescue boat, or land."

"Well that's good." He smiled. "If their souls could be saved."

"You think that's important? A man's soul."

"Of course, doesn't everyone?"

I shrugged. I knew that not to be the case. My sort had been hounded for centuries. A stake through the heart, or beheaded and burned if ever foolish or careless enough to be captured. That was the end of a vampire. His soul would burn in Hell for all eternity. No pearly gates, no chance of redemption, certainly no Heaven. Hell, that was what we had to look forward to. And once there, escape was not an option.

"The soul," Darius went on, "is where the true person is, not the body." He ran his hands down his chest then over his thighs.

I watched him, wondering what it would be like to smooth my palms over his torso and legs. His warm, soft skin held fascination for me and I longed to experience it against mine.

"The body is a vehicle, our transport through life," he continued "We have to look after it, but it's what's up here we really need to care for." He tapped the side of his head.

"I like the way you think," I said, nodding. "Makes sense."

"Not just a pretty face." He laughed.

The sound filled my chest along with a yearning to hear it over and over. "You're definitely not just a pretty face," I said. "There's much more to you."

His cheeks flushed, the blood coming to the surface of his skin, then he turned to the window.

We rode along for a few more minutes, creeping through traffic toward the set-down area at the airport. When we arrived we split the bill as agreed and headed through the revolving doors.

The huge atrium was packed with people. Everyone rushing as if they knew their time was running out.

I paused at Darius's side and studied a huge screen.

Our flight was on time and check-in was at desk forty-one.

"It's this way," I said, knowing the way from previous trips. "Come on."

"Yeah, it is." He adjusted his rucksack, then walked with me.

I was pleased. I wanted to stick with him and continue our conversation, not follow him from afar. This was a much easier way to keep an eye on him, and protect him should anything untoward happen.

Luckily the queue for check-in was short. I gestured for Darius to go first.

"Thanks," he said, stepping forward and rolling his small suitcase behind him.

I watched the woman behind the counter. Her eyes widened and she licked her lips, bringing renewed shine to her glossy lipstick. She pushed her hair behind her ears and sat straighter as she smiled at him.

This man wraps everyone around his finger.

It was clear our cambion had the allure his father did. A demon in full seduction mode was irresistible. Darius just didn't seem to know he could have anyone in his bed, male or female, if he decided to.

Darius spoke to the woman as she checked his passport and handed him his boarding pass. When finished he turned to me. "It was nice meeting you, thanks for sharing the ride."

"No problem." I nodded but couldn't manage a smile. I'd wanted to stick with him, pal up for the entire journey.

He walked away and I stepped up to the desk tugging my phone and passport out of my jacket pocket.

I didn't get the same reaction from the woman behind the desk. She looked at me warily, then frowned when I said I had no carry on luggage and nothing to check in.

"Can I sit next to my buddy?" I said, gesturing to the way Darius had gone.

"Your buddy?"

"Yes, Mr. Linnet." This time I managed a smile and looked her in the eyes.

She held my gaze for a second, just long enough for me to see I'd had an effect on her. "Let me have a look." She glanced back at the computer. "Are you okay with paying for an upgrade?"

"Of course." I passed her a credit card.

After a few moments she handed over my passport, credit card and boarding pass. "Have a nice flight, Mr Yale."

I nodded and headed off toward Security. Darius had gone from sight.

"Benedict's balls," I muttered. Not having Darius close wasn't sitting comfortably with me. But at least I knew where he was going to be in an hour—sitting next to me. And there weren't likely to be any demonic mishaps in such a busy, bright place as an airport terminal.

Ten minutes later I spotted him sipping a coffee and tapping on his phone.

I kept my distance, loitering around the newsstand and pretending to flick through a selection of bestselling paperbacks.

Thirty minutes after that I was following Darius onto a British Airways plane.

Although there wasn't a first class, or even a business class on such a short flight, we were in the premier section at the front with wider seats and more legroom. Which suited me and my long legs.

I hung back with several passengers between us and watched him stow his suitcase in the overhead locker, his biceps flexing and his shoulders bunching as he maneuvered it.

He spoke to a woman he'd had to lean over, and she laughed, batting her hand as if to say he could come as near as he wanted.

I folded my arms, possession coming over me. He was ours, no one else's, certainly not a human female. And Darius Linnet would soon be well aware of that fact.

He sat in the middle seat of a row of three, the window seat being empty, and again looked at his phone. I moved closer, anticipation growing, then sat heavily, my leg brushing his.

He glanced up. His eyes widened. "Oh, hello again." He smiled.

"We should stop meeting like this," I said, matching his grin. "I'm Oscar Yale, by the way." I held out my hand.

"Darius Linnet." He placed his hand in mine.

I'd guessed right, his skin was warm and smooth, a little delicate too, I could sense the bones beneath the flesh. But I knew not to be fooled by that delicateness. Not only could he create lightning from his fingertips, he had an inner strength that had to be respected. Having a demon father did that to a person.

He shook and released. "I hope this plane is on time."

"You have somewhere to be? Work?"

"No, I said I'd go and see my mother, that's all. Her washing machine is playing up again. I'll take a look at it." He shrugged and did up his seatbelt, the clasp sitting over a bulge in his jeans. "If I can't fix it I'll buy her a new one."

"These things can usually be fixed with a bit of know how."

"Yeah, I agree. Shame I don't really know how." He chuckled.

The air stewards ran through the safety routine, then, bang on time, the plane took to the air.

Darius opted for another coffee. As usual I had nothing. What I really would have liked was to have a suck on his neck, find a vein, break it, and let his sweet red nectar fill my mouth. Not lots, not enough to exhaust him, just to sate my curiosity as to what he'd taste like. I wasn't desperate for a feed. I'd taken human blood only a few months ago, when we'd been in New York. George and Rhys had joined me. Lloyd, however, had gone a long time without feeding, longer than the three of us. I'd been surprised he'd managed to hold off when coming face to face, finally, with the man we'd been hunting. It just went to show his self-control was formidable.

"You talked about souls, earlier," I said.

"Er, yeah." He glanced sideways at me, then took a sip of his drink.

"Does that mean you were brought up Christian?"

"Yes, my mother is very religious." He touched his neck, and I noticed a necklace there, and beneath the material of his t-shirt the outline of a small cross.

"But you're not?"

"No, not really. I mean I'll do Christmas and Easter with her, but I haven't been to church for years. Not since I had a say in whether I went or not."

"So she didn't install her beliefs in you?" This had me curious. Had we been right in our suspicions of how a cambion would feel about religion?

He sighed. "Some of them. I mean, half and half."

Well you are half incubus, half human. Stands to reason. I bit on my bottom lip to keep those words in.

"I believe in the concept of souls, and that none are so evil, so far gone they can't be saved," he said.

"Like on the raft. The sailors, even if they killed and ate one another, should they be saved, then they could be forgiven. Is that what you mean?"

"Yeah, but not forgiven by God, or any god, but by other people, and themselves. Where there's life there's hope and all that."

I nodded. I didn't have a human life anymore, but I did have hope for my soul despite my sins over the years.

"Your mother is very important to you," I said, watching him run his finger over the rim of his cup.

"I'm all she's got." He paused. "And to a degree she's all I've got."

"I find that hard to believe. You have this hugely successful career, you must have lots of friends."

"I...yeah, my career is great. But loads of friends? No, not really."

"Why is that?"

"Traveling isn't good for relationships." He turned to me, his gaze seeming to roam my face as if taking in my features, my stubbled jawline, my wide neck. "You're not married are you, Oscar?"

"No." I shook my head.

"Me neither."

"No near misses with pretty models? Thoughts about dropping to one knee and popping the question?" I asked.

"With a girl?"

I hesitated then grinned, already guessing his answer. "Yeah, a girl."

But he didn't give me an answer. Instead he rolled his lips in on themselves then leaned a little closer.

I caught a whiff of not just his cologne, but also the scent of his warm skin.

"Can I ask you something?" he asked quietly.

"Sure."

"You won't be offended?"

I chuckled. "Depends what you ask, Darius."

And if you think it might, you're showing some of that inner strength. It's damn brave to ask a guy like me something that could insult.

"Are you gay?" he asked.

I tipped my head and allowed a small smile to form. "What makes you think that?"

"I dunno." He sat straighter. "Something about last night, when you said you were waiting for a friend. I wondered if that friend was..."

"Male?"

He swallowed and nodded.

I decided to put Darius out of his misery. After all I wanted him to enjoy spending time with me. "Yeah, it was a guy, but not one I'm involved with in *that* way. In fact he didn't stay long, had another place to be."

"Oh, I see."

"I was glad of the room, so close to the airport."

"Yeah, I'm sure."

A silence stretched between us. I decided to break it. "What about you, Darius?"

"What about me?"

"If you're not into girls, are you into guys?"

He closed his eyes and pulled in a breath. "I...I'm not..." He frowned, opened his eyes and set his attention on me. "How did you know you were gay? I mean, when did you find out?"

I folded my arms. "Always. Well, since I was a teen." Which was a seriously long time ago. "And I found out when a sweep I was working with—"

"A sweep?" His eyebrows shot up.

Damn it.

"Yeah, you know..." I paused, remembering the sweet kiss I'd shared with Joe all those years ago, before I'd been turned. We were both chimney sweeps. I'd been scrawny back then. "What I mean is he was a council worker. We were both working on some clean up operation, after a big event, a festival. He went for a smoke at the end of the shift, I went with him." I touched my lips. "He kissed me. In that moment it confirmed to me I was gay, that I'd never want to be with a woman."

"And you never have...with a woman?"

"Actually I have." I smiled. "Family pressure and all that. Trying to be what they wanted, Mom and Dad. It's sweet and gentle with a woman, don't you think?"

Darius pressed his hand to his chest, rubbing his fingers over the slight dent between his pecs. "I don't know."

"Ah, I guess you wouldn't know it's different if you've never been with a man."

"I mean." Again he lowered his voice. "I mean I don't know what it's like to have sex with a woman."

"You don't?" Now that had surprised the heck out of me. Our beautiful cambion was a virgin?

"Oh God, why am I telling you this?"

"Because." I pressed my hand over his, the one resting on the small tray table in front of him. "I just told you something private about myself, Darius. We're sharing."

He twisted his head to peer at me. A lock of hair hung over his eye.

I resisted the urge to smooth it away.

"Can I tell you something else private, Oscar?" he asked, a flash of earnestness crossing his irises and making him appear almost vulnerable.

"Sure."

"It won't go anywhere?"

"No, course not."

"I think I'm gay…no, I *am* gay, that's why I've never been with a woman."

"And you haven't been with a man either, have you?"

His gaze slid downward, over my leather jacket, to my groin, then up again. "No."

Holy cow. This man is a dream come true for us in so many ways.

I leaned closer, reducing the distance between our faces. I could feel his breaths on my cheek, see every eyelash, every dash of color in his eyes. "Have you *kissed* a man?"

He paused, then. "No."

"Would you like me to kiss you? Here? Now?"

"No." He spun his hand, clasping mine in a tight grip. "Not that I don't want you to. I'm sure I'd like it…a lot. But not here. Not with all these people around." He snapped back and released my hand. "I'm sorry."

"Don't be sorry." I'd had many dark moments in the last few centuries, but right now, with this gorgeous creature at my side who said he wanted me to kiss him, I'd forgotten them all. "Just say we can meet up, in London, Darius." I shifted on the seat. My cock hardening at the thought of all I could teach him. "So I can kiss you in private."

Chapter Five

Darius

I walked along the suburban street toward the terraced house I'd grown up in tugging my suitcase behind me. The trees lining the path were coming into leaf, casting dappled shadows over the bins set out for collection and the parked cars pressed nose to tail. It was a familiar stroll. I knew every root that had warped the pavers, every cluster of moss on the walls and fences, and the color of each front door.

The spring air held the scent of blossom and on the ground a few pink petals skittered in the breeze. I'd removed my sweater and shoved it into my rucksack once I'd alighted the double decker I'd caught from the airport.

But despite the warmth a chill kept stroking my neck.

I turned again. I tried not to, but curiosity was gnawing at me.

There he was.

The same guy who'd been behind me since I'd gotten off the bus. He was strolling along on the shady side of the road carrying a soft holdall that appeared to be bulging with tools, or if not tools, something heavy and hard.

He was tall and lean with blond hair cut into a short style with a flick at the front as was the fashion. He wore jeans with frayed rips in each knee and a vintage Beatles t-shirt. There was no doubt about it, he was a great looking young bloke, he could be in the same business as me if he wanted to be. But his bag was making me think he was a tradesman, which was at odds with his shades which looked to be high-end designer.

So why is he following me?

I carried on. The sound of an ice-cream van grew louder, then deafening as it journeyed toward me, stopping only a few yards away to wait for business.

Three children tumbled out of a house to my right, clutching coins and giggling.

My mother's house came into view and I smiled, thinking of how she'd like the macaroons and the perfume I had for her.

Should I tell her?

That thought had come to me several times since my conversation with Oscar. Should I confess to her that I was gay? Come out of the closet, as it were.

The image of her I had in my head changed. It went from smiling to shock, then sadness. She wouldn't understand, I was sure of it. She'd said so many times over the years how I should find a nice girl and settle down. I didn't want to disappoint her. Oscar had talked of family pressure to be with a woman. I understood how he could have gone along that route.

I touched the cross at my neck.

I'd met two men in the last twenty-four hours I could settle down with. Okay, that was maybe stretching it. But both Lloyd and Oscar were hotties. More than that I had both of their numbers and had agreed to meet up with them.

Dates. I have two dates with two sexy as fuck guys!

A police siren sounded behind me. I turned, made a pretence of being interested to see what was going on, but really I had another look at my stalker.

He'd kept his distance; it had barely changed since the bus. That was unusual in itself. I walked fast, with my long legs, and even with a roll along case I'd made short work of the distance.

This man was also tall, true, but he carried a heavy bag and the day was heating up. Most workmen, in my experience, would take their time, stroll rather than stride.

I frowned. I was being overly sensitive to be worrying about a man going about his day job. It was foolish. I guessed my emotions were a little fraught. My decision to be true to myself and follow my desires to be with a man had drained me. Not to mention a bad night's sleep, early start, and a flight which had all played havoc with my energy levels.

I was glad to reach my mother's home. Frustration had been building the last hundred steps, and I really didn't want to get in and immediately have to dispel sparks into the sink. My mother worried when I did that and I would have endless, 'are you sure you're okay?' 'Did something happen?' 'Can I get you some ice for your hands?'.

Ice didn't help, but she'd been doing that since I was small and the sparks had first started appearing, so I went with it.

"Mom," I called, opening the door. "Are you in?"

She appeared almost immediately in the kitchen doorway. She wore her usual pink flowered apron and was holding a saucepan in one hand and wooden spoon in the other.

"Darius. Oh, I'm so glad you're here." She smiled, disappeared, and then returned to the doorway minus the pan and spoon. "I've been making your favorite pasta sauce. I figured you'd have had enough of all that fancy French food."

I pulled her into a hug. Her small frame was light and delicate and I had to be careful not to squeeze her too hard. "I had steak and chips last night. Nothing fancy about that."

"Well that's good." She held me at arm's length and surveyed me. "I don't want you getting anorexic like those girls you work with."

"They're okay," I said. "And that's not likely, I enjoy my food too much." I rubbed my flat belly.

"Just as well it doesn't show." She laughed.

The doorbell sounded.

I shrugged off my rucksack and set my keys on a polished wooden dresser next to the photo she always kept there. It was a strange picture. She'd never really explained why it was of a man in smart polished shoes, a black tuxedo complete with bow tie, the picture ending at the point of his chin.

"Are you expecting someone?" I asked.

She didn't answer. Instead she rushed to the door and pulled it open. "Oh, hello, you must be Rhys Muller."

"That's right. I hope I didn't keep you waiting long, Ms Linnet."

"Marie, please, and no, no, I only mentioned yesterday at the center my washing machine was broken, then I got a phone call, saying there was a scheme for voluntary workers to have a free white goods service." She pulled the door wider. "Very generous of your company."

"We feel you should get something back for generously giving up your time."

"It's most appreciated."

There was a pause.

"Can I come in?" he asked.

"Yes, do. Of course. In you come."

My heart rate sped up.

Stepping into my mother's hallway was the workman who'd been following me. Up close I could see how handsome he was. His youthful skin was flawless, his hair carefully casual, and he had deep navy blue eyes. His lashes were long, he was clean shaven and his lips were almost pouty. I'd been right to think he could be a model—he had the chiseled, manscaped look going on.

No wonder he was following. He was coming to the same address.

His attention fell on me. He didn't appear surprised to see the man he'd been trailing.

He probably didn't notice me!

I didn't like that thought. I'd noticed him. I'd been acutely aware of his presence. And now...now even more so. I could smell his cologne, rich and fruity. His eyes sparkled, and his mouth pulling into a grin made him all the more attractive.

"Hey." His was voice light and friendly. "I'm Rhys."

"Darius. Nice to meet you." I held out my hand. "And thanks for this. I knew the washing machine was playing up, but it's really not my forte. I probably wouldn't have known where to start."

He wrapped his hand around mine, his long, cool fingers squeezing gently. "It's my pleasure." His smile didn't drop and I noticed he had the cutest dimples.

"This way," my mother said, bustling into the kitchen. "It's out the back."

I released Rhys's hand and gestured for him to go through.

The house was designed so the washing machine was in a small utility room behind the kitchen. Once upon a time it had been a downstairs bathroom, but that had been moved upstairs and now it housed a pantry, a washer, drier and a stack of cookbooks on a wonky shelf which I really should fix.

Following Rhys, I found my gaze straying to his ass. His jeans were tight and hugged his rounded buttocks. The pocket on the right side was ripped, the scars of stitches apparent. I guessed it didn't matter to him what he wore for work. Any old thing would do. But still, I liked his look, his casual chic was sexy and it appealed to the fashionista in me.

Sexy.

Yes, he was sexy, very.

Is he gay?

I halted in the doorway, emotion filling my chest. It seemed now I'd admitted it to myself, I was looking at every guy around and thinking about their sexual persuasion. More than that, I was thinking about kissing them, getting naked with them...fucking, shagging, screwing.

Heat traveled up my neck and heated my cheeks. I clenched my hands, willing the sensation not to spread to my arms and fingers.

I blew out a breath, imagining the heat leaving in the expired air.

My mother was talking to Rhys and tapping the top of the washing machine.

He set down his bag then placed his hands on his hips and listened to the problem. Halfway through her explanation about a funny whooshing noise, he turned to me. A smile spread and he let his gaze drift down my body, slowly, as if perusing me, taking in every detail.

The heat came back.

He *is* gay.

I knew that look. Oscar had done the same thing to me in the hotel corridor the night before. That was a man liking what he was seeing and thinking about getting down and dirty.

"I...I...would you like a cup of tea, Rhys?" I asked.

"No, I'm fine, thanks."

"You sure?"

He nodded. "An old towel would be good, in case this leaks when I take the pump out."

"Yeah. I can get that." I turned, keen to hide my hot cheeks and the bulge in my trousers.

I rushed up the stairs and pulled open the door of the linen cupboard. My cock was hardening by the second. An image of Rhys, naked, us alone in the house and all the things we could do to each other filled my mind.

"Damn it." I shoved my hand down my pants and gripped my growing shaft.

But despite my discomfort, my imagination continued to hold me hostage. I thought of his skin, soft and smooth, beneath my palm, my lips, his chest against mine. My chest against his back as I bent him over, spread his buttocks...

"Fuck!"

I'd push my cock into him, giving into what we both wanted and filling his hole. I'd be gentle to start with, then passion would take over and I'd let go of my control. He'd love it, he'd cry out for more. I'd give him everything I had to give and make us both come so hard. We'd be sweating, cursing, and crazed with pleasure.

"Darius, you got that towel?"

"Er, yep, hang on, Mom."

I grabbed one and quickly made for the bathroom. My dick ached but my chest ached more. The burn was there, a furnace inside of me. It had claimed my shoulders and was shooting down my arms.

I angled my right hand at the tub, flicked on the tap, and allowed water to splash to the base.

Gritting my teeth, I released several sparks. They tore the frustration from me. Dragging the need that was almost too much to bear into the open. As they sizzled in the water I managed a few deep breaths.

Get a grip.

My eyes were misty from the effort and my heart was thudding. But my cock, luckily, was deflating.

"Darius."

"I'm coming," I called, flicking off the water and summoning what energy I had. "Be right there." Plastering a smile on my face, I headed down the stairs. My knees were weak. "Here." I passed the towel to my mother.

"You okay?" She frowned.

"Sure. I'll stir that sauce, shall I?"

"Mmm, yes, okay."

I hadn't completely convinced her. She knew me too well. Likely I'd have to confess to releasing sparks later when we were alone. I'd probably tell her something on the shoot had wound me up. Which was true, Amy had. But I wasn't going into the details of why—that she was antsy because I wouldn't date her and wouldn't admit to being gay.

I have. To myself...and Oscar.

It's a relief.

As I stirred the pasta sauce, the landline phone rang. Mom went into the living room to take it. When I heard her say the name Nora, I knew it was going to be a long conversation.

I stared at the doorway to the utility room. Rhys was still in there.

Like a magnet I was drawn to him and I allowed myself to be, not least because I'd released sparks and felt more in control.

Control of what? My attraction to him?

I straightened my t-shirt and wandered into the utility. "Is it the pump?" I asked.

He didn't look up from where he was crouched behind the machine. "Yeah, it's blocked. Easy enough fix."

"Blocked?"

"Probably a penny or a button, they're the usual culprits."

"Oh, that's good then. I won't have to buy her another washing machine."

"You're a good son, if you buy your mother what she needs." His face appeared. He had a streak of dark grime on his right cheek.

"She provided for me for long enough."

"I guess that's true." He smiled then disappeared again.

My line of sight was drawn to his back. His shoulders were wide, his waist tapered and the tight t-shirt showed off the gutter of his spine and his defined lateral muscles.

I tensed my belly and locked my knees. Willed my cock to behave.

"Ah yes," he said. "A fifty pence piece. Got it."

"So that should be it?" I asked.

"Yeah, I'll reconnect it and give it a test. But it should have a few more years left in it."

"That's great news."

He fiddled for a minute then stood and rolled out his shoulders.

"You've got..." I gestured to his cheek.

"What?"

"Here." I wanted to wipe at the smudge of dirt but held back.

"Oh." He laughed and rubbed his cheek. "Dirty bugger, aren't I?"

"Hazard of the job."

"And what work are you in?" A smile tugged his mouth showing off his dimples again. "No, let me guess."

I raised my eyebrows. "Go on then."

"Mmm." He nipped his chin and narrowed his eyes. "Doctor?"

"No, not clever enough for that. Don't much like blood either."

"You don't?" He appeared surprised. "But you're full of it."

"Yeah. And it can stay there. Inside."

"Everyone can afford to lose a little." He licked his lips and his attention seemed to stray from my face to my neck. "How about a tattoo artist?"

"No, I'm not artistic. Well, I'm okay with photographs, I understand them."

"Ah, you're a photographer."

"You're getting warmer." I smiled, enjoying our banter and his easy way.

"In that case...looking at you now, Darius, you must be a model." His gaze landed on my watch. "Yes." He pointed at me. "I've seen you on billboards, wearing *that* Rolex."

"Yeah. You probably have." I rubbed my forearm, above the watch. "Though it's old now. There's a new style out."

"Oh, really?"

"Yeah, I'm doing a shoot for them tomorrow, in Camden. Some antiquated warehouse behind the market."

"Very funky." He nodded and looked impressed.

"Should be interesting."

He stooped and began putting his tools away. The washer was on again, water pumping with no problem.

"My mother is talking on the phone, to a friend. I'm afraid once they start they can chatter all day."

"That's okay," he said. "The washing machine is fixed. That was our main aim. Please give her my best."

"She'll be very grateful."

"Just remind her to empty her pockets before she puts clothes in there. The pump really doesn't like small objects."

"I will."

He stepped closer to me, needing to because of the small room.

I breathed in his scent again and enjoyed the near proximity of our chests, they were the same height and width.

Like upstairs, a sudden vision captured me. It was like a story, flash fiction. Us alone in the house, him on his knees taking out my cock, stroking it, sucking it, making me come down his throat.

"I hope we meet again, Darius," he said, staring into my eyes.

"I...me, too." I swallowed. My balls were tingling, pressure was building in my groin. It was as if he'd seen the vision in my head and liked it.

He smiled. "I'll let myself out."

He stepped past me, a cool gust of air going with him, and slipped on a pair of shades. I'd been right, they were high-end, Carrera, with a slim red line on the frame.

A prick of sweat popped on my brow as he disappeared from view. I leaned heavily against the wall and closed my eyes.

I knew, that night, when back in my own apartment in Chelsea, I'd masturbate again. And now, not only would I have Lloyd and Oscar to think about, I'd also conjure the image of Rhys the sexy plumber. I'd work myself to orgasm and relive all the delicious thoughts I'd had about him...and more.

Chapter Six

George

It had been years since I'd been to Camden Town. It had changed beyond recognition.

On my last visit it had been a quiet, middle class suburb. I'd gone to a music hall. It was a pleasant evening and I'd met a young man named Toby Gent. He was drunk on sherry, and had flirted shamelessly with me; his spirits high despite Queen Victoria having just passed and the nation supposedly in mourning.

We'd gone outside, around the back of the hall, found an alley and kissed. I'd made him come, with my hand, then while he was in the throes of orgasm I'd fed on him. His blood had been sweetened by the sherry, and he was clearly fond of red meat because the iron-taste was strong and heady. So delicious in fact I'd only just stopped myself from draining him dry. Temptation had been a loud cry in my head. But I *had* stopped. I didn't drain my victims unless they were going to die anyway. None of us did. Killing was something we'd all agreed to abstain from because there was enough murder in the world. We'd long since pledged, in front of Master Benedict's effigy at the Worshipful Company of the Ancient Order that we'd respect human life.

After glancing at my pocket watch, I picked my way through the market. The sun was out and the sellers fussed over their wares—slogan t-shirts, London memorabilia, designer knock-offs. The air was full of the scents of street food, and a gull scrabbled on a fence with a half eaten burger bun. I was jostled several times, and always tipped my flat cap in apology, even though it wasn't my fault.

The truth was not much could have gotten me down today, even the crowded market street. It was my turn to meet the cambion, Darius Linnet, and I was impatient to do so.

When Rhys had returned from his guard over Darius late last night, reporting that he'd gone to a swanky apartment in Chelsea, alone, I used his information to make the necessary arrangements for today.

Darius was likely learning right now that Rolex had pulled from the shoot at the warehouse. Instead his agency now had a gig for him with a popular gin company. I smiled at how easy it had been. A few hacks, a couple of emails, a phone call and the company had changed to one that needed two male models and I, too, had myself a job.

It was my turn to keep an eye on our handsome key holder today, and I intended to keep him very close, as close as possible.

I located the warehouse tucked behind the market and found its discreet front door. It was no longer in use for storage and was for sale. The agency Darius was contracted with had sought permission for today's shoot from the current owner. I liked it, it had a nice feel. Reminded me of how the area used to be.

I pressed the buzzer.

A tinny reply came almost immediately. "Hello."

"It's George Bartlett, from the agency. You're expecting me for the gin shoot."

"Ah yes, of course. Come in."

The door clicked open and I stepped into the musty hallway.

After securing it closed again, I glanced around. This section appeared to be offices.

"George."

I glanced upward. A woman stood there, the same one who'd buzzed me in, I presumed. "Hi." I touched the tip of my cap.

"Come on up, we'll be starting soon."

"Certainly."

I took the steps two at a time.

When I came level with her she was studying me. "I think you'll go very nicely with our other male model, I can see why the agency sent you."

"You do?" I smiled and my gaze drifted to a vein in her temple. It stood a little proud and was kinked upward.

"Yes, you both have that sharp, pale look. Still very handsome of course." She smiled and pushed her hair over her shoulders.

"I'm glad you're pleased." I'd been told I was handsome for centuries. This was not news, but I still liked to hear it. And if I complimented Darius, then all the better.

"Make-up is through here," she said. "Everyone else is on set, so don't dawdle, get the costume on and join us ASAP."

"Certainly ma'am."

"Oh, call me Jane." She grinned and scooped up a clipboard. "I'm representing Loyalty and Deceit, by the way."

I didn't reply, even though I knew full well what she was talking about.

"The gin. The two brands we're getting shots for today." She raised her eyebrows.

"Of course." I gestured forward. "I'll go and get ready."

Twenty-five minutes later, I'd had my face made-up, my dark hair scraped back and off my face, and I was wearing a white toga over my white underwear.

I'd worn a toga before, in Rome, not long after I'd turned. It had felt right then. Donning one in Camden was strange.

I spotted the set surrounded by lights and foil reflectors. It was a bed laden with silvery silk sheets and piled high with white velvet pillows. Several people milled around; the photographer, Jane, assistants, and a willowy female model also in a toga, but hers was a very tight body-hugging one.

My attention didn't linger on her. It homed in on the man I'd really come to see.

Darius Linnet.

Like me he wore a toga and his hair had been styled the same as mine. He was beautiful, his face the stuff of fantasies, his body one of dreams. I paused as a wave of awe washed through me.

He's the one.

I knew it. Without a doubt. The others had been right. This was the cambion we'd been searching the globe for. This was the half man, half demon who would save our souls.

Hopefully.

Suddenly he turned to me, as if sensing me staring at him.

His eyes widened and his mouth fell open then he closed it again.

I managed to unglue myself from the floor and walked up to him, ignoring the photographer who was barking at his assistant in a gruff voice.

"Good day," I said, holding out my hand to Darius. "I'm George Bartlett. It appears we're working together."

"Darius Linnet, pleasure to meet you."

He was scanning my face, drinking me in. What was he seeing? And did he like it?

His pupils were wide, and I could make out a pulse in his neck fluttering beneath the surface of his skin.

"Thought I was doing a Rolex shoot today," he said, giving my hand a brief shake. "But it got changed. Unusual to be so last minute."

I slid my fingers over my palm, the spot he'd just held. "It was a sudden call up for me. Luckily I don't live too far away."

"No? Where have you come from?"

"Only Highgate." Truth was, our flat was south of the Thames, but Darius didn't need to know that. Not yet anyway.

"This should be interesting, though," he said. "This gin company seems inventive."

"Loyalty and Deceit." I nodded at his toga and took the opportunity to admire his wide shoulders, perfect skin and the gentle bulge of his biceps. "Interesting combination."

"Hi, you must be our third." The female model shoved herself in front of Darius and gripped my hand. "I'm Amy."

"Hi, Amy." I kept the irritation from my face. After so long looking for Darius, I didn't take kindly to our first conversation being interrupted.

"Oh, you're cold," she said, snapping her hand back.

"Togas are not known for their warmth."

"That's true. But usually I get hot under these lights." She turned to Darius, then leaned close and whispered something in his ear.

"Shut up," Darius said to her with a frown.

She giggled and shrugged. "Just saying."

"Amy, come here please," Jane called.

"What was that about?" I asked, even though I already knew. My hearing was acute, very little could be said within a hundred yards without me catching it. She'd told Darius I was just his type, that he should make a move.

"Nothing, come on, let's get on with this." Darius scowled.

This was interesting. From what he'd told Oscar on the plane, Darius was only just admitting his attraction to guys. Yet this model was teasing him about it, so she obviously knew.

Is he close to her?

"Good, we're ready," Jane said. She nodded at the photographer—a hugely obese man with a gray beard, and hair pulled back into a low ponytail. He wore a tracksuit that could have been bought in the eighties. "This is Mario, he's the shoot photographer today. He's worked with all the big brands, Nike, L'Oreal, Cartier, to name a few and we're thrilled to have him working for Bernard Gin." She paused. "So, our main aim is to get two completely different shots for two completely different gins. Loyalty is a refreshing, simple flavor that can always be relied upon. We're going for the angel image. Thanks to the power of Photoshop you'll all have halos and wings added into the final shots." She pointed at the bed. "You two guys are both in love with Amy. She's the perfect woman, your day and night, your moon, your stars, your everything. You'd die for her. We need lots of adoring looks, wistful eyes, longing caresses for the Loyalty ad."

I looked at Amy. She was examining her nails. I wondered how good of a model she was. She didn't seem interested.

"And for Deceit we want dark, seductive, danger," Jane went on. "This drink is rich and heavy, with notes of spice and chocolate. We'll have different outfits, devilish horns added by Photoshop. Amy and Darius will be on the bed, George at the front not seeing them together behind his back. I'll want you touching, kissing, looking as close as a couple can be."

"Let's concentrate on the first picture." The photographer lifted his camera. "Come on, models, all on the bed."

As I wandered to the bed and sat on the soft mattress, I glanced around. I had to remember my main role here was to protect Darius. His father was dangerous, and if my past conversations with Master Concorde were anything to go by, he was likely getting ready to make a move on his son.

But the room was full of humans getting on with their day jobs, so I relaxed and adopted a pose beside Amy, my arm wrapped around her and gazing at her face as though I worshipped her.

Darius did the same, our hands brushing.

I wished Amy wasn't there. I wished no one was there so I could get to know Darius better, learn everything there was to know about him. I wanted to kiss him, hold him, protect him for all of time.

He cleared his throat and shot me a funny look.

I was stroking my thumb against the delicate inside of his wrist. I stopped. Damn it. He was irresistible. I was drawn to him. My body craved his.

"Guys, you're doing great, don't move." The photographer pointed at Amy. "But come on, girl, you're with your two adoring lovers. You'd trust them with your life. They're faithful little puppies who do anything you ask."

She rolled her shoulders, cupped Darius's chin and rested her hand on my arm.

"Better." The photographer took a few shots. "Now relax your jaw, Amy, you know these men love you, no need for clenching, dear."

I held my position, struggling to keep my gaze on Amy's face when all I really wanted to do was stare at Darius.

I could look at his face forever.

Eventually, and with a sigh, the photographer declared the first image captured.

As he showed Jane the screen of his camera, I stood and stretched out my back. I was glad this wasn't my day job; one experience of being a model would likely be enough.

"We should get changed," Darius said, linking his fingers, then turning his palms to me and stretching out his arms and shoulders. I got a flash of his dark brown underarm hair.

"Yeah, come on." I led the way to the make-up room where I'd seen a rail of clothing.

Two make-up ladies were chatting about babies and pregnancy when we arrived.

"Got the next outfit, Gina?" Darius asked.

"Sure, hon, here you go." She passed him a pair of black silk boxers with a red stripe around the waistband. "And one for you, George."

"Er, thanks." I studied the garment. I was more of a traditional type of guy when it came to clothing. A nice tweed jacket, a pair of pipe-pants, and a waistcoat suited me very well.

"Not as substantial as the toga," Darius said, slipping off his white fold of material.

"Er, no, it isn't."

The make-up lady reached for his toga, then turned back to her friend.

Darius shoved at his underwear. Just like that. Bold as brass he pushed his white boxers to his ankles.

It took a lot to render me speechless. After three centuries I figured I'd just about seen it all. But the sight of Darius's naked body was like a punch to the gut. It stole my breath and made my usually cold skin prickle.

From a patch of trimmed pubic hair his cock hung flaccid. But even so I could tell it was thick and would be long when erect.

I clenched my ass and my balls tightened.

His legs were lean but strong, a little hairy on his calves but not so much on his thighs. He straightened and I got a full frontal view as he pulled the boxers up, covering his cock and setting the waistband over his bricked abdominal muscles. Knowing I was staring, but unable to help myself, I took in his smooth, broad chest, his small dark nipples and the column of his neck.

When I got to his face, I found him staring straight back at me.

"I'm...I'm..." I started.

He glanced at the make-up artists who were taking no notice of us as we changed. "You're gay," he said quietly.

I nodded. "Yes, but please accept my apologies for staring. It was out of order."

"So why did you?"

I swallowed. Normally I was the epitome of control. But now... "You're..." I hesitated. "You're perfect, Darius."

He smiled, and something I couldn't put my finger on flashed in his eyes. "We look similar. Doesn't that mean you're perfect too?"

I wasn't sure what to say to that, which unnerved me as I always knew what to say.

"For the record," he said, leaning closer. "I'm gay too." I'd felt his warm breath wash over my cheek as he'd spoken. I wanted him closer, his lips on me, his hands.

I also wanted to ask if I was his type, the way Amy had suggested, but I didn't. If Darius really was only just coming out, I didn't want to scare him away.

"We should get back to the shoot." He nodded at my toga. "They'll be waiting."

"Yes. I'll get changed." I loosened the material at my waist.

"I'll see you in there." He walked away.

For a moment I watched him, mesmerized by the shape of his back and the gentle orbs of his buttocks, then I dragged at my underwear and switched it for the black silk boxers. It was only then I removed the toga.

"Here, I'll take that," the make-up artist said. She peered at my face. "You haven't sweated, your make-up will do."

"Thanks."

Wearing only the silky boxers, and feeling decidedly underdressed in a room full of people, I went back to the set.

Darius and Amy were on the bed, Jane fussing about their positions; Darius flat on his back, Amy hovering over him. Jane spotted me. "On the stool please, George. You're going to have to look neutral, as if you have no idea what's going on behind you, and grab that drink to hold."

I glanced at Darius.

He was staring straight at me.

I'd sell my soul to be on the bed with him right now, in Amy's place.

It would have taken very little effort to clear the room. One show of my fangs, a few super-human moves throwing furniture around and I'd have Darius alone. But that would terrify him, and as Lloyd had said, there was a possibility he'd turn skittish, disappear and we'd be back at square one.

"Amy, let your weight drop onto Darius a bit more."

"I'm worried I'll squash him."

"You're light as a feather," Darius said.

"And he's a man," Jane added. "He can handle a woman on top of him."

Amy raised her eyebrows at Darius.

He frowned.

"Stop! Stop! This is all wrong." The photographer pushed past me. "You, girl, up here, get on the stool."

"What are you doing?" Jane said, scowling at him.

"You pay me for my artistic genius as much as for my camera, right?"

"Yes, of course."

"Then trust me." The photographer pointed at me. "You get on the bed, with the other guy. Girl model, sit on this stool holding the drink." He turned back to Jane who was looking unsure. "This will work much better. I mean, what worse deceit for a woman with two lovers than to find out they're fucking each other behind her back?"

Jane rubbed her bottom lip and glanced between me and Darius.

A thrill went through me. I was going to switch places with Amy.

"It's a much better twist," the photographer said. "We'll try it, if you don't like it we'll go back to the original plan."

"Okay." Jane nodded. "I do like it."

I slipped over to the bed, passing Amy who now wore a scowl. She'd obviously enjoyed being up close and personal with Darius.

Who wouldn't?

I crawled onto the bed, anticipation rushing through me.

Darius hadn't moved, he was on his back, his head on pillows so his profile was to the camera and his arms at his sides.

"Hey," I said.

He swallowed and then smiled.

"You okay?"

"Yeah." His attention drifted over my torso, settling on the silk boxer shorts.

Fuck, don't do that, I'll get hard.

"Right then." Jane stepped up to the bed. "George, can you lie between Darius's legs, the way Amy was, and rest your chest on his. That way you'll look super connected and we'll get shots of you staring into each other's eyes."

"Yes, I need lust and longing, desire, desperation," the photographer said, his enthusiasm for the shoot apparently growing. "The forbidden touch is always the sweetest, we all thrive on danger."

I moved between Darius's legs. His skin was deliciously warm against mine. Our groins touched, then our abs and finally our chests.

My asshole quivered as I stared into his beautiful eyes. A dragging sensation pinched at my balls and my cock stirred.

"Fuck," he muttered.

"What's up?"

"Something will be."

I smiled and lowered my head. "Just think, we're getting paid for this."

"That's it," the photographer shouted, "perfect, lips hovering but not quite kissing. Hold that pose."

After several seconds, I decided to ad lib and stroked my hand up Darius's arm, absorbing his heat, as I kept my lips a whisper from his. He smelled of soap and blood, a little of charcoal too, I guessed that was the fire in him.

"Model underneath, pull your knees up higher. Grip your lover. Clasp him like you've been waiting to do this all day, biding your time until your femme fatale was out of sight. Let's crank up the temperature. You might get away with it in some magazines, Jane."

"Yes, good, yes...indeed." Jane sounded as excited as I felt.

Darius did as instructed, locking me to him with his inner thighs and knees.

The camera clicked away as the photographer moved nearer.

I held in a groan. My cock was hardening rapidly.

So was his.

I stared at him, our noses almost touching. The urge to kiss him was getting stronger, as was the urge to grind against him, work us both to a frenzy of pleasure.

"Amy, hold the drink higher, stare into space," Jane said. "This is great, keep at it, boys. You look like you're totally in love and lust."

Fuck, lust was taking over. I clenched my ass and pushed into his groin so our hard cocks slid over each other.

He gasped against my mouth. His heart was thudding. I could not only feel it against my chest, I could hear it too.

My mouth watered and my fangs tingled. I wanted to feed and fuck. Damn it, I wanted to fuck. I was becoming mindless with want. Primitive urges were in danger of taking over, both my vampire ones and my needs as a male.

"George," he whispered, the word breathy and quiet.

"Keep still," I said, my lips brushing his, "nearly there."

"Good, yes, that's it." The photographer clapped. "Super work, we'll see what we've got but I don't think anything is going to beat that last shot, you look utterly lost in your own world, the female in the shot is irrelevant to you. And by the time we edit your devil horns in, peeking from your hair, just super. Brilliant."

I tore my attention from Darius.

The photographer was grinning, his beard wobbling. "You guys are hot together. There's tension, interest and wow, some serious sexual chemistry."

Jane rushed to the photographer. "Let me see. Are they as good as I think they're going to be?"

"Hell yeah."

I turned back to Darius. His eyes were sparkling, and the pulse in his cock was vibrating through to my shaft.

"I'm hard," he whispered.

"I can tell."

"I'm sorry."

"Don't be. In case you hadn't noticed, I've got a full blown erection going on too."

He swiped his tongue over his lips. "I *had* noticed." He paused. A rise of color was blooming on his cheeks, beneath his set make-up. "We should move...the shoot is over."

"I don't want to." I smiled. I could stay here all day. Holding my breath, I risked another small push over him.

Pleasure shot through my cock. It must have his, too, because he fluttered his eyes closed and moaned.

"Hey, guys, it's a wrap, in case you hadn't noticed." Amy stood at the side of us with her hands on her hips. "Time to stop doing whatever it is you're doing."

I clenched my jaw. Sometimes it was hard to stick to the rules and not drain humans dry, especially when they were so fucking annoying.

"Yeah, we're getting up now," Darius said, his voice hoarse. He turned to look at her. "Are the pictures good?"

"Good?" she said with a huff. "They're going to set magazines and billboards on fire."

"Fire," Darius repeated, touching my shoulders. "Set...on...fire."

I thought of the sparks Lloyd had seen leaving his fingertips and wondered how they'd feel splashing onto my flesh.

"Yeah, hurry up, you two lover boys can take me to lunch." Amy turned and stalked away, her heels clacking on the hard floor.

Lunch with Amy. Not a chance. I pushed her from my thoughts and smiled down at Darius. I gave in to the urge to touch his hair and stroked a lock hanging over his ear. It was heavy with product but still silky soft. "We really should go and get changed." I wondered if he'd hear the reluctance in my tone.

"Are you kidding? Stand up and let everyone see my boxers tented? I'll look like I've got a banana down there."

"I feel your pain."

A muscle flexed in his jawline, then, "I feel *you*."

"Would you like to feel more?" I whispered. "Forget lunch. We could go somewhere private and I could bend you over and take us both to places that'll feel so damn good we'll forget our own names." I paused. "I'll make you come so hard, Darius."

A flash of excitement seared over his eyes, but then his lips thinned as he flattened them together and turned away.

Damn it. I've pushed too far.

He shoved at me, forcing me to lift from between his legs.

He rolled to his side, knees half drawn up to hide his groin.

"Here." A make-up lady appeared, holding two black robes.

"Thanks." Darius grabbed for his and pulled it on, remaining hunched as he did so.

"I'm sorry," I said. "I just thought—"

He glanced over his shoulder at me. "You thought wrong."

Chapter Seven

Darius

I stared at the framed photograph on the wall of my expensive Chelsea flat. It was of me. I was in Prague on a shoot. I especially liked it. Wenceslas Square was ornate, so much to look at, and the moody black and white shot captured a moment in time. Passers-by went about their business and street artists performed in the distance while I posed, face held to the sky, wearing the latest trendy suit from a high-end designer.

Many of my shots I could take or leave, they were of me, what I saw in the mirror. But Prague had been a great place to visit, and the picture reminded me of it.

I sighed, my thoughts drifting back to George as they had done since I'd met him earlier that day. He was devilishly handsome and he spoke nicely too, confident and sophisticated, with a well to-do accent that suited the way he carried himself. As he'd been nestled between my legs he'd offered me everything I'd been thinking of. Promised to make my fantasies come true. Yet I'd turned him down, walked away. Been quite rude probably.

All afternoon I'd had a semi-erect cock. My first experience of feeling another hard shaft against mine was not something I could forget in a hurry.

I turned from the picture, my thoughts in a jumble. It wasn't just George stealing them, tugging my fantasies and dreams, it was also Lloyd, sexy and mysterious and unperturbed by my sparks. Brooding biker Oscar who'd been the first person I'd ever told I was gay. Then cute Rhys who'd made me think of doing deliciously sinful things to him, *and* made me think he wanted them as much as me.

Damn it, there were four men in my daydreams. What did that make me? A tart? A male gigolo?

"Get a grip," I muttered, wandering into the kitchen. I poured a glass of red wine, it was gone six so perfectly acceptable.

As I took a second sip, my cell trilled to life. The screen flashed Lloyd – Paris, which was what I'd saved him as.

My heart rate picked up. My belly clenched. I was aware of my breath heating in my lungs.

"Hey," I said, trying to sound casual.

"Darius, it's me, Lloyd. You remember, we met in Paris."

"Of course." I paused. "How are you?"

"Okay. Well, actually I'm at a loose end, wondered if you fancied meeting up this evening."

"This evening?"

"No time like the present."

I glanced around my pristine but empty flat. It wasn't as if I had any plans other than watching television. In fact I had nothing going on until the following afternoon when I was doing a shoot in Notting Hill. "I guess you're right."

"I'm not sure where you live, Darius, but right now I'm near Sloane Square. How would that suit?"

Sloane Square was only a short stroll away. "Sure, that'll work."

"Great, there's a bar there, The Pig and Pickle. Shall we say seven?"

"Seven is cool with me." A swirl of anticipation gripped my belly. "I'll see you then."

I ended the call and stared at the screen. Had I just arranged a date with a handsome man I'd met in Paris?

Or was he only seeking friendship?

I hoped not.

He did say I was beautiful.

I tugged my plain white t-shirt off and headed to the shower, undoing my Levi's as I went. If this was my moment, my chance to connect with a guy the way I truly wanted to, I needed to get ready.

An hour later I stood outside The Pig and Pickle. It was a traditional old red brick pub brimming with colorful hanging baskets, and with wooden benches on the pavement outside. The lead paned windows were high, giving no indication as to what was going on inside.

I pushed through the green door and paused for a moment to let my eyes adjust to the dim light.

The bar was polished and set with drafts. There were a few guys sipping beer and talking to a barman. Several patrons sat at tables and two booths were occupied, one with a group, the other with a couple. The farthest booth only contained one occupant.

Lloyd.

Like before he was dressed in a dark hoody, this time the sleeves were shoved up his forearms and the hood was down. Before him sat what looked like a pint of cola.

I nodded and walked toward him, trying to beat down the nerves growing in my guts. He was such a good looking guy. With his crew cut blond hair, his wide, kissable mouth, and blue eyes, he could easily have signed with my agency.

"Hey," he said, making no move as I approached.

"Hi." I stood at the head of the table and twisted my denim jacket between my hands. "Do you, er, need a drink?"

"Nah, I've just got this one."

It didn't appear touched.

"Ah, okay, I'll get one then."

I decided to copy Lloyd and bought a pint of cola. I'd gotten the impression he avoided alcohol, and if he had a problem I didn't want to tempt him or exacerbate it.

Once seated opposite Lloyd, I tried to relax by releasing a breath and willing my core temperature to settle.

"You got back to London okay, then," he said.

"Yeah, easy flight."

"Marvellous to be able to hop around the globe the way we do these days, don't you think?"

"I can't imagine a life without air travel."

He smiled a little. "You've been all over then? With your job."

"Yes, I've been very lucky."

"You got a favorite place?"

I took a sip of my drink.

He spun his around on the small cardboard beer mat it sat on.

"I suppose." I thought for a second. "Some of the European cities are amazing, Prague, Barcelona, Berlin."

"You're a city guy?"

"For now. Maybe when I get older I'll buy a flat cap and live in the countryside with a couple of Labradors."

He chuckled. "I can see you in a flat cap."

"I've worn pretty much everything in my line of work. Today it was a toga."

"Now that I would have liked to see."

His gaze slipped downward, as if imagining me in it.

I squirmed on the seat, remembering George and how he'd looked so regal and hot in his outfit, as though it was something he was used to swanning about in.

"So what was the shoot for today?" Lloyd asked.

"Turned out to be different from what I'd expected."

He nodded and waited for me to go on.

"It was for a gin company, they've got two flavors which represent loyalty and deceit."

"So they had you doing what?" He pushed his drink to the side and leaned forward, his elbows on the table.

I studied his eyes. Like before, in Paris, his face was in partial shadow owing to the low lighting at the back of the pub, but that didn't detract from his appeal.

"I was with another male model and a female, they had us..." I swallowed as I remembered my cock in alignment with George's.

"Go on." He licked his lips.

"They had us on a bed, me and...him...were her loyal admirers for the first shot, and then..." I clenched my ass cheeks. My cock was swelling again. "And then it was just us guys on the bed for the deceit bit."

"So you two were an item?"

"That's what the image is supposed to say."

"And were you still in togas for the second shot?"

I shook my head.

"What then?"

"Black silk boxers."

His mouth slipped into wide smile and his eyes narrowed. "I'd give good money to see you in black silk boxers, Darius."

Whoa.

Okay, that confirmed my suspicions and what I'd hoped this evening was. Lloyd was gay, he was attracted to me, and this *was* a date.

"So who was the other model?" he asked. "Anyone famous?"

"No, new on the scene from what I gathered, but very professional." If getting a hard on and offering to bend me over and forget my own name was professional.

"What's he called?"

"George." I shrugged. "There's lots of models on the circuit though, all gorgeous."

"He's gorgeous?" Lloyd raised his eyebrows.

"Of course, he's a model. But chances of me bumping into him again are slim."

"I dunno. It's a small world." He reached over and touched my right hand with the tips of his fingers. "I've been thinking about what I saw that night we met."

I straightened. "You have?"

"Yeah, those sparks. How the Hell did you do it? A magic trick or something."

I laughed, though it sounded tense even to my own ears. "A magic trick, yep, you caught me."

He traced his finger over my knuckles, his cool touch sending shivers of pleasure up my arm. "You can trust me, Darius. I understand about being different, about living a life less ordinary."

"You do?"

"Yeah." He glanced to the left. "And talking of small worlds, that's my cousin, Rhys, over there."

I turned, but even as I did I had a sense of who'd walked into The Pig and Pickle.

Rhys Muller, the sweet guy who'd fixed my mother's washing machine the day before.

"Rhys," I repeated. "Again."

"You know him?" Lloyd's eyebrows raised, but for some reason I didn't think he seemed that surprised.

"Er, not really."

Lloyd shrugged. "Hey, Rhys!"

Rhys turned and instantly a cute smile grew on his face. "Hi." He pointed between us. "Anyone need a drink?"

Lloyd glanced at my near full drink. "Nah, we're good."

"Do you have lots of family living nearby?" I asked Lloyd.

"No, just Rhys, a few mates and that, but my parents are long dead."

"I'm sorry to hear that."

"It really was a long time ago." Again he swirled his untouched drink on the beer mat. "So how do you know Rhys?"

"He fixed my mom's washing machine yesterday. It was very kind of him."

"He's a kind person." Lloyd was quiet for a moment, then. "You said in Paris your mother raised you alone. Does that mean you know nothing about your father?"

"My father." I was surprised by the question but not offended. "Yeah."

"No, I don't know much. My mother speaks very little of him." I paused and felt a familiar crease form between my eyebrows, as it often did when I thought of my father. "It's almost as if she barely knew him."

"That's the way sometimes."

"I guess. She told me once it was a one-night stand, but I never understood why she didn't find him when she discovered she was pregnant."

"Some people are hard to find."

"More than hard, impossible. She gave me nothing to go on other than the name Mammon. No profession, no nationality, no rough address." I clicked my tongue on the roof of my mouth. "It was worse than looking for a needle in a haystack, it was like trying to find one drop of blood in all the oceans of the world."

"Blood," he repeated. "Yeah, I suppose that would be hard to sniff out. One drop in an ocean."

"Sniff out?"

"Yeah, you know." He grinned. "Like a shark."

"Why are you talking about sharks?" Rhys appeared holding a bottle of beer.

"Ah, nothing," Lloyd said. "Join us."

"Thanks."

I'd expected Rhys to slip onto the bench next to his cousin, but he didn't, he slid in beside me, his shoulder brushing mine, and his leg a hair's breadth from my thigh beneath the table.

He wore the same sexy cologne he'd had on the day before and I breathed deep, aware that my cock was still gently pushing against the material of my pants. Not a full-blown erection, but hardly soft either.

Rhys set his drink down. "Washing machine okay?"

"I don't know. I don't live with my mother." I chuckled. "And I haven't had chance to speak to her yet today, but I'm sure it is."

"You been busy today then?" Rhys asked.

"He's been on a shoot, some sexy advert for gin called Loyalty and Deceit," Lloyd said. "Required him to wear nothing but silk boxers."

Rhys nodded slowly and his gaze slid down my torso as if imagining me wearing just that. "I'll look forward to seeing the finished shots."

The heat I'd been managing to contain spread to my cheeks and a tingle ran over my scalp. It wasn't anything I couldn't handle so I allowed myself to enjoy the sensation. Sitting here, with two handsome guys—two handsome *gay* guys—hadn't been something I'd planned at the beginning of the week. But I wasn't complaining, especially as they both appeared to fancy me.

I fancy them both!

I cleared my throat. "Where do you live, Rhys?"

"Not far from here. Means I often bump into Lloyd."

Lloyd nodded.

I took a deep drink, glad of the sweet, cool cola on my tongue.

A sudden tune rang out. Rhys tugged a cell phone from the back pocket of his jeans.

As he answered it I caught a glimpse of the screen.

George.

"Hey," he said, pressing it to his ear. "Yeah, all good." He paused. "As planned."

George. It was a name I didn't come across in guys of my generation. Was it the George I'd met today? The man who'd turned me on so much with his body and his words I'd struggled to walk.

"Okay, yes, I'll do that. See you soon." Rhys stood.

"Something up?" Lloyd asked.

"No. Got an errand to run for the boss, that's all."

Lloyd didn't appear surprised, and he sat back, arms folded. "Okay, see you around."

Rhys nodded at him then turned to me. "It was really great to see you again, Darius, and hear about your day." He smiled so wide his dimples dented his cheeks. "Perhaps we can meet up again, here."

"Sure. I'd like that." As I'd spoken the words I glanced at Lloyd. Would he object? I did appear to be on a date with him after all.

"Cool." Rhys set his hand on my shoulder and squeezed. His fingers were cool and strong and there seemed to be genuine affection in the touch.

And then he was gone.

Lloyd leaned forward again. "I'm glad we're alone."

"You are?"

"Yeah. Call me selfish, but I found you, I want you to myself."

My mouth dried as I watched him lick his lips. I had an urge to grip his hoody and drag him near, kiss him, shove my tongue into his mouth and discover the flavor of a hot, sexy man.

"Let's get out of here," he said, shoving his full drink to one side.

"Where?"

He stood. "Let's walk. The sun has nearly set."

"The sun?"

"Yeah, the heat has gone from the day."

"It's only March, hardly hot." I laughed.

"I don't like to be hot." He shrugged. "For the record, beach holidays are not for me."

"Ah, now I like a nice beach, a hammock, a few palm trees swaying in the breeze."

"Perhaps I'd find a way to cope, if you were there." He winked.

I smiled and followed him from the bar, admiring his wide shoulders and the slight sway of his hips. He drew a couple of glances, as did I, and for once I didn't mind. We were a handsome couple.

We ambled away from the hustle and bustle of Sloane Square and found a park which hadn't been locked up for the night. After sitting on a dark bench chatting about the trees and the wildlife I checked my watch. I wanted to move the evening on…but not too much. I wasn't quite ready for what George had suggested, I knew that about myself.

"I should get going," I said, standing. "Work tomorrow."

"I'll see you home." He, too, rose.

"I'll be okay. It's only a short walk."

He set me with his gaze. It was full of grim determination. "I'll see you home, Darius."

I chuckled. "I'm not a girl, you know, I can look out for myself."

"I can see you're not a girl." He reached forward and cupped my jawline with his palm. "Though if you were, for the record, it's you I like, what's inside *you*."

"You do?" I whispered, staring into his eyes.

"Yeah, a lot."

"I like you, too."

"That will make this so much easier then." He smiled and dropped his hand. "Come on, I've also got a lot on tomorrow."

We started to walk, Lloyd talking about his job, hunting for missing people. It was all a bit vague but I wasn't complaining, I simply enjoyed listening to his deep voice.

Only once on the stroll home did the other men enter my mind, Oscar, George and Rhys, and I wondered what they were doing. Would Oscar call me? Did fate have another meeting for George and I planned, and would I take him up on any wild, naked offers he made? And sweet Rhys, did he visit The Pig and Pickle often?

Stop it.

I berated myself. Here I was with Lloyd and thinking of other men. It wasn't acceptable.

We reached my apartment block. The entrance was lit but to the right was a set of bushes circling a bike park. I orchestrated it so we used that path to the entrance.

Once in the shadows, by a darkened wall, I halted.

Lloyd turned to me, the glow of a distant street lamp sliding over his features.

"Thank you," I said, quietly. "I had a nice time tonight."

He stepped closer, so close our chests practically touched. "I can make it nicer," he said, sliding his fingers over my cheeks and into my hair so he cradled my head. "If you'll let me."

I knew what he wanted. I wanted it too.

I held my breath. My first kiss. It was time. I nodded.

He slanted his soft lips over mine, they were cool from the night air and held a hint of tobacco.

I moaned and clung to his hoody. His grip on me was strong and possessive. It thrilled a part of me deep down inside.

His tongue found mine. We set up a crazy dance, our chins touching, my breaths coming fast.

Feeling bolder, I slid my hands around his waist and drew him nearer.

Our bellies and groins touched.

The second that happened a flame flickered to life inside of me. Heat welled. Blood shot to my cock, filling it hard and fast.

"Darius," he murmured, clutching my left buttock and dragging me against him. "I want you so bad."

I didn't answer. I was lost to the sensation of our cocks touching through material. I ground my hips, thrusting for more.

"Fuck." He kissed me again. There was a wildness to it. He was as frantic as me.

I clenched my buttocks. The pressure was building and I thrust against him. Soon I'd come. I didn't care.

Our kisses were crazy, almost animalistic. He backed me against the wall, my shoulders slamming against the hard bricks. I was glad of the cool surface on my burning body.

"We need to fuck," he said.

"Yes…no…I'm not ready." I didn't want that, this was all happening so fast. I would want it, but not yet.

"You feel like you're ready," he said. "Damn it, I'm going to come in my pants."

I pulled back and stared at him, though I didn't stop rubbing my cock against his. "Do it, let's come like this."

"Fuck. Okay."

Now that we'd agreed to it, the tempo picked up, as did the franticness of our dry humping. He kissed me, dragging his tongue over mine, our teeth clashing.

And then it was there. My balls tightened, my body was on fire, bright lights flashed and I gave in to a breath-stealing release.

I groaned, pulled my mouth from his and let my head fall back against the wall. My arms ached. They were full of sparks, my fingertips tingled, but I kept the power in, held onto it.

"Ah, yeah, yeah…" he gasped, his mouth trailing over my cheek to my neck. He bashed his cock against mine, shoving it upward in the same movement. A warm sticky wetness filled my boxers.

I was aware of a nip on my neck, a sharpness.

"No." I shoved at him. "No hickies."

"Darius," he gasped, his weight pinning me to the wall. "Just one, I've waited so long for you."

"I mean it." I was panting. "I've got a shoot tomorrow. They'll sue my ass if I turn up with a big suction mark on my neck."

He stared at me. "I can think of other things I'd like to do to your ass other than sue it."

I was breathing fast. A tremble attacked me. "I'd like that."

"When?"

"Give me time. I've only just admitted to myself I want this." I ran my hand over his chest. "That I want a man."

"Can that man be me?"

I swallowed, thinking of the other three guys.

He raised his eyebrows. "Darius, are there other men in your life?"

"I...oh fuck." I paused. "There's no one else like you, but..."

He didn't speak.

I thought of Oscar. "There is someone else I said I'd go out with."

He stroked my cheek. "That's cool with me, so long as we're straight with each other. I have no problem sharing you."

"Have you got anyone else?" I knew I had no claim, but I hoped he didn't.

He shook his head and his gaze bore into mine. "There's only you, Darius. Believe it or not, you're everything I've been searching for and everything I'll ever need."

My chest tightened. He'd spoken with such surety and conviction.

"But right now." He stepped away.

I missed his weight against me.

"I need to go and..." He plucked at the front of his black jeans. "And clean myself up."

Chapter Eight

Rhys

I stood within the branches of a laurel bush holding Darius's forgotten denim jacket. The leaves were thick and glossy and in the dark of the night gave good cover.

Lloyd—the lucky bastard—was ending his evening on a high with the cambion. Right now he had him pressed up against the wall of his apartment block, dry humping him.

My cock was stiffening just watching them. I wanted that with Darius. I'd met him twice and each time fallen a bit more for him. He was handsome and elegant, but also witty, intelligent, and had a strong sense of fairness and willingness to do good. Being in his mother's house with him confirmed this. She was a decent woman and had passed that onto him, not just in his genes but also in his upbringing.

They were talking now, Lloyd and Darius. I didn't know what about, my hearing wasn't as acute as George's. But it was okay, Lloyd would fill me in on the details if necessary.

Lloyd pulled back and tugged at his jeans. I didn't envy him the sticky wetness in his pants.

"Goodnight," Darius said, his voice catching on a breeze and bringing with it his scent.

Lloyd nodded and walked my way.

Darius watched him for a few seconds, then turned and slipped into his apartment building.

"Hey," Lloyd said, drawing level with me.

"Looks like you had fun."

He chuckled. "As much fun as I can have with my clothes on."

"He didn't want more?"

"He's still getting used to having admitted his attraction to men. We can't rush him into bed."

"But we can give him some experiences, right?"

"Of course. So long as we don't scare him away."

"Did he mention me, Oscar, George?"

"He confessed there was someone else he'd promised a date to. I'm guessing that's Oscar."

"Lucky Oscar."

Lloyd pressed his hand on my shoulder. "Rhys, sharpen up. Who is standing here now, with Darius's coat?" He paused and tipped his head. "Go see him. Use it as an excuse to knock on his door."

"He's had enough of us for one day. I'll give him this when he comes out in the morning."

Lloyd huffed. "Whatever. Have a good night, and keep your eyes and ears peeled. His father could appear at any time."

"I know that."

Lloyd adjusted his stance and pulled a face. "I need a shower. I'll see you tomorrow."

"Sure."

Once alone in the shadows, I pulled Darius's coat to my face and inhaled his scent. My belly tightened and the longing that had been there since I'd first laid eyes on him dragged at my cock.

'Go see him.'

Lloyd's words came back to me.

Maybe I should give in to what I wanted. It wasn't like me to be shy or reserved. I took what I desired wherever I was in the world. I seduced who I needed to in order to secure a feed. I won over anyone I had a hunger for. A cute smile, dimples and a body to die for—how ironic was that—could get those results.

I stepped from the bush and stared up at apartment twelve. There was one light on, and I wondered if Darius was in the shower.

If so, I want to join him.

That thought spurred me on. I stepped up to the entrance and pressed the buzzer, hoping he'd answer.

He did.

"Hello."

"Hi, Darius. It's me, Rhys."

A pause, then, "Oh, hi Rhys."

"I've got your jacket, you left it at The Pig and Pickle. I went back later and the landlord gave it to me, figured we knew each other."

"I did? He did?" Pause. "Yeah, you're right. Hang on, I'll come down for it."

"No…I can bring it up. I don't mind."

"Great, I'm just out the shower. I'll pull some clothes on."

He is naked!

The door buzzed and I pushed in. My mouth watered and my fangs tingled. This man had me in knots the way no one ever had before.

Within seconds I was standing at his door.

He pulled it open before I'd even knocked.

"Here." I smiled and presented the jacket.

"Thanks." He took it.

For a moment I stared at him, breathing in his soapy-fresh scent. His hair was damp and his chest bare. He wore navy-blue sweats that sat super low on his hips and nothing on his feet. His body was glorious and utterly perfect. A few veins were visible in his neck and the insides of his arms, and his chest was hairless.

"I appreciate it," he said. "I like this jacket."

"No problem."

"How did you know where I lived?"

"Er, Lloyd. I messaged him to find out."

"I see." He nodded. "I wasn't aware Lloyd knew which number apartment I lived in."

"Ah, I pressed them all. Well, four, then got to you. I don't think I'm popular with your neighbors."

He laughed. "No, I should think not." His smile dropped and he gestured behind himself. "Do you want to come in? A drink maybe after coming all this way."

"Sure, thanks." I stepped in quickly, before he could change his mind. He'd invited me over the threshold after all. Which meant I hadn't broken any rules. Plus, my job for the night was to keep him under surveillance, and safe. What better place to do that than his home?

"Nice place," I said, glancing around. There was only one lamp in the living area, and the white sofa and sleek modern furniture appealed to me. I'd turned in nineteen forty-five and with a country at war it was a time of austerity, so I always appreciated modern comforts. "I like this." I pointed to a huge black and white picture on the wall. It was Darius in Prague.

"Thanks."

"I adore it there," I went on. "You been in the clock tower?"

"No, I didn't get up there."

"It's a lesson in not being too good at what you do."

"Really? I'd have thought that was the way to go." He frowned.

"Not in this case. The government were so pleased with it, they chopped off the hands of the creator so he couldn't make another one like it. They didn't want any other city to have such a beautiful clock."

"That's terrible."

"I think so."

He shuddered. "I'm glad I live in modern times."

"The olden days were grim, I'll give you that. Especially in war time."

He smiled at me. "I wouldn't have put you as a history buff, Rhys."

"There's a lot you don't know about me."

"You're right, starting with what you'd like to drink."

"Whatever you're having."

"I was about to make coffee."

"Perfect."

"Make yourself at home." He gestured to the sofa. "The controls for the TV are there."

He disappeared into what I presumed was the kitchen and I moved across the luxury apartment and sat. The sofa was softly cushioned and exquisite quality.

Flicking on the television, a grip of excitement tugged at my belly when I saw the screen—a still of two naked men kissing beside a lake.

Fuck. He's been watching gay porn.

I glanced at the kitchen. Should I turn it off and pretend I hadn't seen it, or leave it on and see where the conversation would take us?

What would Lloyd do?

Lloyd would leave it on. I was sure of it. He'd tell Darius he also enjoyed porn and suggest they watch it together.

I didn't have long to ponder, because at that moment, Darius appeared in the doorway holding two mugs.

The soft expression he wore switched to one of tension. A line appeared on his forehead and his jaw clenched.

"I...er...just switched it on," I said, resting back and trying to look completely chilled, even though that wasn't how I was feeling.

"I'm sorry, I...here let me." He rushed to put the mugs down then went to grab the controls.

"Hey." I raised my hand so they were out of his reach. "No apologies, I watch this kind of stuff all the time." I peered at the TV. "In fact I think I've seen this one."

"You have?" He swallowed and dropped his arms to his side.

"Yeah, I've got a subscription, you know, so I can indulge whenever I want." I patted the seat cushion. "Sit."

He did as I'd asked.

"There's no man in my life, Darius," I said, then paused. "I'm presuming you guessed I was gay."

He nodded. His eyes were wide and his cheeks red.

"I've been waiting for someone special," I said. "Someone who gives me that fluttery feeling, here, you know." I tapped my chest.

"I understand."

"But I still have needs, Darius, basic desires. So this kind of thing," I gestured to the screen, "gives me satisfaction." I raised my eyebrows. "Beats wanking off to Eastenders."

He laughed softly. "I guess."

"So is that what you do?" I shifted position. My cock was hardening again.

"What do you mean?"

"Do you give yourself a hand-job while you watch it?"

He glanced down at his hands, which were clasped in his lap. The outline of his cock was visible through the material of his sweats. "I haven't..."

"What?" I asked quietly.

"I haven't. I mean this is the first time I've watched it. I mean I've thought about it, a lot, but I just found this and started it and..."

I rested my hand on his bare forearm. "Do you want to tell me why today was the day?"

He looked at me, his neck twisted and his hair flopping forward. "I guess...well something happened at the shoot today."

I knew full well what had happened but I wasn't about to tell him that. "Go on."

"There was this guy, George. We had a connection and it got pretty heated."

"If there's sexual chemistry that's always gonna happen."

He nodded and stared at the screen. "He propositioned me. Offered to take me somewhere private and..."

"And?"

"Bend me over, do things. Things I haven't done before. And I figured." He sat forward, his back hunched. "I figured I should do some research because it's only a matter of time until I do get naked with someone, might not be George or Lloyd but..."

"But someone."

"Yeah, and I don't want to look an idiot," he said. "I'm mid twenties and a virgin for fuck's sake." He shot me a look as if daring me to mock him.

"Hey." I held up my hand. "I was into my twenties before I went with a man."

"You were?" He frowned. "And how old are you now?"

I wasn't going to give him the real answer to that one. "About the same as you." I smiled. "And I'm sure you'll be fine. Once desire, passion and lust kick in, it'll come naturally."

"You think?"

"Yeah." I moved close, still holding the remote. "So how about we watch this together, while we have that coffee."

"You want to watch this with me?"

"Hell yeah. In case you hadn't noticed, Darius, I think you're fucking gorgeous. Watching porn with you is top of my bucket list right now."

"I...well..." He rubbed his temple. "I'm used to being told I'm gorgeous at work and stuff, but by guys who..."

"Want to bend you over and do things to you, not so much, huh?"

A loud bubble of laughter erupted from his chest and filled the room. "Say it how it is, Rhys."

"I'm working on doing that more. Lloyd says I hold back, I should say what I want more often instead of keeping it in."

"If you don't ask, you don't get." His face became serious again. "You really want to watch this?"

"I wouldn't have said I did otherwise." I squirmed and made a show of adjusting my cock through my jeans.

His gaze trailed down my body, then back up again. "Okay, press play."

I did as he'd asked, then silently removed my t-shirt. If I was lucky enough to get close to him I didn't want clothing in the way.

I guessed the on-screen guys had only just started. They were still in jeans and were kissing, their hands roaming over each other's toned upper bodies.

I moved closer to Darius.

"You ever done it outside?" he asked as the men undid each other's pants and shoved at them.

"Yeah."

"You like it?"

I grinned. "I like sex no matter where I do it."

"Oh, I see."

"You'll love it too," I reached for his hand, tugging it from its tight clasp on his other one. "When you're ready."

"I hope that will be soon." He tipped his chin, his attention firmly on the screen.

Two cocks were out now. Each big and hard and glossy in true porn-star style.

The men were moaning, their kisses noisy, as they worked each other's shafts.

For a few minutes we watched in silence as the camera panned around them, giving views of their cocks, butts and faces.

When one man sank to his knees, I moved closer still to Darius. My arm brushed his, so did my leg. Being so near to him thrilled me, as did the solid wedge of flesh tenting his sweats. "Are you enjoying it?"

"Yes." His voice was breathy.

"Me too. The one on the right has a great cock, don't you think?"

"Yes." He swallowed.

"And it's about to get sucked."

He glanced at me, then turned back to the screen. He swiped his tongue over his bottom lip.

The urge to kiss him, hold him, bring him pleasure and taste his blood was almost overwhelming. I reined myself in. "Would you like me to suck your cock?"

He hitched in a breath and his eyes widened as the onscreen cock disappeared into a willing mouth.

"You'll know what it feels like then, Darius. You won't have to imagine."

"You want to…do that to me?"

"Hell yeah." I ran my hand down his warm arm, across his belly, then to his cock. "I can think of nothing I'd rather do." I leaned closer and pressed my lips to the ball of his shoulder.

"Rhys…" He looked at me and touched my cheek.

"No strings," I said. "Just a bit of fun." I paused. "An experience I'd be honored to give you."

His eyes flashed and he rubbed his fingertips together. I wondered if heat was growing inside him, a heat that would result in sparks; I hoped so, I wanted to see them.

"Okay," he said. "I mean, yes please. If you don't mind, I mean—"

I chuckled and brushed my lips over his. "You're the hottest guy I've seen in a long time, and me and you, we'll be good together." Pushing to the edge of the sofa, I then sank to my knees between his legs. I looked up at him as I curled my hands into the waistband of his sweats. "Keep watching the TV and relax. Let me do this. I consider it somewhat of a speciality of mine."

He lifted his hips, allowing me to pull his sweats to his thighs.

His cock sprung free and a wild rage of excitement went through me. This was the man we'd been waiting for, and now I had him. He was mine, for now at least.

I gripped his shaft.

"Fuck," he muttered.

"I'm sorry, my hands are cold."

"It's not that, it's..."

"What?"

"Just having you touch me. Rhys, I..." He rested his hands on my head.

"I told you, relax, and come when you want to." I leaned forward and swiped my tongue over the tip of his glans, gathering up a tiny leak of pre-cum. I moaned and closed my eyes, he tasted divine.

His thighs tensed around me and he gripped my hair.

I opened my mouth wide, forming an 'o' with my lips, and sank onto him.

The noise that peeled from his throat was long and guttural and vibrated through me.

I tipped farther forward, cupping his balls with my free hand and taking him as deep as I could. Once there, I paused.

The sounds coming from the television were sexy as fuck—moans, groans, gasps and unholy praises to God.

I wanted to hear Darius making those noises, so I lifted up and started on a steady rhythm, using my hands, fingers, lips and tongue.

This man is everything I need and more.

"Rhys, fuck, I can't last long." His cock twitched, more pre-cum slid onto my tongue.

I didn't answer, instead I upped the pace, making sure I lodged him against my throat on each downward plunge.

He was shaking, his body tensed to granite. His hips were rising to meet my mouth and he was yanking at my hair following the rhythm.

And then it was there.

He held his breath, froze, and hot cum shot from his cock. His shaft throbbed and his balls contracted.

I swallowed and didn't let up.

He cried out, a long wail of release I knew I'd never forget.

The men on the screen were going for it, flesh-on-flesh slaps filling my ears as they pounded.

Darius yanked at my hair, pulling my mouth from him.

I caught his shaft in my palm and set my thumb over his slit.

He was breathing hard, his face was flushed and his pupils wide. He held his hands out to the sides, fingers splayed on the sofa.

"How was that?" I asked, wiping at a drip of saliva trickling down my chin.

"That was…damn, I should have lasted longer but it felt so good."

"It wasn't a test, it was an experience. You came when you wanted, what's wrong with that?"

He wiped his forearm over his brow then glanced at the TV. "Where's the remote?" As he'd spoken he'd picked it up and turned it off.

"You weren't enjoying it?"

"I've got the real thing, why would I need that?" He smiled. A lovely wide grin that melted my heart all the more for him.

I love him so much.

I studied his groin and traced my fingertip over a vein leading from his abdomen to his right thigh. It was a delicate shade of lilac and combined with the pulse I could feel in his shaft, I had a desperate urge to taste him.

"Just here," I said, looking up at him. "Can I bite you?"

"Bite me?" He laughed, though he was still out of breath and currently studying the ends of his fingers. "What, like a hickey?"

"Yeah, something like that." My fangs were tingling in my gums. "I want to taste you here." I placed the tip of my tongue on the vein. So damn good, so damn close.

"Are you and Lloyd vampires or something?" Darius laughed. "He wanted to give me a hickey too, but I can't have marks on my body, it's my livelihood."

"It would be the smallest mark, two actually, and they would heal quickly." I licked my lips. My fangs were drawing down over my regular teeth. "Say yes, Darius, I don't want to without your permission, you're too special for that."

Confusion flashed in his eyes as he stared at me. "What do you mean two marks?" He paused. "And what's wrong with your mouth?"

I quickly stood and turned. George would be furious if I revealed to Darius what we really were. We'd agreed to pick our moment for that.

"Rhys?"

He was shifting on the sofa, no doubt pulling his sweats back into place.

My fangs retracted and I pulled in a deep breath. Turning back to him, I smiled. "I'm sorry, I got carried away. And yes, I thought a hickey there would be okay. Obviously I was wrong."

Chapter Nine

Darius

I woke alone. Rhys had left the apartment not long after my first blow job, and, exhausted—and for once totally satisfied—I'd flopped into bed.

Judging by the weak light filtering through my curtains, I guessed it was early, but feeling energized I showered, then made eggs on toast.

My agent messaged me the details of the day's shoot and I checked out the address. It wasn't far and as the sun was crawling into a cloudless sky I decided to walk.

At ten a.m. I headed out of the door. The scent of blossom filled my nostrils and I dropped my shades into place. One of my neighbors said good morning as she passed loaded down with shopping bags, so I scooted back to hold the door for her.

"Thank you, Darius," she said with a smile. "Have a nice day."

"You too, Mrs Coleman."

It was lovely to have a spring in my step as I walked. My mind was full of Rhys and how he'd sucked my cock. I'd never felt anything so good, and certainly never had such an amazing orgasm. It was clear a man's mouth was much better than my own hand.

Will I see him again?

A slight frown marred my brow as I crossed the road. I didn't even have his cell number. But I did have Lloyd's, and he was Rhys's cousin.

The frown deepened. Damn it, I was well and truly involved with both men. Not an hour before I'd been thrusting my hips toward Rhys's face, I'd been grinding against Lloyd, kissing him until we were both gasping for breath, and coming in our pants.

I pressed my lips together and shoved my hands deeper into my pockets. I was a two-timer. I'd gone from no man in my life to two.

Turning into a smaller road and away from the noise of the High Street, I berated myself. I'd been caught up in the moment, riding high on the excitement of having found someone, or rather two people, I was insanely attracted to. Lloyd with his sharp features, shorn blond hair and sexy smile had my heart beating faster each moment I spent with him. And Rhys's with his dimples, cutely quaffed hair and young lean body was the stuff of fantasies.

What if I lose both of them?

"Oh God," I muttered. That thought didn't bear thinking about. Lloyd may well be furious I'd had sexy time with Rhys, and the same might be the case vice versa.

I stomped on, into the shadows of an office block. I'd always presumed when I found someone special to be in my life there would only be that one person.

Yet I had two.

And that was before I'd added Oscar, my hot, rugged biker from the plane into the equation. I still wanted to go out with him...I still wanted my promised kiss. What would that stubble feel like on my chin? How would he hold me? Would he want to strip me naked and..."

A heat was growing inside of me. I knew what it was. It had happened too many times in my life, and the scorching sensation was unmistakable.

I pulled my hands from my pockets and spread my fingers, allowing the breeze to slide between them. But it was only a delaying tactic. The burn in my chest was spreading over my pecs to my shoulders. My belly was tight, my skin tingling and the hair on the back of my neck standing up as if an electrical storm was about to kick off.

One glance at the sky told me that wasn't the case, it was still a perfect azure blue.

Oscar. Lloyd. Rhys.

How had I got myself into this mess?

Frustration and confusion swirled within me. I tried a few deep breaths, worked on keeping my thoughts calm, but it was no good. I'd have to release sparks.

I glanced around. The back street wasn't busy but there were too many pedestrians around for me to fire a few even at a drain or the gutter. Plus there were high windows, anyone could be looking out.

'Never let anyone see your special trick, Darius.'

My mother's words came back to me, but also an image of Lloyd walking toward me, hood up, eyes flashing. He was the only other person to have ever seen the power leave my fingertips.

I spotted a narrow alley, one which had a large green wheelie bin at the end and what appeared to be an abandoned bike, minus one wheel, half blocking the entrance. I slipped down it, and out of the sunshine. It wasn't quite wide enough to fit a car along and stretched for about fifty meters.

Glancing over my shoulder, I guessed I'd soon be away from prying eyes. If only I could hold off until then. The blistering pain in my arms was becoming unbearable. It was as if boiling water was being splashed onto my skin.

The arrival of a sudden cloud crossing over the sun was a welcome reprieve from the heat in the air, as was a sudden cool gust of wind. It lifted my hair and pressed my t-shirt to my chest.

"Fuck," I muttered, speeding up. Soon I would be out of view of the office windows, just another few steps.

I stepped over a cardboard box, bursting at the seams with household rubbish. A few flies buzzed around it.

My stomach was tight. Nausea gripped me. I stopped, leaned against a cool, gritty wall and raised my right hand. A bitter taste had lodged itself in my mouth and unease was making me shake.

But I was out of sight.

There was no one here but me.

I was alone.

Wasn't I?

A glance around confirmed there was no one else with me. The wind picked up swirling litter near the box, a couple of crisp packets, and several dry leaves caught in an upward spiral.

I couldn't hold in a groan, the pain was extreme. I flicked my wrist forward, sending the agony down my arm, over my palm, through my fingers and out of the ends. A shower of golden sparks splashed over the cobbled ground and crackled against a wall. I released more, then added my other hand. There were so many. Each was a release of the discomfort, each ripped a moan from my throat.

A sudden, huge clap of thunder mixed with my final cry of relief. It rolled overhead, seeming to land in the alley and vibrate through me.

I sent more sparks toward the wall. They skittered over the floor, brilliant and bright.

The whirling litter lifted higher. Added to it now was more trash, floating and spinning like ugly confetti. The flies from the household rubbish were swept up in its cyclone.

The bitter taste intensified. Another bellow of thunder shook my ribs, seeming to shake the breath from my body. The ground beneath me trembled.

I scanned my surroundings. The sensation of not being alone was increasing. The whirling litter was getting closer, like another being stalking me.

I dodged it, pressing against the opposite wall as it flittered past me. The swirling air was cold, ice cold, and smelled of damp earth and rotting foodstuff.

Above me, the sky was black, as if night had suddenly dropped over the alley. The whirling litter was increasing in diameter, a tornado that was nearly touching each wall. I pressed against the brickwork, both mesmerized and fearful of the turbulent air. There was something ethereal about the way it was spinning—an energy growing by the second and darkening too.

"Darius."

I was gripped, tightly, on my right upper arm, then yanked to the side and away from the twister.

"What?" I tore my gaze from it. "Oscar?"

"We have to get out of here," he said, continuing to tug me toward the end of the alley. "Now."

"Why?"

"It's not safe for you." He threw a glare at the tube of spinning trash which was howling now, the way wind does in horror movies.

"It's weird, look," I said, falling into step with him, which was hard as his strides were long and fast and I was trying to look behind myself. "What is it?"

"Not something we want you around." He was all but dragging me.

"We?"

Reaching the end of the alley, I found myself bathed in sunshine again. It warmed my chilled cheeks and shoulders. The hairs on my forearms were standing on end, as were the ones at the nape of my neck. I tried to look back but the large bin was in the way. I turned to Oscar who was swinging his leg over a huge black motorcycle. "What are you doing here, Oscar?"

"Get on."

"But—"

"I don't wanna have to make you, Darius, but I will." He frowned and slammed on a helmet. "So do it now. On!"

I quickly reached for the helmet behind him and rammed it over my head. There was something in his tone, and the way he was looking at me, that gave me a thrill. It also told me he was deadly serious about us going for a ride...now.

I climbed aboard, the leather seat warm against my jeans, and slid my hands around his waist.

He revved the engine once, then tore away from the curbside. I gripped him tight, fearful of sliding off when the bike almost went onto its back wheel.

As he slalomed past several cars, I rested my cheek against his soft leather jacket and closed my eyes. The twister was all I could see, as if it had burned onto my retinas. The rancid scent lingered in my nostrils and I swallowed to get rid of the bitter taste.

Oscar took a left, then made a set of lights just before they switched to red. He zoomed past a bus then rocketed up the gears, plunging us into a tunnel and out the other side.

My heart was pounding. Being on the bike was thrilling. Thoughts of my shoot faded into the distance. Now all I could think of was Oscar, and being with him, and where he taking me.

'Not something we want you around.'

What had he meant by that?

Eventually he began to slow, as if he'd finally decided the Hounds of Hell were no long snapping at the back wheel. He took a turn toward a park, then drew the bike to a halt in an empty lot.

Without the sound of the engine my ears rang. I released my tight grip on him, flexing and unflexing my fingers as I straightened.

"Where are we?" I asked, removing my helmet.

"Somewhere I used to come as a kid." He kicked a stand into place.

"Oh, okay." I slipped off the bike. My heart was thudding and my body buzzing from the fast ride through town.

Oscar stood next to me and removed his helmet. He then took mine and balanced both on the seat of the bike.

I allowed myself a moment of admiration. His black leathers hugged him in all the right places, and the guy was huge—a good couple of inches taller than me and considerably wider. He wore clumpy biker boots, and his dark hair was messy with a few strands stuck to his head.

I cleared my throat. "I'm supposed to be heading to work."

"Yeah, sorry about that." He didn't seem it. "But that alley was no place for you to be."

"How did you know I was there?" I frowned.

"Let's just call it luck."

"What does that mean?"

His eyes narrowed and his jaw tensed. He stepped closer, fast, then loomed over me with his shoulders hunched and his breaths coming quick.

I stared up into his eyes. My hands itched to touch him again, feel that leather jacket and explore the way it stretched over the damn fine muscles of his chest and biceps.

A tendon twitched in his jawline, beneath his thick stubble. He cupped my face, the material of his jacket bunching at the tops of his arms and creaking softly.

What's going on?

He was all I could think of. He was so damn handsome in a rugged, dominant, don't-mess-with-me way. My cock twitched, my breaths were becoming harder to catch.

Then his mouth was over mine. His cool lips exerting a firm pressure as his tongue delved between my teeth.

I groaned and clung to his thick forearms. I opened up and let him in. He tasted of everything I'd thought he would, man and danger, sex and lust.

His chin abraded mine, and our noses touched. I groaned into his mouth and closed my eyes, lost to the power of his kiss.

Eventually he pulled back but kept my face cradled in his hands. "Now that's out of the way we can talk, babe."

Babe!

I swallowed. "Yeah. Okay, we can talk."

The right side of his mouth twitched and his eyes narrowed. "You taste good, Darius. You should know I'm gonna need more of that. More of you."

"I can handle that."

He twitched his eyebrows. "You reckon?"

I gulped. The thought of Oscar unleashing his passion, combined with those muscles and that strength was as nerve wracking as it was alluring.

Damn it.

I suddenly remembered Rhys and Lloyd. If I'd been feeling bad for two-timing before, now I was three-timing.

"Why the frown?" he asked.

I bit on my bottom lip, reluctant to confess there were two other men in my life.

"Darius?"

I glanced away.

He turned my face back to his so I was forced to look into his eyes. "I only want what's best for you, you should know that. You can tell me anything. Absolutely anything."

I cleared my throat and decided to change the subject. "What was that back there? Some freak weather occurrence?"

"No. That was evil, pure evil, and I didn't want you anywhere near it. That cross around your neck, it won't protect you."

"Protect me from what?"

He glanced up at the sky and released my face. "We should get going. The sun is getting high now, too high for my liking."

"Get going to where?"

"To see the others...it's time."

"What others? And time for what?"

"Time for you to know the truth about who you really are."

Chapter Ten

Lloyd

I spun the glass of cola on the beer mat. As usual it would go undrunk, but it didn't look right to sit in a pub with nothing. Besides, they'd probably kick us out if we didn't spend.

"They should be here by now," Rhys said, fidgeting on the seat next to me.

"Don't concern yourself." George pulled his pocket watch out, studied the face then slipped it back into the innards of his waistcoat. "It's only a few minutes past Oscar's estimated time of arrival."

"There was a bad feeling in the air this morning, around the corner from his apartment." I frowned. "As if his father is getting closer."

"I think it's safe to presume that is exactly what's happening," George said. "And it's why we must be vigilant."

"We are being, or at least I am." Rhys glanced at the door.

"You certainly kept a close eye on him last night." I raised my eyebrows at Rhys. He'd told me how he'd sucked Darius off while they'd watched porn. I couldn't help a small tug of jealousy, but equally I was pleased they were getting closer and Darius was learning to trust us. Besides, I'd had my fun with him outside. True, we hadn't got naked, or even undone our zippers, but our cambion was one heck of a kisser, and pretty damn reactive to some pump and grind of my groin against his.

I squirmed on the seat, my cock hardening at the erotic memory.

"You two are the lucky ones. Oscar too, probably." George huffed. "I haven't had a moment alone with him."

"You will," I said. "And then you'll fall for him hook, line and sinker the way we all have."

"He's impossible to resist," Rhys said. "It's as if there's magic between us and him. A magnet drawing us together."

"Well he is our savior." George touched his cap as if checking it was on correctly. "So there must be some kind of connection."

"And we *were* drawn to his location," I added, then looked at the door as it opened. Oscar's wide frame was instantly recognizable, and next to him stood Darius. "They're here." I sat a little straighter.

"Good." George ran his finger around the collar of his starched shirt. "Now play it cool, okay."

"Of course." I frowned at him, then tried to relax my brow. That wasn't how I wanted Darius to see me.

The two figures moved into the pub. Oscar had his arm partially around Darius as if steering him to us.

Two guys at the bar threw the couple a wary glance; Oscar did that to people. Built like a mountain and looking ready to snarl at any moment, his good looks were definitely of the badass biker variety.

As they drew closer I studied Darius's face. He appeared relaxed enough, until, that was, he saw the three of us seated in a darkened booth with a high window behind us.

He stopped dead in his tracks. His eyes widened and his mouth fell open. He closed it again, then moved his attention from me to Rhys, to George, and finally to Oscar at his side.

"What are *they* doing here?" he asked.

Oscar nodded at a space on the bench beside me. "Sit and we'll explain."

"Explain." Darius made no move to sit. "I didn't even know you *knew* Rhys and Lloyd." He pointed at George. "And how come the guy from my shoot is—?"

"I told you, sit and we'll explain, babe."

Babe! Since when did Oscar ever call anyone babe?

"All will become clear." George smiled; a devastating smile I'd seen him use to win over many men and, on occasion, women.

"But?"

"It's okay," I said, also smiling. "We're here to help you, Darius."

He swallowed, his Adam's apple bobbing low, then he sat.

I could feel his warmth diffusing onto my cool skin as he perched on the edge of the seat, his back rod-straight and his hands clasped in his lap.

I itched to touch him, comfort and reassure him, but I didn't want to scare him away. "It really is okay," I said in as gentle a voice as I could muster.

"Did you tell them?" He turned to me. Pain and confusion flashed in his eyes.

"Tell them what?"

"You know what." He waggled his fingers beneath the table so only I could see.

"I didn't need to."

"What does that mean?" He scowled.

I could resist no longer and I pressed my hand over his. "Darius, we know you're different, the way we are too. We're *all* different."

"You mean?" He stared at me for a moment then glanced around. "They can all do what I do?"

George leaned forward with his chin tilted. "If you're talking about generating fire from the power of your emotions then no, we can't do that, Darius."

"Oh." His shoulders slumped. "It's just when Lloyd just said you were all different, I hoped..."

"I'm sorry," I said. "This must be confusing."

"Too right it is."

He nibbled on his bottom lip and I ached to kiss him again, the way I had the night before.

He turned to me. "So you did tell them about the sparks."

"I didn't really have to." I hated the in his eyes, and the thought of him believing I'd betrayed him. "We've been looking for you for a long time, Darius, and when I saw you in Paris, creating sparks, I knew you were the one."

"The one?" He shifted his hand so it was no longer in mine. "I'm guessing you don't mean 'the one' as in the love of your life, Lloyd."

"Fuck, yes, actually I *do* mean that." I grabbed his hand again. "You have to understand you're special to us, *very* special."

He froze, as if the intensity in my words had stunned him.

George tapped his fingers on the table, thumb to pinkie finger and back again, an annoying habit he had when concentrating. "Darius," he said. "When Lloyd said we'd been looking for you for a long time, he meant it."

"How long?"

"Me, personally?" George shrugged. "Over three centuries."

"Three centuries!" Darius said loudly. "Are you mad?"

"No." George smiled and shook his head. "Just patient and persistent." He nodded at me. "And also grateful that Lloyd here made the connection."

"And why were you looking for me for three bloody centuries?" Darius huffed as if the question he'd posed was preposterous to his ears. "I was only born twenty-five years ago."

"I know that now," George said with a smile.

"We hope you can help with something," Rhys said. "Something very important to us."

Darius stared at Rhys. I wondered if he was remembering having his cock sucked the night before. His first experience of a blow job had been with possibly the cutest damn vampire on the planet.

"And what's that?" Darius asked quietly. "That you want help with?"

"You hold a key," Oscar said gruffly. He'd sat on the same bench as me and Darius, as if blocking him in.

"A key? The only key I've got is to my apartment." Darius tapped his jeans pocket.

"Ahh, that's where you're wrong," George said, finally stopping the awful tapping. "You have something in here." He touched his temple. "That will unlock our future and free us from an eternity in Hell."

"An eternity in Hell." Darius laughed but the sound didn't hold humor. "I think you're being a bit fucking dramatic."

"We're not," Rhys said earnestly. "There's an old fable, they talk about it at The Worshipful Company, about a cambion who...ouch!" He glared at George. "What did you do that for?"

George didn't reply.

"What's a cambion?" Darius asked, swinging his gaze around us all.

George sighed. "Do you want a drink, Darius?"

"No, not really. I'd much prefer some sodding answers. Starting with what's a cambion, then moving onto how do you all know each other? Have you been following me?" He turned to Oscar. "And what the heck was that bloody thing in the alley this morning?"

"There was something in the alley?" I directed at Oscar. "Like what?"

Oscar frowned. "He was there. The evil was palpable, the air thick with it."

"Who was there?" Darius asked.

No one spoke.

"Who...was...there?" he asked again.

George folded his arms and sat back. "Your father most likely, Darius."

"My father!" Darius mimicked George's posture. "Now I know you're off your head. Not only do I have no idea who my father is, I was also alone in that alley until Oscar turned up. God only knows how he found me there."

"Think about it," Oscar said. "In the alley, that whirlwind of energy, it was growing stronger by the second. It was pressing you against the damn wall. The sky had turned black and you couldn't tear your attention from the swirling air."

"It was a dirt devil, that's all."

"Devil is a good description," Rhys said, shaking his head. "We should never have allowed him to get so near."

"No, we shouldn't." I threw a glare at Oscar. The demon had had Darius pinned to a wall! That was way too close for comfort. Another few minutes and he could have possessed him.

"Hey," Oscar said gruffly. "I got him out of there, didn't I?"

"Thank goodness," George said.

"I told you, I have no idea who my father is, and there was no one in the alley." Darius tensed his jaw.

"What did your mother tell you about him?" I asked, squeezing his hand in the hope that would calm him.

"That..." he paused, and touched the cross at his neck. "She had a one-night stand. All I know is his name was Mammon, not sure if that's a first or second name, and before you ask, no I haven't ever found him."

"Mammon," George nodded. "Sounds about right."

I had to agree with that. Mammon was a name the devil and demons often went by.

"How is that right?" Darius asked.

I pulled in a deep breath. "Because, Darius, your father is an incubus. He seduced your mother. He tricked her into having sex with him and—"

"An incubus? What the Hell is that? And of course he tricked her. My mother is a sweet woman but very gullible, it's why she's so devout to God, He gives her direction."

"That picture," Rhys said, leaning forward. "In your mother's hallway."

"What about it?"

"Don't you think it's odd?" Rhys asked Darius. "A man in a smart suit with no head, no face."

Darius shrugged. "It's always been there. Mom says she likes a man in a tux." He paused. "So she had a one-night stand with a guy in a tuxedo, so what?"

"She had a night time encounter with an incubus in a tuxedo," George said. "Who seduced her for his own evil gain."

Darius turned to me. "What is an incubus, Lloyd? Tell me."

I didn't like being the bearer of bad news, but it seemed I had no choice. "A demon. Your father is a demon, Darius, and you're the product of his coupling with a human woman, making you a cambion, a very special person who has powers and a key to the future of our kind."

He stared at me, then slumped back, but only for a second because then he pushed to standing. "Excuse me, Oscar, I have some place to be. Work, actually. I need to go get a cab. All this nonsense has made me late."

"Sit." Oscar didn't move. "We've not finished this conversation."

"Please, get out of my way."

"No." Oscar wrapped his huge hand around Darius's arm. "We care about you. There is no way we're going to let you leave here upset and confused."

"And you have nowhere to be," George said. "I cancelled the shoot."

"You did what?" Darius sat again, much to my relief, and stared at George.

"I...we...knew you'd need some time to get your head around this," George said. "Work is the last thing you need today."

Darius reached for my cola and took a long drink. When he'd replaced it on the mat he pulled in a deep breath. "Let me get this straight. I can make sparks because my father was a demon—"

"Is," I said. "Your father *is* a demon. He's still out there."

Darius nodded. "Okay, he's a demon. And you're telling me I hold a key in my head that will save you all from Hell, and that thing in the alley this morning was my father, the demon, coming to visit me."

"Yes," George said. "We believe that was him. He has evil intentions with your physical being and your soul."

"Why, what does he want to do?"

"We believe," I said, then glanced at George.

He gave a small nod.

"We believe," I went on, "he wants to possess your body and use it to procreate, make sons, many sons, who he can control and use to carry out his evil plans."

"Possess me? Evil plans?"

"We don't know what these plans are for sure," Rhys said. "But we know they'll be harmful for anyone who gets in the way."

"And not just a few people—potentially millions," George said. "Evil men have a habit of getting great power if one looks through history. All they need is for good men to do nothing."

"Fuck!" Darius glanced at the door. "Do you think he's in here now? Or waiting outside? I don't want to be possessed, and I certainly don't want to have anything to do with unleashing evil into the world. I try to only do good, and if I can't do that, then no harm."

"It's okay." I squeezed his thigh. "He isn't here. We'd feel his presence, it's too powerful to ignore."

"And you're safe with us," Oscar said.

"Yes." George nodded. "We won't let any harm come to you, we promise."

"Well thanks, I guess." Darius paused. "And is that because of what I supposedly know?"

"No," George said. "If you didn't hold the key we'd still..." He frowned.

It wasn't often George was lost for words. I raised my eyebrows at him.

"We'd still," he carried on, "Have this insane attraction to you, a *need* for you. That's how it works for our sort. Cambions are irresistible."

"Irresistible." Darius said, cocking his head. "To your sort. And what exactly *is* that sort?"

Chapter Eleven

Darius

I looked around the table. The four handsome faces—all different but equally appealing—were rendered in shadows and their attention set firmly on me. It also appeared no one was going to answer my question about what their sort was.

"Look, guys," I said. "I haven't got time for this. I really have to go to work. Or to the agency at least to see what's going on."

Rhys leaned across the table. His cute smile dropped and a seriousness came over his eyes. "You see, the thing is, Darius, we're..."

"What?" I asked, feeling the color draining from my face. A memory of last night, his mouth changing shape, top lip protruding and him wanting to bite me, flashed through my mind. "What are you?"

Fuck! I know what they are.
No. That can't be true.
What if it is?

"We're vampires," Rhys said. "All four of us."

"Vampires," I repeated as my belly clenched and my knees shook. It made sense now. Lloyd trying to give me a hickie, Rhys's behavior, Oscar standing outside my door in Paris all night.

I set my focus on George, though my sight was a little blurred as a million thoughts spun through my head. "So that's how come you've been searching for me for centuries? You're that old?"

"Yes." He nodded. "I turned, became this way, before Lloyd, Rhys and Oscar. And ever since I heard the fable I've been on a mission." He smiled. "I can honestly say it's a relief to have finally tracked you down."

"So there's only one of me, one cambion?"

"In Europe, that we know of," he said. "At this present time, yes."

I folded my arms, slotting my hands into my armpits and hunching my shoulders forward; a tension knot was forming at the base of my neck.

"You okay?" Lloyd asked. "This is a lot to take in."

I didn't answer.

He set his hand over the discomfort growing at my nape and rubbed. His cool palm was soothing.

Vampires. I'm surrounded by vampires.

So why wasn't I terrified? I was aware of many emotions swirling inside me, but not fear. I didn't think these men would hurt me. If anything they all seemed to be as attracted to me as I was to them.

Rhys was studying me with narrowed eyes. We'd had fun the night before, lots of delicious, hot, orgasmic fun. I wanted that again with him. And Lloyd, he did funny things to my belly when he kissed me and created a longing in me for more, much more. Oscar, too, fascinated me. What would he be like in bed? Would he be able to control his strength, and just how big was his cock? I wanted to find out.

"Darius," George said. "Much as I'm keen to spend time with you, get to know you, and talk about the key, I think you've had enough to contend with today. The last thing we want is for you to be emotionally exhausted."

"I'm fine." I might not be muscle bound but I wasn't that much of a wimp.

"I know you are," he said. "You've taken this news amazingly well. But still..." He paused. "We all know what it's like to find out life is never going to be the same again. It takes everyone a while to adjust no matter how strong they are."

"I guess." He was right. Of course he was. I'd gone from a regular guy with a single mother and a few sparky problems, to a demon's child—a rarity apparently—who held the key these sexy vampires wanted so they didn't spend eternity burning in Hell.

"Oscar," George said. "Take Darius back to his apartment and stay with him."

"With pleasure." Oscar stood.

"And what will we do?" Lloyd asked George.

He'd sounded a bit disappointed and I wondered if he'd wanted to come back with me. I glanced at Rhys. He was staring at me too, almost longingly.

I swallowed and looked up at Oscar. His jaw was set determinedly and his fists were clenched. I had no doubt he'd defend me from my demon father, but still, a tremble went through me at the thought of being alone with him in my apartment.

"We," George directed at Lloyd, "have something to do."

"Okay then." Lloyd nodded though a frown remained on his brow.

"We need to check out that alley," Rhys said. "See if there are any clues, or anything in particular that called the demon to it."

George pulled out a pocket watch, glanced at it, then slipped it away. "Keep your phone on, Oscar, we'll be in touch."

"Right you are, boss." Oscar held out his hand to me. "Come on, we'll get you home. You're white as a sheet."

"I am?" I pressed my hand to my cheek.

"Yeah," Lloyd said, stroking his hand over my hair. "Go and rest, eat something. We'll see you later."

I turned to him. "You will?"

"Yes." George stood. "Now we've found you, Darius, we'll never be far, and if you want us, any of us, we'll always be there for you." He smiled, a wickedly sexy grin that made my cock twitch and reminded me of him pressed over me at the shoot, skin to skin, dick to dick. "We're here," George went on, "to bend to your will, service your needs, and ensure your constant happiness and satisfaction."

"Fuck," Oscar muttered. "I'm trying to stay in control here. Come on, Darius. Time to go."

He slipped his arm around my waist and steered me from the pub. I glanced over my shoulder, taking a last look at the three devastatingly good-looking guys all following my every move.

I want them all.

The thought hit me like a punch to the guts as we stepped outside. It was like running through a stop sign, then another and another. How could I be so turned on by so many men? So completely enraptured, drawn to, obsessive about.

"Here." Oscar handed me a helmet. "Let's get out of this place."

I didn't answer as I put the helmet on. Was it a problem if I wanted them all? It seemed not.

'If you want us, any of us, we'll always be there for you.'

George's words came back to me. Could I really have any of them whenever I wanted? Would Lloyd mind if he knew Rhys had sucked my cock the night before? Would it matter if Rhys knew I'd kissed Oscar in the park, or that George had turned me on so much at work I'd hardly been able to walk?

"Hey." Oscar placed his hand on my shoulder. "I don't know what's going on in that pretty head of yours, but let's go to your place, then we can talk some more."

"Yeah. Okay."

He nodded then swung his leg over the bike.

I did the same, once again wrapping my arms around his waist and clasping my fingers. Only this time, as he pulled away, the engine roaring, I knew I was riding pillion with a vampire. This was no ordinary journey home, and as it happened, *I* was no ordinary guy.

We reached my apartment block quickly. I'd enjoyed having the drive to concentrate on for a few minutes, and giving my mind a chance to slow slightly.

I opted for the stairs up to my apartment, aware as I went that Oscar was behind me, and, judging from the tingles on my buttocks, staring at my ass.

By the time I unlocked the door, my mind was twisting and turning again. I held it open and gestured for him to step inside.

He stopped and looked down at the threshold; a slim brass bar which separated my carpet from the hard flooring of the corridor.

"Oscar?" I asked, confused by his hesitation.

"You have to invite me in."

"What?"

"Say it." He shrugged.

"In." I nodded at the hallway.

"Properly." He smiled, just a small tilt of his sexy mouth. "Otherwise I can't."

"Okay, er…Oscar, please come into my home. You're very welcome."

"Thank you." He stepped in, walking straight through to the huge living area, glancing around as he did so.

I toed off my shoes and hung up my jacket. "Do you like it?"

"Yes, he's not here."

"Who?"

"Your father."

I raised my eyebrows. "You can tell that?"

"Kinda. It has a nice vibe to it. No evil here." He turned to the window as if admiring the view. "Only good."

I took the opportunity to admire his pert ass encased in shiny black leather.

"If you have questions I'll do my best to answer them."

"Thanks," I said, stepping up to the window. A small black fly was on the inside, trying to get out. I opened the catch and shooed it into the fresh air. "First things first, Oscar, would you like a drink? Tea, coffee, a beer?"

He turned to me and swiped his tongue over his bottom lip. "I don't drink."

Damn it. Was he the same as Lloyd and struggling with an alcohol problem? "I've got juice, or cola if you'd prefer."

"I mean I don't drink regular drinks." He shoved his hands into his pockets. "I don't drink anything you just mentioned."

"Ahh…yes." I swallowed. "Vampire. Just blood, right?"

Fuck. Did he want *my* blood? What if he attacked me and sucked me dry? Sure, he'd been a good guy up to this point, saved me too, apparently, but what if…?

"Hey." He frowned and stepped close. "Calm down, babe."

"I am calm."

"I can tell by your face you're having some damn scary thoughts." He cupped my cheeks and stared into my eyes the way he had at the park.

I tried to stop the tremble in my stomach, and I locked my knees. He had dark rims around his irises, and this close I could see every bit of stubble over his top lip and jaw. Beneath that top lip, hidden away, were fangs.

Fangs!

"What you have to know, right now, Darius, is I will never hurt you. None of us will. Our mission is to protect you, care for you, and ensure you only ever feel good. Please don't think for one second any harm will come to you at our hands. We would never do that."

"But you do drink blood, human blood."

"Yes." He nodded. "Not often. We can go months, even years without feeding from a human, Lloyd especially."

"And do you…" I struggled to find the words. Was I dealing with murderers here?

"Do we kill our victims?"

I nodded, not sure if I wanted the answer.

"Not unless they want to die, or death is imminent, because draining them of the very last drop of their blood turns them into vampires. Becoming a vampire, with a fate of burning in Hell for eternity isn't something to be taken lightly." He slipped his palms from my cheeks to my neck. "Mostly, we take our fill, then leave the human to continue on as normal."

"It doesn't affect them?"

"Not in a bad way. In fact, as a rule they enjoy it. There's something in our saliva that induces euphoria."

"Euphoria?"

He lowered his face a little. "Yeah, euphoric, orgasmic, really fucking good."

"Orgasmic."

"Mmm..." He brushed his lips over mine, his prickly chin scratching my flesh.

I kissed him back, but just when I thought things might heat up, he pulled away. "You should eat, or get a drink," he said, stepping back.

"I'm not hungry or thirsty." I missed his body so close to mine.

"In that case you must have questions, right?"

"Yeah."

He sat and crossed his right ankle over his left knee, his arms out to the sides, fingers spread on the white sofa. "Fire away."

He looked so big, and gorgeous and tough, and with his taste on my lips I had to stop myself asking when he was going to fuck me.

"Okay." I sat opposite him. "If my father is an evil demon, does that make me evil too?"

"No."

"How do you know?"

"Darius, you just let a fly out of the window rather than kill it. I suspect you've never killed anything in your life."

"Well no, I haven't."

"And you've always done your best to help others."

"A little kindness goes a long way, or so my mother brought me up to believe."

"And she's right, and also the reason why you have such a good kind heart and soul."

"I don't understand."

"Your father's choice of mother for his child went against him. Your mother is pure and just. You have that in you, and she nurtured it as you grew. We believe that's why you've been able to evade him for so long."

"But I'm not as religious as her. In fact I struggle to understand the strength of her belief sometimes." I rubbed my cross, then tucked it beneath my t-shirt when I saw Oscar staring at it with narrowed eyes.

"Demons have no respect for God. They cannot be exorcised. Religion and religious artefacts have no meaning to them. It's not surprising, despite your mother's influences, you struggle with the concept."

"What about you? Do you believe in God?"

"I believe in Hell."

"And you don't want to go there, right?"

"Not particularly." He glanced away.

"Can I ask you something more personal?"

"Of course, anything."

"How did you turn into a vampire, Oscar? Was it one of the others?"

"No." He sighed and a sadness came over his face.

I was silent, waiting for him to continue.

"One hundred and eighty years ago I was working in a coal mine in the north east of England. Like I told you before, on the plane, I was married. We had no children. My wife and I rarely had sex, it wasn't something I enjoyed with a woman but being married was the done thing. I'd had a poverty stricken childhood but even so my parents took me to church and Sunday school, so back then yeah, I believed. Didn't know it was an option not to."

"And your wife, what happened?"

"What happened was I became a vampire. November third. I was down the pit, there was a collapse, me and another guy, Jack, were trapped. I'd broken my leg. It was grim with no water and intense heat. We were there for four days and I was slowly dying. I began to accept that and was glad it was Jack with me. I'd always got on well with him, thought him a good chap, and he was handsome and strong, something which appealed to me more than my wife's delicate curves. But the weird thing was he wasn't getting sick like me. Having no food and water, the thinning air, it didn't affect him. Neither did the heat. He didn't even have sweat patches. And he never seemed to sleep. I was delirious, going in and out of consciousness. I knew the end was coming. It was then he asked if I wanted him to bite me. I had no idea what he was talking about, but when his fangs sank into my neck this wonderful sensation came over my body. I presumed I was dying and going to Heaven. It went on and on, my cock was hard, my stomach felt full, the hunger and thirst left me. No longer burning up on a hard rocky floor I was gaining strength, as if death had given me a new powerful body."

"He'd turned you into a vampire."

"It was his only option to save me. He could have lived for centuries down there. My time was running out."

"So then what happened?"

"When he'd finished explaining what I was, we fucked. And we fucked hard for two weeks before deciding to dig our way out and leave our old lives behind."

"You fucked for two weeks?"

"Yep." He huffed. "It had been a long time coming, being with a guy, and Jack made me feel invincible. Heck, I was."

"And where is…" I trailed off. I'd thought Oscar and I had something starting, but if Jack was in the picture that might never happen.

"Jack?"

I nodded.

He closed his eyes and squeezed the bridge of his nose. "Jack is gone."

"Where?"

"To Hell."

I sat forward. "What do you mean?"

"He was killed." He opened his eyes and set his attention on me.

"But I thought you were immortal."

"Immortal, yes. We don't age, and neither will you for that matter."

"What?" *I won't age?*

"But," he went on, "we can be killed. Stake through the heart, decapitated, burned, that'll do it. And then our cold souls go to Hell."

"Someone put a stake through Jack's heart? Who?"

"Not who, what." He folded his arms, his biceps bulging. "Shifters."

"Shifters?"

"Wolf shifters. We were in Canada, roaming, fucking, taking the occasional drink from loggers we came across, then the Carlton Pack picked up our scent."

"The Carlton Pack?"

"Long time enemies of vampires, they're men who can shift into wolves. They've had some success at reducing our numbers over the years. Jack and I knew this, and we tried to shake them off. But we became complacent and Jack was caught." He paused. "By the time I'd tracked him down it was too late. They'd killed him, his head was off and burned and his heart staked."

"Oscar, that's awful." I switched sofas and sat next to him, rested my hand on his wide upper arm.

"Yeah, it was. Took a long time to get used to him not being around."

"I'm so sorry."

"No. You're the last person who should be sorry. It wasn't your fault, and you have the power to help stop that happening to Rhys, George, and Lloyd, the three souls in this world I still truly care about. They're like brothers to me, I don't want them to burn in Hell and suffer the way Jack is for all eternity."

"And you, surely you don't want that for yourself."

He glanced away. "I wouldn't choose it, but…"

"But what?"

"If it meant I could see Jack again then perhaps it's an option."

"No." I slid my hand up to his shoulder. "I never met Jack, but if he loved you the way you clearly loved him, I'm sure Hell isn't something he'd want for you. After all, it's not something you'd wish on your worst enemy, let alone a lover."

He stared at me. "I've never thought of it that way."

"Perhaps you should start." I smiled sadly. "I'll help in any way I can. I'm not sure what you all want me to do, or what I know, but I'll try to give you a key so your souls won't suffer the same fate."

"I know you will." He unfolded his arms and wrapped one around me, tugging me close.

I pressed up against his hard leather-clad body and stared into his eyes. "When did you last drink blood, Oscar?"

His eyebrows raised, as though I'd surprised him with my question. "A few months back, in New York."

"Did you fuck too?"

His eyebrows raised higher still. "No, there's been no one since Jack. I couldn't bring myself to, and then I met George at the Worshipful Company and he asked me to join him in his mission to find you, so I…" He paused. "I thought I'd wait for you, Darius. It seemed like the right thing to do."

"You've been waiting for me? All that time."

"Time doesn't have much meaning."

I swallowed. "So do you want to fuck now?" Jeez, had I really just asked that? Yes. I had. I wanted Oscar, there was no question about it. I wanted to get naked and have him do all the things to me he and Jack did, in that two weeks down in the mine, and when they were roaming around Canada.

"Ah, sweet Darius." He kissed the tip of my nose. "I want to fuck you so badly, but my big cock shouldn't be the one to take your virginity, and I have been known to get carried away."

"I've told you before, I can handle it."

"I'm not sure you can...yet. But you will. We'll work up to it."

"But—?"

"I've promised not to hurt you, and I intend to keep that promise, even though I'm not particularly comfortable right now." He squirmed on the seat.

"So do you want to drink?" I asked, my mouth drying at the thought.

"Taste your blood, Hell yeah." He rolled his lips in on themselves. "If you're offering that I'll take it."

"Don't vampires just take it anyway, without asking?"

"From humans, yes. But you're not human, are you?"

"So I've been told."

He reached for the base of my t-shirt and pulled it up. "Take this off."

I did as he'd asked.

Within seconds it was off and he was tugging at his leather jacket. Once removed he tossed it to the floor, then added his t-shirt to the pile.

I stared at his naked torso. His skin was taut over dense, hard muscles, and his nipples were small and dark. He had a patch of chest hair which ran downward, thickening beyond his navel before disappearing into the waistband of his leathers.

"Your skin is a beautiful color," he said, tracing from my left nipple to the right. "The veins are most visible here." He stroked up to my collarbone, then my neck.

"Where do you want to drink from?" I asked, a fizz of nerves winding through me.

"Wherever you'll let me." He ran his hand over my shoulder then down my arm. His huge palm was cool and a little rough. His gaze followed his own movements.

"Here." I held up my wrist, exposing the delicate underside to him.

"Good choice." He smiled then cupped my forearm.

I gulped.

"Don't be scared, it will feel good, like I told you it would."

"I'm not scared."

"Then you're a braver man than me, I'd have been scared if I hadn't been nearly dead and Jack told me he was going to bite me."

"Jack drained you."

"For my own good. We need you very much alive and as human as you can be, Darius. This is purely for pleasure, mine and yours."

He peeled back his top lip, exposing his teeth, then his eyes glazed slightly and two sharp teeth slid downward. His top lip settled again, protruding the way Rhys's had the night before.

"Are you ready?" he asked.

I nodded.

He hovered his mouth over my wrist for a moment, then drew it close and sank his needle-sharp fangs into it.

There was no pain, just prickly heat which surprised me knowing how cold he was.

And then it washed over me—a wonderful euphoria that grew with each tug of his mouth. The gentle suction flooded me with a sense of pleasure, and desire. I gasped and closed my eyes.

My cock hardened, straining against my pants, and my balls tightened.

"Oscar," I managed, settling my hand over his head, his thick, dark hair slotting between my fingers. "That's so fucking good."

He didn't answer, just continued gently drinking my blood.

The pleasure grew. I clenched my ass, thoughts of sex sweeping over me. More blood pumped through my shaft and I groaned, amazed at how hard I'd gotten so quickly.

After a full minute he pulled up, setting his thumb over the two tiny puncture marks he'd left.

I was high on bliss, ecstasy flooding my veins. Whatever was in his saliva was potent stuff.

"I told you you'd enjoy it," he murmured against my lips.

"Yes. Fuck yes." My dick ached. I needed to masturbate. "But...damn it." I glanced at my groin.

"I see the problem." He slid his palm over my tense abdomen then popped open the button on my jeans. "And I have a solution."

"Oscar," I gasped as he shoved at the material, quickly exposing my cock.

"That's it, let me..." He wrapped his hand around my shaft. "Relax and let me finish this."

"Fuck," I muttered, gripping his wide, chilly shoulder and fisting my other hand over a cushion. "I'm gonna..."

"Yeah, you're gonna come fast, real fast and real hard." He started pumping me, root to tip. "My saliva in your veins will do that."

I stared at his hand working up and down, the end of my cock, already glossy with pre-cum, peeking out on each stroke. It was one of the most erotic sights I'd ever seen.

I raised my hips as the pressure grew, lifting my ass from the sofa. He stayed with me, his breaths coming as fast as mine. My balls retracted, my belly tensed further. "It's here."

He didn't answer.

"Fuck!" I came, long and hard, holding my breath as spurt after spurt of cum landed on my belly.

He rubbed steady and firm, extending the bliss.

I cried out, dug my nails into him, and arched my back as sweat popped on my forehead and armpits.

"Ahh...yeah...that's it." I slumped and he stilled.

My belly was basted with pearly fluid. A strand had caught in my pubic hair, stretching up to my navel. Another drip remained balanced in my slit.

"Did that feel good?" he asked, kissing my cheek, then my lips. His fangs had retracted.

"Couldn't...you tell?" I panted.

"Yeah." He smiled. "And that was just my hand. Think what my cock will be like when we get to that point."

Chapter Twelve

Oscar

I stared at Darius. He was breathing hard, his cheeks were flushed and beads of sweat sat on his top lip. He looked more beautiful than I could ever have imagined. We were so lucky to have found him.

I stroked his cock. It was still hard, the pulse throbbing against my palm. He was so responsive, so utterly open. A blank page when it came to sex. Which was why I couldn't fuck him, not for some time. Jack and I had been wild together. But he'd been a big, tough unbreakable vampire. Darius was a delicate half human. A wild session with me would not only hurt him, it might also scare him away from us all.

"Was it good for you? The blood?" he asked.

"Perfect." I licked my lips, gathering up the last of his taste. "You're all I'll ever need. Your blood is strong and delicious."

"Good, I'm glad."

"We were meant to be, Darius," I said. "All of us."

Something flashed over his eyes.

"What?" I asked.

"You keep talking about *all* of us and..."

I released his cock and slid my hand up his body, enjoying the delicate contours of his abdomen and chest. "Tell me."

"Do you really mean *all* of you and me?"

"Yes."

"Even when..."

I raised my eyebrows.

"Even when I tell you Rhys gave me a blow job last night?"

I smiled. "Your first blow job, congratulations."

"And Lloyd kissed me, outside, and we..."

"And you had a good time together. I understand, we all do. You're our cambion, and it's going to take all of us to protect you and see that you're kept happy and satisfied."

"So you don't mind, none of you, if I...?"

"Have sex with us all? No, we don't mind."

"What if it goes deeper?" He cupped my cheek, his hand pleasant and warm. "What if I fall for one of you, Oscar?"

"We hope you will fall for us all." I moved closer to him, feeling his breath on my skin. "It's what we want, to love you and have you love us in return."

"Vampires can love." He hadn't said it as a question, more of a statement to himself.

"With fierce passion and frightening intensity. We love with a determination that will blow your mind, Darius." I paused. "Just give us a chance. I promise, we won't let you down."

"I want that." He rested back as if exhausted. "I want to give you all a chance. This is so new, but also exciting and a little scary, if it's okay to say that."

"Of course. I want to know how you feel, so I can make it right if it's not. And if there's anything I can do to make it less scary you must let me know."

"Being with you, all of you helps with that."

"I'm pleased that's the case." I paused. "I should get something to clean you up." I nodded at his sticky belly.

"Yeah, thanks."

"And then something to eat and a rest for you."

"Shall we order takeout? What do you fancy?"

I reached for my t-shirt and tugged it on.

"Pizza, Indian..."

"Whatever you want, babe."

"Ah, fuck." Darius frowned. "You don't eat, do you? Sorry."

"You'll get used to it."

The afternoon turned to evening. Darius ate pizza—a huge amount for someone so lean in my opinion—then made a call to his agent and a photographer. I didn't know why he was bothering. George was one step ahead of his schedule and would adjust it to suit our needs over the coming weeks and months. Darius's safety and finding the key was our priority, not him getting his photograph taken over and over. It wasn't as if he would ever need the money, we had more than we could spend between us. And now he'd reached adulthood he'd never age. Modelling was something he'd be able to do for as long as he wanted providing we could conceal his youthful appearance.

I watched him move across the room with his cell pressed to his ear. He was chatting to his mother, his daily catch up, he'd said.

Even the way he walked appealed to me, his back straight, his long limbs elegant, and knowing his skin was warm and soft beneath his clothing made my cock tingle with a hunger to be close to him. And he was so damn beautiful. It was hard to believe a demon had anything to do with his creation, but of course that had been part of his father's evil plan, to create a human no one could resist, everyone wanted to feast their gaze on, and ultimately be with.

When it darkened outside, I pulled the curtains, relieved the sunlight had gone from another day. I sent George a text, letting him know all was calm. He replied saying they'd found nothing in the alleyway.

"What do you want to do?" Darius asked, setting his phone aside. "Go out, stay in? Are we waiting for something?"

"I'd rather stay in, I don't think we'll get any visits from your father in here."

"Why not?"

"It's too..." I struggled to find the right words. "It's too nice, too full of warmth and good."

"Good." He frowned. "Surely my mother's house was the same, when he visited her that time." A slight rise of color grew on his cheeks. "When he came to seduce her and create me."

I thought for a moment. "Yeah, I'm sure you're right. George and I talked about it. I think the difference is she was longing for a man in her life, a special someone and he knew that. It made her vulnerable and that's how he wormed his way into her dreams and her bed."

Darius ran both of his hands over his hair, tugging his bangs back from his face. "It's kind of sick, don't you think?"

"Evil has a habit of playing that way."

"You said earlier I wouldn't age. What did you mean by that?"

I shrugged. "Exactly that. Time has no meaning in demon worlds, or vampire worlds. You don't need to worry about your body growing old and wrinkled, you'll stay in the prime of your life, forever."

"Forever." He blew out a breath. "Fuck, that's a long time."

I stood and went to him, cupped his elbows. "Is it long enough if you're with someone, or a few someones, you love?"

"Well I..."

I smiled. "You're stuck with us, for as long as you want us, even if that means centuries...millennia."

He glanced away.

"What?" I frowned.

"Unless you get staked or burned like Jack did. Unless the Carlton Pack, isn't that what they're called, get a hold of any of you?"

"That won't happen." I'd spoken in a gruffer voice than I'd intended. "The Company keeps a close eye on the movements of the Carlton Pack now, and on top of that we're careful to avoid them. I learned long ago they should never be underestimated."

He set his gaze on mine for a moment, then turned away, forcing me to drop my hands. "I've never fallen in love, Oscar, or even had a relationship, you know that."

"I do."

"But you've all wriggled under my skin so quickly." He rubbed over the tiny bite marks on his wrist. "If I'm not thinking about you, I'm thinking about Lloyd or Rhys or George."

"That's fine by me, by all of us."

He was quiet for a moment, then, "I really hope I can help with the key, so you can all live in the knowledge you won't burn in Hell if something does happen."

"You will, the fable tells us so." I pushed thoughts of Jack from my mind. There was nothing I could do to save his soul. I'd beaten myself up enough over the whole sorry ordeal. "And it doesn't matter how long it takes. There's no rush, and no pressure."

"I'm trying to get my head around it." He turned. "But thanks, Oscar, for what you just said."

I nodded, then sat.

"I'm going to take a shower." He gestured toward the bathroom, flexing and unflexing his fingers as he did so.

"I'll be here."

He glanced around. "You're sure my demon father won't show up?"

"As sure as I can be, but we're not taking chances, which is why you've got me in your apartment and not outside your door like in Paris."

"So back then…" His eyes widened and he clenched his fists. "You were…"

"Keeping you safe, yes. Lloyd had just found you after our long search. There was no way we were going to risk anything happening to you."

He paused for a moment, then nodded and headed into the bathroom.

He pushed the door up but didn't shut it.

Water splashed onto the shower tray and I closed my eyes, imagining him stripping off, the mirror steaming up, and the confusing thoughts running through his mind. He'd taken it incredibly well. The things he'd learned today would have had mere mortals running for the hills. An average guy could be forgiven for having a nervous breakdown, losing the plot, spiraling into a tailspin. But not our cambion, he was taking it in his stride.

Or was he?

He'd just stood before me flexing his fingers, fidgeting on the spot and heat growing in his cheeks.

Suddenly I was compelled to check on him. So I moved to the door of the bathroom and peered through it.

Darius was in the shower, his perfect skin dotted with droplets as though he'd been sprinkled with diamonds. He had his back to me and my cock twitched as I studied his ass—it was high and pert with two small dimples at the base of his spine.

He's so gorgeous.

He held his face to the water. A groan echoed from the shower cubicle as his arms straightened, the muscles in them flexing and straining.

And then the room lit up. A burning bright orange and the air seemed to crackle. Sparks flew from his fingers into the shower tray, bouncing up the glass, steaming against the water.

I held my breath, mesmerized. I'd suspected he'd released sparks in the alley, when he had his close call with the demon, but I hadn't seen them. Now I was witnessing the power he had inside in all its stunning glory.

On and on the brilliant starbursts of sparks flew from his fingertips. The cubicle was full of life and heat. He moaned as though the effort of releasing them pained him, or exhausted him, one of the two.

I wanted to go to him, but stopped myself. I got the feeling releasing sparks was a very private thing for Darius. He'd left me in the living room to do it.

But he hadn't shut the door.

My feet twitched, wanting to step into the room. I stopped myself. Our relationship was new, delicate, and of the upmost importance. I'd already drank his blood and given him a hand job—probably done more than I should have so soon into our meeting.

At least I didn't fuck him.

I shoved my hand down the front of my leathers and adjusted my cock. The temptation to go in there, bend him over and introduce him to man-on-man sex was almost too much.

The sparks stopped, and the sound of hissing was replaced with the splash of water again.

I ducked away from the doorway, not wanting him to see me watching. After pacing to the window I looked out.

Lloyd was at the corner of the street—hood up, leaning on a wall, one knee bent and smoking a cigarette. Two girls, arms linked, walked past him, veering closer to the curbside as they went.

I didn't blame them. Dressed all in black, and with his dark eyes, Lloyd was handsome, sure, but more dangerous than they could ever know. Not that he'd ever been into women, unless it was for a much needed drink.

Glancing around, I wondered if I'd spot Rhys or George. I didn't. They were either out of sight or at our apartment. Two of us keeping guard over Darius was enough…in theory.

The sky was full of stars; a sparkling blanket spread over London. I was pleased because when the demon had come he'd brought storm clouds with him. Day had turned into night, the wind had whipped up, and I'd been surprised not to hear the crack of thunder and witness bolts of lightning. Seeing a clear sky and stars allowed me to breathe a little easier. The demon was out there, but he wasn't close.

"Hey," Darius said behind me.

I turned. He wore a pair of tartan pyjama bottoms with Calvin Klein written around the waistband.

"You alright, babe?"

He smiled. "Better for a shower."

I pressed my lips together, not wanting to admit I'd seen him releasing sparks.

"I'm gonna..." He pointed at the bedroom. "Get some rest."

"Want company?" I asked.

His gaze slid to my groin.

"I just wanna be close," I said. "Like I mentioned, we've got all the time in the world for the full on physical stuff."

His shoulders relaxed, then he stifled a yawn. "I'm still getting my head around the immortal thing."

"It's a lot to take on board." I sat and removed my boots. "Can I take a shower too?"

"Of course." He raised his eyebrows.

"What? You thought vampires didn't shower?"

He laughed suddenly, a lovely soft sound that erased the worry from his features. "I don't know. I guess I'd never thought about it."

I stood, undoing my pants as I straightened. "We've got a lot to learn about each other."

"I've got a lot to learn about *all* of you."

Chapter Thirteen

Darius

I lay on the bed, listening to the shower and staring at the ceiling.

I'm not going to age.

Or at least not the regular way of getting old and my body giving up. There was always the possibility of my demon father getting possession of my physical self and leaving my soul to rot—which actually sounded like a worse deal than the rest of the human race. I'd take wrinkles, dementia and incontinence any day.

Holding my wrist up, I studied the tiny fang marks over the pale blue vein on the inner side. The minute scabs appeared to be healing fast. There was no bruise. I guessed Oscar was well practiced at sucking blood, having been around so long and it being the only sustenance he had.

The shower turned off and I rolled over to face the window. The curtains had been drawn and light from the bathroom shone onto their silky black material.

Within a minute the bed dipped behind me. The scent of soap swirled around and Oscar's hard body pressed against mine.

"You okay for spooning?" he asked, sliding his arm over my waist.

"Haven't tried it before, but I'm willing to give it a go." I rested my hand on his thick forearm.

"You'll know I'm here, looking after you, if you stir in the night."

He'd spoken by my ear, his breath chill on my neck and cheek.

"No one and nothing will harm you, Darius, not on my watch. Get some sleep." He paused. "I don't sleep, so have no fear I'll miss anything."

"You don't sleep?"

"No, and would you believe, it's one of the things I miss the most. Those few hours of oblivion. A break from thoughts. Pure blackness."

"You're lucky if your nights were like that...before...you know."

"Why do you say that?"

"My dreams are vivid. *Too* vivid."

"Why? What happens?"

I hesitated, not wanting to tell him that I dreamed as a woman. That my body morphed into a female with breasts and a pussy. That men in my dream drank me in with their eyes, kissed me, touched me, and on occasion brought me to orgasm.

"Don't worry about telling me now," he whispered. "Sleep."

I closed my eyes and exhaled. It had been a long day with lots of revelations.

Within minutes I was slipping into slumber. My thoughts fragmented and my body sagged into the mattress and against Oscar. I wasn't used to sleeping with someone else, but far from being strange it felt right, comfortable, as it should be.

Soon I was where I'd expected to be, standing on Tower Bridge looking down at the Thames. I stroked the curves of my breasts, then the dips of my small waist, ending on a slide over the flare of my feminine hips.

Overhead, ravens circled. An old fashioned car went past, and an urchin held his hands forward, reminding me of Oliver Twist, then evaporated. The familiar, unpleasant smells filled my nose and I grimaced, waiting for a breeze to slide them away from the air around me.

It did.

On the river the usual small rowing boat was making its way along the muddy waters. Holding three men, one a bound prisoner, it made steady progress. Again I was drawn to the prisoner, as if I knew him, as though he was important to me somehow. But how could I know him? How could he be anything to do with my life? This was a scene from years ago. Not only that, it was a dream.

Compelled to get closer, learn more, I made my way over the bridge with the intention of getting to the water's edge. If only I could see his face clearly, perhaps that would give me a clue as to who he was and why he was so prominent in my psyche.

A sense of urgency besieged me. I began to run, aware of my breasts jiggling against my dress, the voluptuous flesh wobbling for all to see.

And look and stare they did.

I left the bridge, rushing down the steep slope toward the prison walls and the riverbank.

He had something for me, I didn't know what.

The key.

In that dreamful moment the realization came to me. I'd known the prisoner was important. All along that sense had been with me at this point in the dream, and now it was confirmed somewhere deep in my mind. I had a surge of energy, rushing closer to the prisoner with each step, and then he was there, not the prisoner…the handsome stranger, smiling and holding a bunch of red roses.

"Hey, pretty lady." His smile widened. "Here, for you."

I didn't take the flowers, instead I rested my hand on my chest, my breaths coming fast and the rest of London fading around me. I scanned the river, looking for the boat and the prisoner.

"Take these, my love." The stranger was close, so close he crooked his finger beneath my chin turning my attention back to his face. "And now that I've found you I'm coming for you…soon."

There was something dark and dangerous in the depths of his eyes that chilled me. I shuddered and tried to step away from him.

"I'm coming for you soon," he repeated.

Part of me knew I'd wake now. This was the point the dream ended and even in sleep I was aware of that.

"No," he said, "do not be afraid, Darius, I will care for your beautiful body in its male and female forms. You have nothing to fear."

"Leave me alone." I tried to twist from his touch but his grip on my chin was like a vice. Panic grew inside me. He was so strong, so evil.

"Just let it happen, do not fight." He came closer, a strange murky scent filling my nose that made me want to gag.

"No!" I pushed at him, putting all of my strength into the shove. He didn't react. It was as if I'd done nothing.

I was scared now. London had evaporated, the prisoner had gone. My chances of getting the key had slipped from my grasp.

"Surrender to me," the stranger said, fire glowing in his eyes. "And I will make it as painless as possible."

"Step away from him."

A new voice entered my head. It was deep and authoritative, and blasted around us as if it had arrived with a bellow of hot air.

The devilish stranger turned, fury twisting his mouth. "Benedict!"

"Yes, it is I."

I stared at the man, knowing it was the prisoner from the boat. He was bedraggled, his hands still bound, and he wore a tattered cape with a fur collar. His beard was thick and matted, his hair long, but his eyes were full of passion and determination.

"Leave, now. This is no concern of yours." The stranger left my side, much to my relief, and rushed to Benedict. He seemed to float rather than walk, and dry leaves swirled around him.

"This is my concern. *Darius* is my concern," Benedict said.

"No, no he's not. He's my son. Now go. It's my right to possess his earthly body."

The two figures merged, as though they'd turned into black smoke and were twirling and twisting together. A weird howl rang out, an ear-splitting scream that chilled my bones. It was hard to breathe, and my heart was thudding.

"Darius."

Someone was speaking my name.

"Darius, wake up."

I spun around to the blackness. The bridge had gone. Everything had gone.

"Darius."

Oscar?

The scream continued, loud and frantic. I flailed my arms and kicked my legs, desperate to get away from the swirling evil.

"Darius, babe, it's okay. I've got you."

Strong arms tightened around me and my back was pressed against a hard chest.

It was me making the awful screaming noise.

"Shh," Oscar said into my ear. "It's okay, calm down. It's all okay."

I clamped my mouth shut, but immediately a sob bubbled up. Adrenaline was surging around my system. The need for fight or flight had well and truly taken hold. Flight, it would have to be flight—I could never fight the stranger. He was too strong and too wicked. More than I could take on.

My father.

I opened my eyes. The enormity of who he was bowling through my emotions so violently it was like my thoughts were skittles, scattering every which way.

I snatched in a breath.

It had been him, all along, in my dreams. He'd never been far away despite what I'd thought. My father had been with me, at night, for years.

"That's it, just relax, relax and breathe," Oscar whispered. "I've got you, you're safe. You're safe here with me."

"I know," I managed. "Thank you."

"Well done." He held me tighter, wrapping his thick legs over mine and curving his body around my back and ass. "It's over now."

"But...but it's not," I managed. "This is just the start."

"What do you mean?"

"I told you I had vivid dreams, right?"

"Yeah."

"Well this one was more vivid than most, and it's a recurring dream."

"So you're used to it."

"I was...but it's just changed." I gripped him tighter.

"Go on." His voice was deep, as though laced with a new concern.

"I..." I paused. "I just saw my father."

"Your father?"

"Yeah, in my dream, and what's more..."

"Tell me."

I was aware of the tension radiating from him. He was worried.

Are my dreams important to the vampires?

"You have to tell me, Darius, it's the only way we can protect you."

"My father is getting ready to possess me, and Benedict was trying to stop him."

"Benedict?" He sat, tugging me with him. "You dreamed of Master Benedict?"

I nodded and squeezed the bridge of my nose. "Yes, that's the name of the prisoner in my dream. He's been in it all along, from the very first time I had it, but I've only just learned his name."

Oscar stared at me with his eyes wide and his lips in a tight straight line.

"What does it mean?" I asked.

"It means we need to call the others and get them over here now."

"We do? In the middle of the night?"

"Night is when we function best, and let's face it, we'll hardly wake them."

"I guess."

He stroked my cheek. "I'll call them, then you can tell them everything. This is getting serious, Darius. Thank goodness we found you when we did." He paused. "Time is running out, and that's something I never thought I'd say."

Chapter Fourteen

George

Ten minutes ago I'd been relaxing in our apartment, laptop closed for once, and listening to the sound of the city at night—sirens, fox calls, drunken voices below and in the distance a car alarm.

Now I was sprinting through the streets with Rhys. Darius filled my thoughts. I ached to see him, to be with him, to confirm to my inner self that he was okay.

If he isn't I may as well go to Hell now.

He was our savior, the ethereal man who could save our souls. If there'd been one thing that had kept me going all of these centuries it was knowing he was out there, somewhere.

And Lloyd, clever bugger, had found him in Paris. I wished it had been me, but I'd pushed those thoughts aside. We had him in our sights and that was all that really mattered.

Rhys's shoulder brushed mine as we ran. Our speed was swift, likely humans in our midst would only see a blur of light and feel the gust of air as we passed. Usually we were more careful to be completely inconspicuous when running but Oscar's phone call had rid us of that need.

One priority—Darius.

When we reached the threshold of his apartment we both hesitated.

"I've already been invited in," Rhys said. ·

"So go." A twist of hurt curled in my belly. I was the last of us to have any intimate time with Darius. And I longed for it, my body screamed for it. My cold, dark heart bled for it. Would it ever happen?

Oscar pulled open the door. "Good, you're here."

Rhys stepped inside then turned to me. "I'll get him."

I nodded, thankful he understood my predicament.

"It's okay, I'm here."

Darius's voice washed over me. It was like music to my heart, a breeze in my ears, which were always so acute. His voice, the depth, the way it vibrated through his throat, was something I could listen to for always.

His gaze connected with mine and he blew out a breath through pursed lips. His arms hung at his sides, his torso was bare, and some kind of clan tartan adorned his nightwear.

I licked my lips, not daring to imagine his flavor—the taste of his kisses, his cock, his blood.

I want it all.

Our gazes locked then he nodded and gestured for me to enter his home. "Come into my home, George. We were waiting for you."

Oscar curled his hand over Darius's shoulder, as though giving him strength.

"Thank you." I stepped in. An unusual sense of urgency had invaded my thoughts. It was strange when I was used to time being so fluid, like a tap that would never switch off, a bird that would never stop singing. But here it was...time running out.

Darius walked, looking like an Adonis, into the living area and sat on a seriously large and expensive looking white leather sofa. He crossed one leg over the other and spread his left arm over the back of the cushions.

Oscar sat on one side of him, his dark features brooding. Lloyd hovered behind him, pacing with his hood up and his arms crossed. Rhys had pulled back a curtain and was looking out of the windows as if expecting a demon to slam into them at any moment.

I pulled in a deep breath then walked into the room and perched my butt on the low oak table in front of the sofa.

Leaning forward, I took Darius's right hand in mine. "Start from the beginning."

"The beginning beginning?" he asked, allowing me to hold his hand in both of mine.

"Yes, that will do." I nodded.

He pulled in a deep breath, his lips pursing a little. "In that case we'll have to go back to when I was about thirteen."

"We can do that." I managed a small smile, hoping that would reassure him.

"Okay." He glanced at Oscar, then at Lloyd.

I was glad he was getting comfort from them, but equally I wanted him to know he could trust me, and that I, too, would always protect him and be there for him. His best interests, his body and soul, were my priority now.

He has to know that.

"When I was thirteen," he said. "The dreams started."

"You can tell us everything," Oscar said, his deep timbre echoing around the room.

"Yeah, I know." Darius nodded. "When I was thirteen my dreams became weird."

"What do you mean?" I asked.

"They became more vivid, more full of color, and I could remember them the next day, as if they were coming back to haunt me."

I resisted sharing a look with Lloyd. This was something we'd talked about. Darius being so in tune with the underworld, whether he knew it or not, was going to manifest somehow. Dreams were an obvious choice for his demon father to contact him through as he waited for adulthood.

"Go on." I tilted my head, keen to hear every nuance in his articulation.

"But it was the same dream nearly every time," Darius said.

"Recurring?" Rhys raised his eyebrows.

"Yeah." Darius glanced at him, then back to me. "Since I was thirteen, over and over, practically every night."

"Can you describe it?" I asked.

He glanced at his chest and ran his hand over his pecs. "I'm on Tower Bridge and there's this prisoner in a boat being taken toward the Tower of London." He shook his head. "Before I couldn't…see the prisoner, his face that is."

"But now you can?" I asked.

His gaze connected with mine for a second then he shook his head. "Yes, and I know his name."

"And what is it?"

"Benedict."

A surge of energy went through me. Master Benedict was in Darius's dreams…what the heck?

"But more than that," Darius went on, "I know who the other man standing close to me is."

"Other man?" Lloyd asked, and looking as shocked as I felt at the mention of Master Benedict.

"Yeah," Oscar said. "The *other* man in his dream."

I nodded, a frown creasing my brow.

Who the Hell is it? This other man standing close.

Darius clenched his fists. "It's my father."

"Fuck, what!" Rhys snapped the curtains closed and flicked his attention around the room, corner to corner, wall to wall. "Where?"

"In his dream," I said. It was as though a jigsaw puzzle was coming together in my brain. All the things I'd learned about the fable were slotting into place. "So let me get this straight. In your dream you're back in time, in London, by the Tower, and there's a prisoner and your father with you."

"Yeah, that's the dream." Darius sat forward, a new energy coming to him. I wondered if sparks were pricking at his fingertips.

"Can you tell us more?" I asked.

He glanced at Oscar, then over his shoulder at Rhys. "I can. I think."

"We're all here for you," I said. "You have to believe that."

"I do. And I believe you're all here for my protection *and* to serve yourselves." He glanced down at his feet.

"Hey!" Lloyd said. "Serve *ourselves*?"

"Yeah." He pulled his hand from mine and twisted his fingers together. He was still looking at the floor. "Save your own souls."

"Saving our souls is important." I grabbed his hand again and caught his cheek in my palm. "But saving you, and your soul is *more* important. You have to believe that."

He frowned, but at least he looked up at me.

"In all our history," I said, gentling my voice. "A cambion would be the freerer of souls, the key to escaping an eternity burning in Hell. You are he, Darius. We would be selfish individuals if we let anything happen to you when you have so much to give."

He turned away.

Damn it. Now I sound as if I don't care about him.

"Please." I sank onto my knees and rested my palms on his thighs. "We love you. We have since the moment we saw you. You're all we want, you have to believe that."

I didn't look at Rhys, Lloyd or Oscar. I was always the capable one. The guy who had it sussed. Dropping to one knee and begging wasn't on my usual to-do list. It didn't suit me, but needs must.

"Darius," I went on. "The key you have, the gift, and the beauty inside and outside of you is a rare thing. More than rare, it's a once in a lifetime thing for us to experience, even a very long lifetime. Please, let us help you...let us in."

He locked his gaze on mine again. "Let you in?"

"Yes. Into the darkest parts of your mind, into who you really are in your soul."

He glanced at Oscar. "Can you handle it?"

"Try us." Oscar folded his arms and his mouth twitched as if they'd shared some secret.

Darius swallowed. "Okay." He pulled in a breath. "When I dream…I'm a woman."

A silence descended.

I was aware of Rhys and Lloyd sharing a look

I kept my expression neutral. This was more than even I could have imagined. "Physically or mentally?" I asked.

"Physically." He frowned. "I'm always the same mentally….aren't I?"

"Yes, I suspect so." I smiled, hoping I didn't give away my surprise at his revelation.

"It makes perfect sense," Lloyd said. "His father could switch between incubus and succubus depending on who he was seducing. The female and male forms are easy to switch from one to the other for a demon."

"But…" Darius gestured to his groin.

I felt a small tremble in mine.

"But," he said again, "I'm very much male." He glanced at Rhys, Oscar and Lloyd. "As you can all testify."

Again a twist of jealousy caught me. I soldiered on. "Yes, you're male. But until you hit puberty I suspect you could have chosen between the two genders."

"What?" His eyes widened. "I could have chosen to be male or female?"

"It's just a guess," I said, "but an educated one, going on what I know about incubi."

He tugged his hand from mine, folded his arms and slotted his palms into his pits.

Oscar wrapped his arm around Darius's shoulders and pulled him closer so their bodies touched.

Darius didn't resist. In fact he kind of wilted against him.

"You can switch between genders, much like your father can," I said. "Or at least you could have, until you reached puberty. Had you known that, perhaps you'd have become a woman."

"No, I don't think so." He paused. "Is that why I'm gay? In my dreams when I'm a woman, I've, on the odd occasion the reoccurring one hasn't happened, dreamed of being with a man...intimately. Is that why I'm into men and not women? It's the female in me?"

"I have no idea." I smiled. "Why is any one of us gay? I'm sure it's for many different reasons."

Everyone was silent.

Darius blew out a breath, then, "I can't cope with being half female and half male on top of having a demon father, being immortal, and holding the key to saving vampires from an eternity burning in Hell." There'd been a shake in his voice.

"Shh." Oscar stroked his hair. "It's okay, babe.'

Fuck! Oscar is the toughest hard nut around, yet for Darius he's turned sappy.

But seeing the look on Darius's face, I wasn't complaining. Oscar's touch seemed to be soothing Darius's anxieties and easing his nerves. The last thing we needed was for him to freak out.

"George," Lloyd said, nodding at the kitchen. "Can we..."

"Yes. Of course." I caught Oscar's gaze as I stood.

He nodded a little letting me know Darius was okay in his arms while Lloyd and I spoke.

"We need to go to the Tower," Lloyd said, as soon as we stepped into Darius's sleek, modern kitchen.

"I know." I placed my hands on my hips and frowned. "This is reaching a tipping point. Darius's father isn't afraid to let him know he exists in daylight and at night."

"Which means he's preparing to possess him. Once that happens, Darius will have a fate worse than death."

Just hearing those words was like having a stake driven through my heart. I swallowed as nausea churned my belly.

Lloyd grimaced, as though experiencing the same discomfort.

"We should go to the Tower now," I said. "Right now."

"I don't like risking him, but it makes sense." Lloyd pulled out a pack of cigarettes. He tapped the base of the box and took one between his lips.

"Not in here." I frowned. "This is a nice place."

"Fuck," he muttered, slipping the cigarette away, then the box. "I don't like this, any of it."

"Me neither, but if we're at the Tower, all of us together, and he turns up, we have a chance of defeating him. If he catches Darius in the day again, when only one set of eyes are on him, our odds are significantly decreased."

Lloyd nodded. "Yeah, it'll take all of us."

"He's going to be really fucking determined."

"And pissed that he can't get the body he wants and has been waiting for."

I glanced over my shoulder at the living room. "Benedict is in his dream, Lloyd."

"Were you expecting that?"

"No, but I always had an inkling he had a role in delivering this key."

"So what does it mean?"

"It means we have to learn more about Master Benedict, perhaps delve into Darius's dream a little deeper, find out what his intentions are, what he says."

"One thing is for sure, he's leading us to the Tower of London."

"With our cambion." A steely sense of determination speared through me. "So we have to go through with it and see what happens."

Lloyd nodded. His eyes were narrowed, his jaw tense.

"It'll be okay." I clasped my hand on his shoulder. "This is what we've been waiting for."

"But there's so much to lose. That beautiful man in there is innocent. If anything happens to him…"

"It won't. Don't think like that." I pulled in a breath. "We have to be strong for him, and don't forget we're a formidable group of guys when we've got our minds set."

"And they are set." He tilted his chin. "On protecting the man we love."

"And finding the key so we can all be together, forever."

He nodded and I saw the fight in his eyes. Lloyd wasn't going to let anything happen to Darius, he loved him as much as I did, that much was clear.

Chapter Fifteen

Darius

"We're going to the Tower of London...now?" I said.

"Yes." George nodded. "We need to face this head on and find out all we can while it's fresh in your mind."

"But..." These guys were nuts. Wandering around the banks of the Thames after midnight wasn't a sensible idea.

"You have nothing to worry about." George smiled, his handsome face lighting up. "You have four vampires with you, who all love you and would do anything for you. No mortal would stand a chance if they so much as looked at you the wrong way."

"It's not mortals I'm worried about," I muttered as I stood.

Oscar rose too. "You don't have to worry about anything."

I did, and I was. There was heat in my chest and in my shoulders. The familiar ache which turned to hot pain had spread down my arms. I was thankful I'd released sparks earlier in the shower, it meant I'd have control over them for the next few hours. "I'll get my jacket."

While riding on the back of Oscar's bike through the dark, I summoned my courage. My dreams had all been leading to this moment and it was time to face it head on.

But that didn't mean I was looking forward to it.

Maybe nothing would happen. Perhaps we'd just have a night time stroll, see the moonlight on the river and spot a few bats swooping low for bugs.

Oscar pulled the bike to a halt on Tower Bridge at the point I'd told him the dream began. Rhys, Lloyd and George were already there. I had no idea how they'd arrived so fast, Oscar said they'd run, but that was super-human speed.

They are super-human.

I climbed off and removed my helmet. It was strange to be in a place I'd only ever dreamed of. Although I'd lived in London for years, this bridge was out of my way and I'd only ever been over it in a cab.

"Are you okay?" George asked, stepping near and stroking my upper arm over my denim jacket.

I enjoyed his touch and his closeness. George fascinated me. He was obviously highly respected by the others and the great length of time he'd had on Earth had given him a wisdom which shone from his eyes. Eyes that looked fresh and young—like his handsome face—yet were really centuries old.

"Yeah," I said. "I'm okay. I just want to get this done, see if we can find out more about the key."

"And your father," George said. "I'd very much like to take him out of the equation. That would protect you for always."

"How do you intend to do that?"

"The only way to truly defeat a demon is to show him that love and goodness is your armor, that way he'll give up."

"Even one who wants his son?" After all this time of not having a father, it was strange to talk of one in connection to myself.

"Darius," Lloyd said. "Do not make the mistake of having affection for this demon. He created you for his own evil ends. He did not love your mother. In fact, he is incapable of love. He can't and never will love you. It's your perfect body he wants to inhabit. He does not care for your soul."

I shuddered. The whole idea of a demon possessing my body was beyond horrible. And George was right, the sooner he was out of the equation the better, then we could concentrate on finding the key. If we found that, and got rid of the demon, it would mean we were all safe from burning in Hell.

I stepped up to the stone wall at the side of the bridge and looked down at the water. The silvery light of the moon shimmered off the gentle ripples.

Finding myself rubbing my chest, I realized how used I'd become to seeing this sight as a female, with breasts, curves, a vagina. Now in my male form, it suddenly felt odd.

Rhys stood next to me. His usually smiling face had been deathly serious since he'd arrived in my apartment. "Is that where you see the prisoner?" He pointed downward.

"Yeah, he's in a small wooden boat with two other men. One is rowing, one appears to be guarding him."

"And is he bound?" Oscar asked, moving to my other side.

"His hands are shackled. I know now he wears a big cloak with a fur collar."

"That's definitely Master Benedict." There was surety in Lloyd's voice. "He was known for that cloak, in fact at The Company his statue shows him wearing just that."

"It does." George ran his hand down my back to my ass. "Usually you're female when you're here and the dream starts?"

"Yeah."

He stroked my butt.

I let him, enjoying the way his caresses soothed my mind and calmed my heart rate.

"And then what?" he said by my ear. "Then what happens?"

"There's an old-fashioned car that goes past and a child begging." I paused. "But it's the prisoner I'm drawn to, so I walk down there." I pointed at the steps leading to the bank of the river. "Only in my dream it's more of a bank, and it's cobbled at the base."

"Come on, then." George slid his hand upward to my waist and circled it. "Let's go that way."

I allowed him to tug me close and steer me to the end of the bridge. A night bus drove by; a flash of red, its engine loud. Behind it was a black cab, its yellow light on, showing it was available.

As we went down the stone steps, a sense of *deja-vu* washed through me. I'd been here so many times, but never in reality, or at night...or with vampires.

"And what happens here?" Lloyd asked, coming to a halt as I did.

"This is where I lose track of the prisoner and a man appears, a truly handsome man with an alluring smile and red roses for me."

"Red roses?" Oscar said with a sharp laugh.

"I'm female, remember." I paused. "And what have you got against red roses?"

He shrugged with a half smile still on his face. "Nothing if you like them."

I didn't answer, instead I stared at the spot my father always appeared. Now it was a neat gravel path with a small wall on one side leading to a grassy bank. Gone were the cobbles, the dirt, and the ravens overhead.

"He shows up here." I pointed. "And distracts me. In my last dream he told me he's coming for me soon. It was the first time he's ever said that."

"Let him fucking try." Rhys folded his arms and glanced around. "I dare him."

"Rhys," Lloyd said. "Be careful."

"Well, the sooner it's done, the better." Rhys huffed.

"Darius," George said, "in your last dream, you mentioned Master Benedict—was he on the bank or still in the boat?"

"Just here, with my father."

All four vampires stared at the point on the ground I'd indicated.

"He stood *there*?" Lloyd said. "Master Benedict."

"Yeah."

"Wow." Rhys nodded. "Cool."

"And can you remember what he said?" George asked me. "If anything."

"Yeah, kind of." I rubbed my forehead. "My father said he would make it as painless as possible for me if I surrendered. I guess he was talking about possession." I gulped. "Benedict appeared and told him to step away from me."

"I take it that didn't happen," Lloyd said. "A demon doesn't obey instructions."

"Actually it did happen, because Benedict argued with my father when he said I was of no concern to him."

"Oh?" George raised his eyebrows at me.

"Yeah, he said Darius *is* my concern."

"Master Benedict actually said your name?" Oscar asked.

"Yep, and then my father rushed to him, or something did and they appeared to fight, but it was like that swirl of air in the alley, Oscar, a twister or a cyclone type thing, made of black smoke and roaring."

"Fuck," Lloyd muttered.

"Yeah, fuck. Master Benedict is trying to protect Darius for a good reason." George stared to the left and frowned. "What's that?"

"What?" I asked.

"Over there, I can hear something."

I strained my ears. Nothing.

"Shit, he's here." Oscar suddenly stepped before me, his broad back blocking my view of the Thames.

"Surround him," Rhys said, hemming me in against Oscar, Lloyd and George.

"What's happening?" I asked, but as I'd said the words I knew. Clouds had masked the pale light of the moon, the temperature had dropped and a shroud of heavy darkness had fallen.

"Your father is here." George clasped my arm. "Do as we say, we *will* protect you."

Fear gripped me, and my belly tightened. A gust of wind skittered dust and litter around my feet. I clenched my fists, heat building in my chest and arms. A nasty taste filled my mouth again, and a rancid scent invaded my nose—I recognized both of them.

"Over there," Rhys said. "Look."

I glanced over his shoulder. The same twisting swirl of air I'd seen before was growing, and it was getting bigger by the second.

"You got a plan here, George?" Oscar shouted above the noise of the howling wind.

"Keep him locked between us," George said. "He can't penetrate our love for his son. He'll feel that and give up."

"It's going to get pretty damn violent in a minute," Lloyd yelled as the whirl doubled in size, gathering up gravel and stones from the path so it was hard and lethal. "Protect his head."

George rested his hands on my crown. Oscar reached behind himself and gripped my waist.

I was cushioned between their hard, tall bodies. Protected by their strong hands and limbs. The noise of the whirling wind was becoming deafening, I could sense it growing too. Heat and power coming off it and filling the air around us. Trees nearby shook, the ground seemed to tremble and a horrible fizzing sensation filled my ears as if the pressure had changed.

"Fuck!" George muttered. "How much bigger is this thing going to get?"

Several stones were flung our way, moving like bullets and bouncing off Oscar and Rhys.

"It's okay," Oscar said. "Keep him tight between us."

The heat inside my chest was boiling now. Growing to furnace levels. My arms hurt with the scorch in my nerves. I flexed and unflexed my fingers then slid my hands over Rhys's left shoulder.

I couldn't contain the boiling surge in my veins, and with a moan I let it fly, blasting sparks toward the stony twister.

"Darius," George gasped. "What the...?"

"We need...to get rid of him..." I managed. "Once and for all."

I shot more sparks at the coil of rapidly spinning debris. They hit the stones, sending them flying out to the sides and rolling onto the ground. The thing stopped growing as I fired more sparks, brilliantly bright and orange they lit up the air and twisted with it in a dancing flame.

A loud roar of thunder rolled overhead, then there was a streak of lightning, cracking from east to west as if trying to rip apart the night sky.

I was breathing hard with the effort of releasing yet more sparks. The taste in my mouth was so revolting I had to stop myself from vomiting.

Lloyd broke away, then raced toward the stony wind. He stood before it, chest puffed up, arms held high. "With the glory of love and respect, your evil will not reign. Be gone, demon. There's nothing for you here, and I say that from my heart with the unwavering support of the mighty Master Benedict who stood in this very spot with the same message for you."

Thunder bellowed again, ringing through my ears and vibrating through my chest. George had his arms around my body now, holding my back to his chest. His cheek was against mine.

I dropped my hands, exhaustion flooding me.

Suddenly the howling wind stopped. The remaining stones fell to the ground, rolling and rattling over the pathway and grassy bank then coming to a halt.

"Go. Do not return," Lloyd shouted, triumph filling his voice. "There is nothing here for you."

"Everything is here for me!"

My father's voice, full of rage, screamed through the air.

And then silence.

Stillness.

"He's gone," Oscar said. He was breathing hard.

"Don't fucking come back!" Lloyd shouted at the sky, then turned to us.

"Darius," George said against my ear. "Are you okay?"

"Yeah, but it's hard work...releasing all that energy."

"It leaves you drained, doesn't it?" he said, spinning me to face him.

"Yeah." I wrapped my arms around him, glad of the support his strong, solid body gave me.

He set his lips on the side of my head. "I've got you, it's okay. Lean on me all you want, my love."

I closed my eyes and pulled in air, steadying my breathing and waiting for the ache in my arms and chest to subside. He smelled of soap and it was the perfect scent after the stench of my father's energy.

"Everything is here for him," Rhys said. "Did you all hear him say that?"

"Yeah," Oscar muttered. "He'll be back for the body he wants."

"But can't have," Lloyd said, his voice nearer now.

"Was that always the plan?" I asked.

"What do you mean?" George said, cupping the back of my head and holding me closer so my face was against his neck.

"To surround me. To use love to protect me."

Silence.

I raised my head and looked at George. "It's a nice idea and might keep him away from me, but how will that defeat him?"

George sighed. "How can we fight wind and stones? Our speed, strength and fangs aren't effective against that."

I shrugged. It had been my sparks that had gotten rid of him, I was sure of it.

If I hadn't done that, would he still be here?

"We need him to come in a physical form to defeat him once and for all," Oscar said.

"A body?"

George nodded.

"But he hasn't got one," I said, "isn't that why he wants mine?"

"Yours is different, yours is perfect, the one he's designed for himself," George said. "We need him to get another host and come for you then we can kill it *and* him."

A wave of shock filled me. "But that means another person has to die to save me. I can't have that. I...that goes against everything I believe in, everything I was taught about right and wrong. We have to—"

"Shh, it's okay, we'll figure it out." George held my face in his hands. "I promise, we'll work it out. No one innocent will die, Darius."

"How can you promise him that?" Oscar huffed.

"I can and I have," George said, lowering his face to mine. "I will not let your pure soul be tarnished, Darius."

"*We* won't let it," Lloyd said, clasping his hand on my shoulder.

"We should get out of here." Rhys stepped away and glanced at the messy scattered stones, then the river. "Master Benedict isn't here. There's no lingering energy."

"No, but he was." Lloyd pointed at the prison. "He was incarcerated in there before he was hung, drawn, and quartered, and his heart staked for the ravens to feast on."

"I hate that." Oscar pulled a face. "Don't you?"

"Yeah," Rhys said, folding his arms. "But it's history, and a history we seem to have been drawn into."

"We'll come back in daylight when it's open for tourists," George said. "Get inside and see what we can find out."

"Master Benedict's death is well documented at The Order," Lloyd said. "Do you really think we'll find anything new?"

"We won't know if we don't look." George wrapped his arm around my waist. "But right now, we have to get our guy home to bed."

Half an hour later I was in a lush penthouse apartment in Greenwich. It was sleekly designed with heavy black drapes, black pile carpet and dark walls. The lighting was muted, the kitchen devoid of any implements, gadgets or food. The only organic thing in the place was a spider plant set in the middle of a glass table.

"Come through here," George said, tugging me to a doorway. "You need to rest."

I wasn't going to argue with that. It was the middle of the night and due to that and the release of sparks, I was tired.

He shut the door on Oscar and Rhys. Lloyd was loitering outside the apartment, keeping a watch out for danger.

"Do you all live here?" I asked, looking at the large bed covered in pristine black silk sheets. It looked as though it had never been used.

"When we're in London."

"It's nice. Dark, but nice."

"We like dark." He chuckled. "Suits us."

"I guess." I removed my jacket, then stripped off my t-shirt.

"Fucking Hell." George stared at me.

"What?"

"You have no idea, do you?"

"What?" I tossed my t-shirt onto a chair.

"The effect you have on me, on all of us." He gestured to my body. "You're all our dreams and fantasies wrapped up in one glorious package. And the fact we've waited so long for you, it just makes you more enticing, even more fucking sexy."

The longing in his voice was obvious and my cock stirred. Ever since I'd been close to George at the photo shoot I'd had a craving for him. We'd touched, our cocks pressed close, lips hovering, but it had been so teasing, so elusive. The promise of pleasure had been very much there, but there'd been no satisfaction.

"You're not so bad yourself," I said, popping open the button on my jeans and not hiding my appreciative perusal of his body, head to toe and up again.

"I'm glad you think so." He pointed to the bed. "Shall we?"

I swallowed and clenched my ass as a shiver of desire traveled the length of my spine.

"We don't have to do anything," he said. "But I would like to hold you." He smiled. "Perhaps steal the kiss that nearly but not quite happened."

I nodded. "Yes, I'd like that."

He pulled off his waistcoat, setting his pocket watch on the bedside table, then removed his pristine white shirt.

I drank in his body. His torso was similar to mine. In fact, everything about him physically was similar to me. Lean and strong, skin a little pale, only the smallest smattering of body hair. We'd look good together on the campaign shots for Loyalty and Deceit, that was for sure.

"You orchestrated it that day, didn't you?" I said, removing my jeans.

"What day?"

"At the shoot. I was supposed to be working for Rolex."

He smiled and pointed to the corner. Another glass table held a slim silver laptop. "Marvellous invention, the world wide web."

"But how...?"

"The advantage of not sleeping is it gives you plenty of time to learn. I chose to learn about computers, hacking, using information technology to my advantage. It suits us well, it means we always get what we want."

I was impressed even if it wasn't particularly ethical.

"Are you complaining that I was your co-model that day, Darius?"

"No." I tugged at my socks. "The only thing I'm complaining about is it took this long for us to be alone together."

He stepped up to me wearing only tight white underwear, which did nothing to disguise an impressive wedge of flesh beneath. "It makes me so happy you feel the same as me, Darius."

"Which is?"

He hesitated with his palms resting on my shoulders. "Attraction, longing, desire."

"Love?"

"Yes, and love. At least on my behalf."

I stared into his eyes, remembering the promise he'd made me, and how he'd protected me down by the Thames, *and* how long he'd been searching for me. "My love is growing for you, for all of you."

He closed his eyes, inhaled, then opened them again. "You make me happier than I ever thought I would be again."

I smiled, leaned forward and kissed him. It was a gentle kiss, exploring the sensation of his lips on mine, his taste, and how he moved his mouth in time with my own. I slid my tongue in, found his, and tangled it gently, loving the slow pace in which he kissed me back. It wasn't frantic, it felt indulgent and dreamy as though we had an eternity to kiss each other.

"Let's take this to the bed," he said, hooking his hand beneath my elbow. "It's been waiting for you."

"What has? The bed?"

"Yes. Why else do you think we bought it? It's all for you, Darius. All of it."

"Oh, I see."

He lay down and I did the same. He hovered his face over mine and set his palm on the center of my chest. "I love to feel and hear your heartbeat."

"Hear it?"

"I have very acute hearing. I'd hear the heartbeat of a mouse on the other side of the apartment."

"Wow, that's incredible."

"You think?" He swirled his fingertip over my left nipple.

My flesh tightened beneath his touch.

"It's a pain in the neck," he said. "Hearing everything all the time is noisy. I crave silence."

"And do you ever get it?"

"Yes. We've got a place in Russia. Siberia to be exact. In the winter we spend time there. For miles around nothing but snow which falls almost silently. Perhaps you'd like to see it."

"Sounds cold."

"We'd light the fires if you were there."

"You don't for yourselves?"

"No." He brushed his lips over mine and moved his attentions to my other nipple. "We're always the same temperature, no matter where we are or what we're doing." He kissed me again, slipping his tongue between my lips.

I closed my eyes and gave myself up to him. George's kisses were intoxicating and his body touching mine had given me a serious hard on.

He slipped lower, tracing a circle around my navel, then sliding his hand over my boxers.

I groaned, his cool palm on my cock was exactly what I wanted.

"You were hard like this on the shoot," he murmured.

"Yeah, for you." I began to explore his body; the width of his shoulders, the shape of his biceps, the dip of his back and the curve of his buttocks.

"I thought I was going to come in front of everyone," he whispered. "Right there, on top of you, everyone watching. I wouldn't have cared, I'm a believer in doing what feels good."

"It did feel good. *Too* good."

He squeezed my shaft, his thumb tracing my slit through the material of my underwear.

I groaned and my balls tightened.

"We need to get naked," he said.

Suddenly he shifted upward, whisked off his boxers and then mine. "That's better."

The sheets were smooth on my bare ass and my cock so hard it felt like granite.

"What do you want to do?" he asked.

I beat down a wave of nerves. "Whatever you want to do."

"Good answer." He grasped my cock. "Your dick is amazing."

"So is yours." I glanced down and saw his hard on tapping up against his belly. I gripped it the way he was mine. It was the first time I'd held another guy's penis.

"Mmm," he moaned as I stroked his shaft. "More, yes, fuck yes, more of that."

I copied what he was doing, masturbating him, working him root to tip.

Within a minute I was battling not to come. It was so erotic to have George responding with gasps and groans with each tiny movement of my hand.

We kissed, harder now, and a mounting sense of urgency.

"For the love of Benedict," he said, pulling up and clasping his hand over mine, stopping my movements. "I'm going to spurt if you keep doing that."

"Isn't that the idea?" My belly was quivering, and my balls retracted. My orgasm was really close. I just needed a bit more…

"I want to come inside you," he said, his gaze trailing my body. "If you're willing to bottom, that is."

My cock twitched and my asshole trembled. "Come inside me?"

"Yes, in your sexy ass, Darius."

I stared up at him. This was it. The moment I handed my body over to another man and lost my virginity.

"I know," he said, kissing the tip of my nose, "that you haven't done it before."

I exhaled, relieved I wouldn't have to confess.

"Oscar told me," he said. "And I'd be honored if you'd pick me to be your first."

"I guess it's only a matter of time before we all fuck, right?"

"Well, you—it's only a matter of time before we all fuck you. We don't screw each other."

I raised my eyebrows. "Not even when you're horny?"

"No." He downturned his mouth. "They're like brothers to me, that would be weird."

"So just me, right?"

"Yes, just you. Prepare to be pleasured whenever and however you want to be."

"Starting with..." I stroked along his collarbone, and then settled my finger at the hollow of his throat. "You fucking me now."

He was silent.

"I want it," I said. "But—"

"But you're scared. That's understandable."

"No, I'm not scared. I want it, I want sex with you, with all of you."

"So what is it?"

"I'm worried I might not do it right, that I might disappoint you."

"Darius! You could never disappoint me. You're everything I want and more."

"But what if I do it wrong?"

"There is no wrong." He slid his hand over my cock again and then scooped up my balls. "There is only pleasure and satisfaction."

"Show me."

He smiled and his eyes flashed. "Of course, my love." He stretched one finger lower and skimmed it over my asshole.

I gasped at the intimate touch.

"Bend your knees and widen your legs."

I did as he'd instructed as he reached behind himself for a bottle of massage oil.

"This will help," he said, dribbling it onto his fingers.

"Help with what?"

"Help with getting me inside you." He stroked over my hole again, this time circling it, then pressing at the center with his slick finger.

My breaths were shallow, my abdominal muscles rigid.

"You feel amazing, so warm and tight," he murmured against my lips. "Now just relax so I can..." He invaded my asshole with his fingertip.

There was no pain, but it was a little odd to be touched there, and it made my cock jerk.

"Breathe," he said.

"I am." I rested my palm on his cheek and stared up at his face. "Give me more."

He pushed in higher, knuckle deep.

I groaned. So this was it. This was what I'd been craving all that time. It felt fucking amazing.

"Touching you like this is going to make me orgasm," he said breathily. "I've wanted to pleasure you for centuries, the perfect beautiful soul that you are."

"Please, do it, fuck me."

"Not yet, I have to prep you."

My asshole stretched as he added another finger. I curled my toes and my legs tensed.

"That's it, good," he said against my lips. "So good. You're doing so well."

"Fuck!" I bucked upward. Whatever he'd just touched inside me was intense and sent an incredible wave of pleasure through my core.

He laughed softly. "That's your hot-spot, Darius. Feels nice, doesn't it?"

"Oh bloody Hell." I was shaking and my cock was leaking pre-cum. "I can't describe it, it's..."

"The best feeling ever."

"Er yeah, probably."

"Wait until it's my cock stroking over it, and not my fingers."

I groaned and closed my eyes. He was massaging me inside, not enough to make me buck from the bed again, but enough to stoke the need inside me.

"You look beautiful like this," he said. "All pliant and responsive. I'm so happy it's you." He kissed me. "I love you."

I was gasping now, beating down the need to let my release surge. "George, please, fuck me."

"Okay."

He slid from me. "Turn over." As he'd spoken he'd nudged my left hip. "Show me your ass."

My tiredness was a distant memory, and I turned, rising up onto my hands and knees as I did so.

"That will do nicely," he said, setting the oil bottle to one side again. "Now keep still while I lube up."

"Be quick." I stared down my body. My cock was rock-hard, the end slick. A tremble of need started in my nape and flowed to my asshole. I clenched it, missing George's fingers there.

"Relax now," he said, gripping my hips. "And bear down."

"Bear down?"

"Yes, it will open you up for me."

I clenched my hands, fisting the sheets, and braced my spine.

"Relax, I said." George kissed the dip of my back, his breath washing over my hot skin. "I'm not going to rush this, or pound into you the way Oscar would. Your first time is sacred."

"Thank you." Impatience was burning me up. "But, please, George. I need you."

"And I need you."

The cool, smooth dome of his cock tip pressed against my hole. It felt impossibly wide and hard.

"Get used to the feel of it first," he said. "And visualize where I'm going. Imagine me filling you."

"Yes. Yes, I can do that." Hell, it was all I could think of.

"And now accept me, make it real."

He pushed forward, holding me still and tight.

I arched my back and raised my head as my hole opened, stretching around his glans. On and on I accepted him until there was a stitch of pain.

"Oh, oh, it's too much..." I squirmed.

"I'm in, you've done it. You've taken the entire tip of me." He stilled but kept a strong hold of my hips. "That's as wide as you have to take."

"Okay." I closed my eyes and waited as the pain dulled and in its place came the wonderful sensation of cock in my ass.

"How is it now?"

"It's good, real good." I was breathless.

"Now take my length. My cock is the same size as yours, Darius, so you know what you have to cope with."

He pushed forward. The sensation became dense and all consuming as my innards received him.

"Ah, yeah, fucking Hell," he groaned. "Better than I could ever imagine. Fuck, Darius, you're incredible in here."

I answered with a groan of my own. My balls were so tight, my cock seeping pre-cum.

"Can you feel me on your hot-spot?" he asked.

"Yes, yes I can."

He bottomed out, his sac pressing against mine.

"You're not a virgin any more, my love. You've taken my cock, full depth."

"So use it," I said, twisting to glance over my shoulder. "And fuck me good and proper."

"You're demanding I fuck you good and proper on your first time?" He laughed, though the sound was strained. "You're a wild one, Darius. How are we going to keep up with you?"

I made a strange growling sound. I wasn't sure where it had come from. Desperation. Longing. Need.

"It's here, for you, always and only you." He withdrew almost out, then eased back in, his cock driving over my prostate.

Again a wonderful dense pleasure claimed me.

He hit full depth, paused for a heartbeat, then repeated the action. The lube he'd coated his cock and my ass in eased the way, and the coolness of his skin made it so acute where he was inside me.

I adored it.

I adored him.

"Darius," he gasped. "Come when...you need...to."

I screwed up my eyes and tried to hold off coming. I didn't want this to end.

Heat grew in my chest and seeped over my shoulders. My dick felt as though it was on fire, the pressure in it so great.

On and on George fucked me, slowly and steadily driving his cock in and almost out.

I became lost to it. Nothing else existed. Only George and his wonderful cock and what he was doing to me.

Sweat laced my body, my breaths were shunting in and out of me in time with George's thrusts. "I need to come," I gasped.

"Yes, come, come with me."

The heat in my chest was spreading down my arms. My biceps were burning up. So were my forearms, my palms.

Fuck. No. Not now.

"I'm coming, oh, come with me," George cried. "Darius."

I allowed my climax to take hold. My asshole clamped around George's concrete-hard cock, seeming to drag him higher and harder onto my hot-spot.

I cried out as my dick surged, shooting pearly ropes of cum from the end. My balls retreated so far into my body they ached. Fire burned inside me, and shot down my arms to my hands. My heart thudded and my brain turned to mush as pleasure took over.

"Yes. Yes. Yes." George punctuated each word with a thrust. "It's here."

I wailed as he filled me with cold release. It seemed to wash through my insides and created more waves of glorious orgasmic pulses.

I'd never felt so alive, so wild with ecstasy.

George slowed, then stilled. He leaned forward, shifting his cock inside me, and kissed between my shoulder blades. "That was incredible."

"Yes, it was." I was breathing hard.

"And I can easily buy new bedding."

"What?" I opened my eyes. Had my cum made that much mess?

"Don't worry about it." Very gently he pulled out.

My hole clamped shut and I trembled. It was then I saw what he was talking about. "Fuck, I'm sorry, I—"

"Don't mention it, it's sweet." He flopped onto the bed with his head on the pillow.

"Sweet?" I stared at the singed silk sheets around my hands. They were still smoking. "This bedding must have cost a fortune. I'll pay you for it."

"No you will not. Cost has no meaning to us," he said, running his hand down my arm. "I told you that."

"But still, it's yours and I wrecked it with my…" I sat back on my heels and stared at my fingertips.

"With your passion? Your emotion? Your incredible orgasm?" He reached for me and pulled me into an embrace. "To think that our first time together, your first time *ever* was so good you could be yourself entirely and release sparks makes me very happy."

I rested my head against his shoulder and bent my leg over his. "Thank you for accepting me as I am. I never thought I'd find anyone who would."

"You've found four of us who do."

Chapter Sixteen

Rhys

Knowing Darius was in the bedroom and most likely having his virginity taken by George made it impossible for me to relax. Add in the fact he'd had two near misses with his demon father in twenty-four hours, and I was most definitely on edge.

"Would you sit down," Oscar grumbled. "You're beginning to piss me off, Rhys."

"I'm sorry." I sat and gripped the arms of the chair.

"And *try* to relax."

"Like you are?" I frowned at Oscar who was perched on the edge of the couch, arms folded, and his booted feet flat on the floor. He appeared ready for action.

"Yeah, well, George won't be keeping an eye or ear out for demons, so someone has to."

"Lucky George," I muttered.

"Rhys," he said. "We all agreed we'd share Darius. His power is strong, and his energy vibrant. He can juggle us all, and our needs for blood and intimacy with him. He's no ordinary guy, he's special. The only thing we have to control is our jealousy."

"I'm not jealous," I said quickly. "I'm glad he and George are having time together and..."

"Fucking."

"Yeah, that too, if it's what's happening behind that door."

"I think we can safely say it is." Oscar tilted his chin.

I glanced toward the bedroom. "Yeah, I'd agree with you there, Oscar." Would George top or bottom with Darius? What would Darius have a preference for? I hoped he'd like both, giving and receiving. That would suit us all.

He does suit us all. Perfectly.

"And the other thing we have to control," I said, shaking my head to rid the image of Darius naked so I could think straight, "is his father."

"We have to defeat him. It's the only way the danger can be eliminated."

"Of course we do." I stood again and walked to the window. My legs were as restless as my brain. I pulled back the curtain and glanced up at the starry sky. The moon hung like a giant silver coin to the west. I was pleased there were no clouds around, stormy or otherwise. "And then, when his father is out of the equation we'll have a much bigger danger to face," I said. "You do know that."

"We're not a foursome to be messed with," Oscar said gruffly.

"I know that, but there are many vampires at The Order who will seek Darius for themselves if they discover he's the cambion of the fable."

"Which is why we must protect him, for always." Oscar linked his fingers and squeezed his fists together. "And keep who he really is a secret."

"And we're going to start that process tomorrow," I said, straightening the curtain and turning back to Oscar.

He raised his eyebrows at me.

"We have to go to The Order and speak to Master Concorde."

"You think we should tell him?" Oscar raised his eyebrows. "I'd rather tell no one. It's the safest way."

"But if we tell the head of The Order and then stake our claim on Darius as our human mate, we can legitimately keep him at our sides, feed from him when he'll allow it, and protect him without raising suspicion."

"George has spent centuries, Lloyd too, looking for the cambion and that fact hasn't been kept a secret," Oscar said. "Them turning up with a lover will immediately raise suspicions as to who he really is."

"Which is why we need to speak to Master Concorde and *claim* Darius in private, not in the usual ceremony."

"But what's the point of that? No one will see, no one will know he's ours."

"But it will be documented, that's what's important going forward. And there's no reason we can't go down into the dungeon with him, let a few people see that he is with one or maybe even two of us, preferably not George or Lloyd."

"The dungeon? Fuck, it's been a long time since I was there." Oscar huffed. "Had a great time, though, that place seems to bring out the sex beast in me."

He grinned suddenly and I matched it, remembering my last trip to the basement of The Order. It was a place for dark pleasure, where anything went; feeding, fucking, flogging and forgetting everything and letting ecstasy take over.

Oscar sighed suddenly and scrubbed his hand over his messy dark hair. "I agree with you, Rhys, but we should concentrate on the demon first, don't you think?"

"I think other vampires wanting a taste of our man is as dangerous as the demon. Especially when you consider they'll all want to save their souls the same way we do."

"But we don't even have the key yet, or understand what it is exactly. I'm scared you're jumping ahead with all this talk of taking Darius to The Order and then down into the dungeon."

"I've spoken to George and Lloyd about it."

"You have?" He raised his heavy black eyebrows.

"Yeah. They seemed keen on the idea."

He was silent. Which was never a good thing with Oscar. It meant stubbornness was setting in.

"Don't you see?" I stepped up to him. "We're so near, so close. Master Benedict is talking to us through our lover's dreams. No one,

I repeat, no one has *ever* been where we are. We're a whisper away from salvation. This is big."

"I know it is." His jaw tensed and then he stared at the door again, as if he could see Darius and George on the other side. "Can you smell burning?"

I sniffed the air. "Yeah." I stepped forward, fearful the demon had slipped past us while we'd been talking.

"No." Oscar was behind me. He set his hand on my shoulder and squeezed. "Darius is probably releasing sparks…as he comes."

"Fuck, do you think so? As he orgasms?"

He shrugged. "Every chance, and if so, we really shouldn't burst in there. They shut the door for a reason—privacy."

I swallowed and closed my eyes. An image of Darius's beautiful face contorted in ecstasy as his cock spurted and sparks flew out of his fingers held me hostage. I longed for more intimacy with him and to feel as though his warm body was part of mine.

Be patient.

"Sit down," Oscar said, "Read or something."

"I might go out and check the corridor, the elevators and the lobby."

"Yeah, good idea." Oscar sat again. "Get out of my hair for a bit, kid."

I headed out of the apartment with a scowl. I was nearly a hundred years old, I wasn't a kid.

Though in Oscar's eyes, I guessed I always would be. As the youngest of the four of us, and the youngest as I'd turned at just twenty-three, I did tick the youth box in our definition of the word.

When the sun began to stroke shades of peach and lilac on the London horizon, Lloyd and I went back into the apartment.

Oscar was in the same position I'd left him in, perched on the edge of the sofa and staring at the bedroom door.

"All okay?" Lloyd asked, shucking his hood back and running his hand over his crew cut.

Oscar nodded.

"Any more burning smells?" I asked.

Oscar glanced at me. "No, nothing. Silence."

"You sure they're in there?" Lloyd frowned.

"Nowhere else they could be." Oscar stood. "But it's time for us to go."

"Where?" Lloyd asked.

Oscar nodded at me. "Rhys here thinks we should take Darius to The Order, present him to Master Concorde."

Lloyd was quiet for a moment, then, "Yeah, and I think that's a good idea."

"So does George apparently." Oscar folded his arms and rocked back on his heels.

"What do I think is a good idea?" George said as he pulled open the bedroom door.

I wasn't surprised he'd heard us talking. In fact, he'd probably heard everything we'd said earlier too, if he hadn't been in the throes of ecstasy that was.

"About going to Master Concorde," I said. "Today."

He nodded and pulled the door closed. "Yes, I do think it's a good idea. It will give Darius an introduction to The Order, and he can be seen as a human mate."

"So we're going to present him as all of ours?" Oscar asked.

"No. Just one of us. It will be hard to hide the fact we're all in love with him, but we need to try." George rubbed his chin. "And we need to make sure only one of us is with him in the dungeon."

"So you think the dungeon is a good idea?" Lloyd said. "I thought you weren't sure."

"I've thought about it. Rhys is right. We have to treat him how all vampires treat their human mates, and that means sex in the dungeon, a private room most likely for a first visit."

"And who will be the one?" Lloyd asked.

Me. Me.

Oh, how I wanted to be with him—to hold him, touch him, have him touch me.

George glanced around us, then nodded at Oscar. "What do you think?"

Oscar huffed. "I'd like to say myself, but Darius isn't ready for me. I think it should be Rhys."

I turned to Oscar. "You do?"

"Yeah, kid. I do."

"Oh, okay." I glanced at Lloyd.

"I'm a patient man," he said. "You know that. And I'll have my turn with our guy when the time comes."

I shoved my hands into my jeans pockets and shifted from one foot to the other. "Okay. I'll take one for the team." I grinned.

"If…" George stepped past me, "he's up for it, Rhys. To be honest, I think I may have worn him out."

"Is he still sleeping?" I asked.

"He's stirring. I've come out to make him a coffee. Someone tell me we have some."

"Fuck knows," Lloyd said. "But I'll go to the shop if not. Won't take me long."

"Bet you can't get to the shop and back before the kettle boils," I said with a grin, feeling suddenly buoyant and excited.

"You should know damn well never to bet me anything." Lloyd's mouth twitched into a half smile. "Go put the kettle on."

An hour later I was heading down the large sweeping street that housed The Worshipful Company of the Ancient Order. The terraced houses were tall with sash windows and the brickwork painted white. Each had a pillared porch leading to a shiny black front door. Railings, to match the color of the doors, protected basements, and a few had gates leading downward. None of the houses were homes, mostly they were offices.

Darius walked at my side. He knew the plan was to speak to Master Concorde honestly about our situation, but outside of the Master's office he would be primarily at my side, as though we were a couple.

We walked into the high-ceilinged hallway of the reception area then drew to a halt. The walls were sectioned in half by a wooden dado rail. Beneath was painted startling red and above the rail a pale cream. The floor was parquet and another huge door ahead was of the same dark polished wood.

A woman sat at an empty desk. She was stunningly beautiful, immaculately made up and wore a scarlet blouse that matched her lipstick. She smiled warmly. "Hello, George. It's been a while."

"Yes." He touched the peak of his cap. "I trust you are well, Samree."

"I am." She sniffed the air and looked at Darius. "You have a local with you?"

George nodded. "Can he sign him in?"

"Of course." She placed a thick leather-bound book on the desk and added a feather-tipped pen next to it. She didn't take her attention from Darius, as though like us, she was drawn to his beauty.

"All visitors must sign into the Company," I said, picking up the pen and passing it to Darius. "It's policy." A wave of protectiveness came over me. Samree would take her fill of Darius's blood if she were given half a chance.

"That's fine with me, Rhys." Darius opened the book and began to write his name.

"Are you going to chambers?" Samree asked.

"Perhaps," I said. "We have a meeting with Master Concorde first."

"You do?" She raised her eyebrows and glanced at George. "Concerning what?"

"Samree." George leaned forward with his hands on the desk. "Do you *have* to know everything?" He smiled then swept his tongue over his bottom lip.

She frowned and cleared her throat. "I was only asking, that was all."

George chuckled and straightened. "It's simply to offer him use of our cabin in Siberia. I know how he likes it there."

"Oh yes, he does." She picked up the book and pen which Darius had now finished with. "That's very kind of you." She turned to Darius. "Welcome to The Ancient Order, I hope you enjoy yourself."

"Thanks," Darius said. "I'm sure I will."

She narrowed her eyes and studied his face.

I stepped closer to him, my arm brushing his.

"You're..." she paused. "Exceptionally beautiful for a human."

Darius laughed. "So I've been told." He nodded at the door we'd just come through. "And it's why I'm on several billboards across the city and gracing two magazine covers this month."

"Ah, you're a model?"

"Yeah."

"That explains it." Her features relaxed as if she'd solved a puzzle.

"Come on." I wrapped my arm around Darius. "Time to show you this place."

The first room we came to after Reception held a sweeping staircase and a large stone sculpture of a bearded man in a ragged fur cape. It was Master Benedict, and he stared downward with his lips pulled back in a grimace. He'd come to a bad ending, and the creator of this sculpture had captured an element of that, despite him being a good vampire who only wanted what was best for others who'd turned and the humans they lived amongst.

"It's him," Darius said, coming to an abrupt halt. "The man in my dreams."

I shared a look with Lloyd.

"Good," George said. "That confirms it then."

Darius stared up at the statue. "He's a principled, kind man, I can feel it, despite him looking like a...caveman."

Oscar laughed. "Yeah, he does a bit."

"He was one of the longest living vampires ever, if living is the right word," I said. "And the fact he's coming to you in your dreams is more important than you can possibly imagine."

"Shh," Lloyd said, glancing about. "The walls have ears, Rhys."

"There's no one here," George said. "Not that I can hear anyway. Come on, let's go to Master Concorde's office."

I had a familiar gush of nerves going into the Master's suite of rooms. There were a couple of the senior ranking vampires who gave me the creeps. A woman, Elfrida, and a man with a long white beard who always stared at me for longer than was necessary. I wasn't sure if he disliked me or wanted to get to know me better.

Master Concorde was standing beside a window, staring out at the street below.

We came to a halt, in a row, and I took Darius's hand in mine.

Master Concorde turned. He swept his gaze over us all, his attention ending on Darius. "I've been expecting you."

Chapter Seventeen

Darius

I swallowed down a fizz of trepidation. The Ancient Order was huge and grand with many winding corridors, giving the impression of a rabbit warren—each burrow full of vampires I didn't know. It also felt otherworldly which I guessed it was. And Master Concorde, he could have been a friendly grandfather, except he was dressed in a medieval style cape held on with ropes over his chest and he held a golden stick with a wolf's head on the top—a head that appeared to have been severed, ripped off. The wolf had no eyes, just black holes.

"You've been expecting me?" I asked, squeezing Rhys's fingers tighter. I was glad of his return tightening. Master Concorde's words had surprised me.

"George said he would find you. It's not often my son doesn't achieve what he sets out to." He stepped up to George and kissed each of his cheeks.

His son?

"You're too kind, Master." George inclined his head. "As always."

I looked between George and Master Concorde. There didn't appear to be any family resemblance.

"And where did you find him?" Master Concorde set both of his hands on the top of his stick, covering the wolf's decapitated head.

"Paris," George said. "Lloyd made the final discovery. As you know we'd been making headway over the last few years."

"Well done, Lloyd."

"Thank you, Master." Lloyd bowed his head.

Master Concorde's eyes narrowed, deep lines shot from the sides to his temples, and he stared at me.

I resisted the urge to squirm or fidget—I was used to being stared at.

"You could almost be a vampire," Master Concorde said, "Quite impressive work for a demon." He snapped his head to George. "You have told him, haven't you?"

"Yes, of course." George nodded. "He knows everything. We thought that was only fair."

"It's certainly safer." The Master set his attention on me again. "Mmm, apart from a rise of color on his cheeks, the pulsing of neck veins and the sound of his heartbeat...*almost* a vampire."

"Cambions are rare," Lloyd said. "It's not often an incubus can impregnate a human woman."

"Don't I know it," Master Concorde huffed.

"Which is why we're here," George said. "We need to protect him. If the fable is true, if we find out what the key is, then all the vampires on the planet will want to know it. They'll all want Darius for themselves."

Master Concorde rubbed his chin. "Yes, we've had the same problem with Bombays for years."

Rhys turned to me. "Humans with Bombay blood type were almost wiped out by vampires unable to control themselves with their obsession for it. Now there's only a handful left. Master Benedict's ancestors had to put in vampire laws to protect them."

I nodded, hoping there'd be some kind of law to protect me if necessary.

Master Concorde reached out and put his hand on my shoulder. "Darius, you're safe here in this room, you're amongst friends, and I suspect, lovers."

I glanced at George, the gorgeous man who'd given me a tender and beautiful first time then held me close all night. My heart tripped over itself. I was falling for him hard and fast. Everything about him seemed so right for me, as it did with all my vampire protectors.

"But out there." Master Concorde nodded at the door. "You're not so safe."

"Can I ask a question, sir?" Oscar spoke for the first time.

"Of course, Oscar."

"The fable suggests that Darius holds the key to our salvation. How come you do not want him for *yourself*?" He folded his arms and looked down at the older man standing before him.

Master Concorde was quiet, then, "That's a good question, Oscar, and one that should be asked." He paused. "I met a cambion, many years ago, in Kathmandu. I was with a friend, another vampire who is sadly no longer existing but his soul is relaxing where he deserves to be for he was a good man."

"I don't understand," Oscar said gruffly. "Where he deserves to be?"

"Yes. We both drank from a cambion in a sacred place, and it set our souls free from eternal damnation. So you see, I have no need of your cambion—I've had my own. But I believe I'm the only one here at The Order in that fortuitous position, unless others have kept it quiet for the sake of the one with the key."

There was silence for a moment, as though my vampires were letting the new knowledge sink in.

"You *drank* from him in a sacred place?" Lloyd asked eventually. "That was the key?"

"Yes, it was a temple in Patan Durbar Square in Kathmandu. Drinking his ethereal blood at a certain date and time on the Magh Nepali calendar—they're decades ahead of us—was the key to our salvation."

"You drank his blood and it saved your souls?" I asked. Was that really the key? My blood?

"A cambion's blood is delicious, much more so than regular human's blood," Master Concorde went on. "Like Bombay blood, it's rich and power-giving, I guess a little like having beluga caviar instead of roe. But it's more than the taste—it's magical, it's literally soul-saving if consumed by a damned soul according to the rules of the key."

"So we can take Darius to this temple in Kathmandu?" Lloyd said, his eyes widening. "And if we drink from him there, we'll all be together forever, our souls saved? There'll be no Hell, no limbo, no parting, ever." He smiled at me, his eyes sparkling with excitement. "We can be together without fear."

"I'm afraid it's not that simple." The Master shook his head.

"Why not?" George asked.

Lloyd frowned.

Oscar tutted.

"The temple is no longer there. It was flattened by an earthquake several years ago."

"But there must be something, ruins perhaps," Oscar said.

"Maybe, but the date was significant, too. And like I just said, they go by a different calendar in Nepal." He looked at me. "I'm afraid you're going to have to figure out the key Darius's dreams hold for yourselves. From what I gather, each cambion in history—and there have only been a handful—have their own place, date, and time where drinking their blood is sacred."

"So it's in here." I touched my head with my free hand. "The key to saving the souls of these men." I glanced at Oscar, Lloyd, George and then Rhys. "My mind holds the place, date, and time they must drink my blood?"

"Yes." He stepped close again and rested his hand on my shoulder. "And I have no doubt that between you, you'll figure it out."

"Darius is a good man," Rhys said. "There is no demon in him."

"Of course not," Master Concorde said. "Good always prevails over evil, and Darius's maternal bloodline is one of great purity of the human soul. The demon slipped up there in his choice, but that is to your advantage."

"Can I ask something?" I said as thoughts rattled around my brain.

"Of course."

"The cambion you fed off, Master Concorde, where is he now?"

He inclined his head. "Yes, you, out of everyone, Darius, have a right to know that." He sighed and adjusted his grip on his stick. "He's still alive. He lives in Tibet as a monk. There they do not question his great age or wisdom."

"Did you love him?" George asked.

"Yes, of course, he's a truly wonderful person." Master Concorde smiled. "But I am not a vampire who has ever wanted physical pleasure with another man, indeed not often with a woman. It's the price I paid for turning late in life. So I gave him a promise of anonymity and that I would never tell a soul his name. We parted ways after our other friend left this Earth."

"How long ago was that?" Lloyd asked. "If you don't mind me asking."

"Nearly five hundred years ago." He turned. "It was a difficult parting, but I was called here, to carry on Master Benedict's work and maintain an Order in London."

I spotted Lloyd and George looking at each other. Lloyd nodded.

"Master Benedict has visited Darius in his dreams," George said.

"I'm not surprised." Master Concorde smiled. "He works in mysterious ways, and although he's gone, his energy was so powerful it still weaves around us. It's why we take comfort in his teachings and follow his guidance to this day." He smiled at me. "You are most fortunate to have a direct pathway to him, however surreal it must be for you."

"Yes. I understand that," I said. "I think."

George cleared his throat.

"Yes, George?" Master Concorde turned to him.

"Would it be possible to do a private claiming ceremony for us all with Darius so we have made our position known that he belongs to us?"

"Four of you? That is most unusual? Two perhaps for one mate, but four?"

"Which is why it should be private," Lloyd said.

"No. That will bring far too much attention to all of you, and that's the last thing you need right now."

"But it will be something for us to fall back on, and it shows we have the support of the Masters," George added. "And besides, no one else will know unless it's necessary to tell them."

"As I've already mentioned, I'm the only Master here you can truly trust, George." He tapped his stick on the floor, not impatiently, but as if thinking. "What you need to do is a keep a low profile. Let others believe you are still searching for the cambion." He raised the stick and gestured to my hand linked with Rhys's. "Let it be known that young Rhys has found himself a human mate, nothing more than that. A human mate who will accompany you on your continuing search."

Everyone was quiet. I wished my heart rate would slow and my mind would stop twirling with thoughts of blood, and dreams, and being a key.

"It's not ideal," Oscar said. "We all share Darius, we're *all* in love with him."

They all love me.

I couldn't hold in a small smile of pleasure as my heart swelled in my chest. These men, these vampires had quickly become my everything, my entire world.

"I can see that." Master Concorde took a step back and sat on a plush red chair. "And it's understandable for many reasons. But in order to protect your special human here, you're going to have to play along with him belonging to Rhys. No one will take any notice of him if you do that." He paused. "Well, there are bound to be some comments on his beauty, but I guess you'll figure that out." He sighed and rested his head back.

"Yes, we'll figure it out somehow." George nodded. "Thank you, Master, for your time."

"I will perform a claiming ceremony in Chambers on Monday, for Darius and Rhys. Because tonight it's the spring equinox service and I will be busy." He nodded at the door. "If you're still in London and wish that to happen, that is."

"We do. We appreciate your wise words and advice, Master. We only want the best for Darius." Lloyd set his hand on my shoulder. "Thank you."

Oscar muttered his thanks.

Rhys tugged me toward the door.

"What's the equinox ceremony?" I asked as we stepped through it.

"Equinox happens twice a year, spring and autumn, and it's when day and night are of equal length."

"And that's tonight?"

"Yes. Vampires prefer the winter when the nights are long and dark. It suits us better. There are always ceremonies when the days lengthen and shorten. It's our way of marking the year. It's not as if we follow any religious calendar."

"Oh, I see."

We walked back through several windowless corridors. I was well aware of the tension coming from George, Lloyd and Oscar, though Rhys seemed pretty relaxed, which tended to be his usual state.

"George. Lloyd."

I stopped and turned, as did the others, at the sound of a deep voice.

At the top of a steep bank of stone steps stood two men and a woman.

"It's been a while." The man who'd spoken had hair similar to Lloyd's—super short and blond— and he was grinning broadly.

"Hey, Ryle." Lloyd held out his hand. "How's things?"

"Good. Just back from a trip abroad."

"Did you have fun?" Oscar asked.

"To a certain degree. It's a very long story," the other man said, his voice upper class, his vowels rounded. "We'll tell you sometime."

If Ryle reminded me of Lloyd, this guy bore a resemblance to George; his smart but outdated clothes at least.

"You met Bea?" Ryle asked, slipping his arm around the woman between them.

"Haven't had the pleasure." George nodded. "Pleased to meet you, Bea."

"And you." She smiled, her pretty face lighting up. Even in the shadows of the chamber we stood in, I could see her cheeks were rosy and her eyes sparkled. She also had two sets of small bite marks on her neck.

"Young Rhys has a mate," Lloyd said. "Aimery, Ryle, meet Darius."

Both men set their attention on me. The taller, older looking one, Aimery, swiped his tongue over his bottom lip. "Welcome to The Order, Darius. We're always happy to have human mates join us."

"Do you have family?" Ryle asked me.

I was surprised by his question. "A mother, that's all."

"Ryle," Oscar snapped, his deep voice rattling around the high ceilings. "Is that necessary?"

Ryle held up his palms. "Keep your hair on. I was only asking." He nodded at Rhys. "Congrats, have fun in the dungeon, we just have." He set a kiss on the side of Bea's head. "Come on, let's go and get you some tea."

"Mmm." She smiled up at him as she linked her hand with Aimery's. "That sounds good."

They wandered away, toward an archway leading to yet another corridor.

"I bet she's Bombay," Lloyd whispered.

"You can't presume that," Rhys said with a frown.

"I can." Lloyd huffed. "And I bet I'm right."

"Yeah, you probably are," Oscar said quietly, "the last time Aimery and Ryle both claimed the same female human, she was Bombay, and they kept her to themselves for the span of her life."

"If that's the case," George said, "good luck to them. Protecting Bea will be a full time job." He pointed at the steps leading downward. "It sounds like there's a lot going on in the dungeon."

"Is there?" Rhys tugged me a little nearer. "We should go down then. Get started."

"What...what exactly is it?" I asked, eyeing a set of large oak doors at the base of the steps. "The dungeon, that is." From behind it I could make out faint sounds; cracks, cries, gasps and groans.

"It's a place of pleasure," Rhys said, his breath breezing on my cheek as he moved close. "A place where vampires and their mates indulge in a feast of carnal desires."

"Don't worry," George said, "even if what you see appears kinky, or sadistic, everything is consensual."

"Sadistic?"

"Yeah, you'll understand in a minute." Rhys urged me down the steps then pulled open the doors. "You're with me, only me, remember." He set a light kiss on my cheek. "We belong to each other."

"Yes, I remember." I smiled at him, enjoying the excitement in his eyes. He was clearly enjoying having me at his side and that made him all the more appealing—it was thrilling to be so wanted, so desired.

As we stepped in I caught the scent of fresh sweat, log fires, and arousal.

"We like to keep it warm down here for the humans," Rhys said. "Because generally they're naked."

I nodded, my attention drawn to a large bed in front of me. Several bodies writhed and thrust, groaning and gasping as they did so. The flicker of candlelight over their flesh showed me exactly what they were doing...fucking. A woman had two men inside of her, ass and pussy, another man had his cock at her mouth and she was sucking eagerly on it as they all moved to an erotic rhythm.

"Bloody Hell," I muttered, amazed at the scene. A shiver of desire went through me. I wished I was her and was being penetrated every way I could be. How would it feel? How hard would I come?

"Group sex is fun, huh?" Rhys grinned then pointed to the left. "Look, there's two guys."

I stepped with him as we moved deeper into the shadows. I was vaguely aware of Lloyd, George and Oscar behind us, but they'd allowed a distance to form.

Before a fireplace alive with glowing embers stood a large table. Over it a man was bent double with his forehead resting on his folded arms. His cock was hard and tapping against his belly. His knees were locked straight and his pale ass offered up.

Another wave of desire crashed through me, and fascination. What was going on?

"Have you seen what's on his ankles?" Rhys asked.

My attention drifted lower. Fastened between his ankles was a thick black bar.

"It's a spreader," Rhys said. "Keeps his legs apart so his lover can play."

"Play?"

"Yeah, with silver. Watch." He stepped behind me and wrapped his arms around my waist, his cheek settled against mine and I was aware of his hard chest on my back.

There was a sudden loud smacking sound. I jumped. The man bending over the table cried out and jerked forward.

His lover, a guy in black leather trousers, bare chest and with two nipple piercings had just delivered a swift spank using a shiny bat. Within a second he did it again and after the strike he rested the bat against the buttocks of the recipient.

A yelp was followed by a long, low moan which curled around us, mixing with the seductive atmosphere.

"The bat is made of silver," Rhys said. "The only substance on Earth that can truly cause a vampire pain."

"He's a vampire, the one bent over?"

"Yeah." Rhys paused. "The other guy, with the piercings, is human."

"Really?" I stared as another set of swift spanks were delivered. Each one had pure male muscle behind it and the sound of flesh being whacked sung around the dungeon.

The vampire, spread-eagled with his buttocks vulnerable, writhed and yelled. His cock seemed to surge upward and he went onto his toes, almost dancing on them as the silver bat hit.

My buttocks tingled as I watched the pale skin take a beating. Sensual pain wasn't something I'd experienced, but these guys were making it look seriously hot.

"You've had enough for today, Gaspare," his lover said, discarding the bat and smoothing his hands over the vampire's buttocks. "It's time."

What is it time for?

The human dragged at the poppers on his leather pants, and pulled out his cock. Quickly he lubed up, then set the tip at the other man's asshole.

"Oh, jeez, is he going to...here?" I muttered. "In front of everyone?"

"Yeah," Rhys said against my ear. "He's going to fuck him, good and hard, sink his cock deep and make them both come and we're all allowed to watch."

"Fucking Hell." My belly tightened, and my dick swelled. Sure I'd watched porn, heck, I'd watched it with Rhys, but this was real, and personal, and up close.

"His skin, although it's not red, will be burning from the silver," Rhys said, "His human mate will satisfy him well now that he's so turned on."

The vampire cried out and raised his head as he was thrust into on a swift plunge.

A few other spectators stood around, and I noticed a couple opposite exploring each other's bodies as they watched.

"It's so..."

"What?" Rhys asked against my ear. "It's so what?"

"Erotic," I whispered.

"Yes, yes it is. That's what the dungeon is for. It makes us vampires feel so alive, so in tune with our humans. We don't have any inhibitions, we just do what feels good."

I nodded and clasped my hands over Rhys's. I was beginning to have space issues in my pants.

What is wrong with me?

I'd gone years with no sex, yet now it had started it was like a floodgate had opened. I wanted it again, I wanted more. With all of them, even Oscar who'd said I wasn't ready for him. I wanted to be fucked by all of my men.

Desire washed through my veins as I watched the two men fucking hard and fast, clearly oblivious to everyone watching. Satisfaction was their goal and their bodies were behaving as one as they thrust and bucked at a frantic pace, shoving the table legs over the hard floor.

"I want you to do that to me," Rhys whispered, his groin pressing against my ass.

I swallowed. "With the silver bat?"

"Maybe not the first time." He kissed the shell of my ear, then nibbled on the lobe. "But I want that, me bent over, you fucking me as if nothing else exists."

"*Me* fucking *you*?" That surprised me. I'd presumed he'd want to put his cock in my ass.

"Yeah, I like to bottom. It's the way I am." He paused. "Can you give me that?"

"Er, yeah, I reckon." A new fizz of excitement besieged me. Bend Rhys over and take him…like that.

Hell yeah.

"I'm going to bite you first," Rhys said, "while we watch. It will turn us both on even more."

Bite me.

"And then," he said, licking the small patch of skin behind my left ear, "we'll go into the private room behind us and do what they're doing. *Exactly* what they're doing."

"Rhys." I curled my toes in my shoes and clenched my buttocks.

"Say yes," he whispered. "We'll have so much fun, and everyone seeing us go in there, together, will protect you. It's what human and vampire mates do. No suspicion will be aroused."

"Yes. Yes. Okay." I tilted my head, hoping the biting sensation would be the same as when Oscar had drunk from me—heady, euphoric, arousing.

Rhys kissed down my neck, then his mouth landed over my jugular.

I tensed, nerves getting the better of me.

A vampire is about to feed on me.

A rush of pleasure accompanied the heated nip of his fangs.

I stared unblinking at the fucking men.

Excitement grew with each gentle tug of his mouth. My cock surged and my heart rate sped up. I gasped and leaned back against him. "Rhys. Oh, fuck…I need you."

He didn't reply, just continued to drink.

Heat grew inside me, my mouth dried and my balls tightened.

Pleasure grew, but it was a pleasure that would need to reach a climax and find release. It couldn't be contained.

As the men in front of me reached a noisy, almost violent orgasm, Rhys pulled up and placed his fingertips over the small puncture wounds I knew would be on my neck.

I was high on bliss, yet desperation flooded my veins. I couldn't even find the words to articulate what I wanted.

"This way," Rhys said with urgency in his voice. "Come on."

He half pulled, half dragged me to a darkened room on our left.

Oscar stood at the doorway, in the shadows, with his arms folded and his expression stern.

Rhys slipped past him, tugging me along in his wake, then shut the door, giving us privacy. "Come here," he said, pulling me close. "Fuck, I love you. Everything about you. I really fucking love you."

His mouth hit down on mine, giving me an intense kiss that tasted slightly metallic.

I tangled my tongue with his, and tore at his t-shirt, wanting it off. I was in love with him too. There was no point denying it or trying to hide it.

He did the same to my t-shirt and our mouths broke apart as we stripped off our clothes.

For a moment we paused.

Candles on wooden pillars were set beside the gray stone walls, their flames sending a gentle light flickering over Rhys's torso. He was such a beautiful man, with defined muscles and a delectable trail of hair running from his navel to his waistband.

I watched, mesmerized, as he toed off his shoes then quickly removed his pants and underwear.

When he stood before me naked, pre-cum seeped from my cock tip.

This man is mine.

I need to claim him.

In the center of the room stood a black leather bench. It appeared soft and just the right height for me to bend Rhys over.

"Yes," he said, as though reading my thoughts. "That's what it's for."

"So do it." I began to undo my pants, enjoying the new confidence running through me. "Show me your ass."

He grinned. "Yes, sir."

I groaned. I didn't know where the sound had come from, but him calling me sir had hit a chord inside me I hadn't even known was there.

He smiled, a cute as fuck, sexy smirk that had me shoving my pants and boxers off completely and stepping out of them. Had he known that would turn me on?

"Do you want me like this?" he asked, tipping over the bench so his ass was offered to me, the way the vampire's butt in the outer dungeon had been presented to his mate.

"Legs apart." I tapped my toes on each of his ankles. "Wider."

He did as I'd instructed, and I traced my finger down the cool, smooth cleft of his buttocks.

He trembled, the shiver going up his spine and his shoulders quivering. "I want you so bad, Darius," he said breathily.

"You're going to get me." I spotted a bottle of oil to my left and reached for it. After pouring some on the tip of my finger, I found his asshole and stroked over it.

He groaned and gripped the bench. "Please, I don't need slow. Ohhh…"

I'd pushed two fingers into him. The sensation of his tight ring of muscle and the soft chilliness inside him had a fresh rush of blood surging to my cock.

"Yes, yes," he hissed. "More."

With my free hand I gripped my shaft, lubing it up with some of the oil. I needed to sink deep. It was the only thing that could happen next. I was almost frantic with lust and only just controlling myself. I needed to know what fucking Rhys would feel like. I wanted it so bad.

"Darius," he groaned, arching his back. "Do it."

"It's here." I scissored my fingers, stretching him further.

"Oh, fuck." He went onto his toes. "I'm gonna come too soon."

"No, you're not." I slid out, and replaced my fingers with my cock. "It's here, and it's all for you."

"Yes, fuck me. Fuck me now. Hard." He was squirming before me, his fingers gripping and ungripping the bench and his hair stroking the nape of his neck as he tilted his head up.

I pressed one hand on his left buttock, pushing it outward so I had a good visual, and with my other I grabbed his right hip. I knew he was strong, seriously strong, but right now he was allowing me to own him, control him, and that was a heady, thrilling knowledge in itself.

I pushed my cock forward. I was so damn hard, and his asshole opened eagerly around the tip. I kept on going, his band of muscle sliding down the length of me like a dense stroke as I penetrated deeper.

He was quiet and still as if holding his breath and lost to sensation.

Finally I reached the hilt. I'd sunk into him all I could. Our balls pressed together, and his butt hit my lower abdomen.

I blew out a breath and gripped his left hip so I was holding both of them. I'd never felt anything like it. To be inside another being, to have him beneath me, needing me. It was powerful but also came with great responsibility.

"Take me," he said, twisting slightly, "please, now."

"Okay. Hold on tighter."

I watched him grip the bench, then I drew back, groaning at the sensation of his asshole around my cock. When I was almost out I paused, then plunged in fast.

He cried out, a bliss-soaked noise that went straight to my heart.

"Rhys!" I withdrew almost out again. "Are you…okay?"

"More. I can take it, all of it." He moaned, rested his forehead on the bench and arched his back. "Take no notice of my cries, I love it."

"In that case…" An image of the vampires and humans fucking in the dungeon came to me. I set up the same frenetic, animalistic pace. Driving in and out of him, relishing the tightness of his ass on my cock. So much better than my own hand, which was all I'd had for so long.

I was breathing fast, panting. Rhys was bucking backward onto me, impaling himself on my cock each time I forged into him. I was lost to it. Lost to him. He was all I could think of. The pressure was building. Growing too big and fast. My balls shrunk into me. I clenched my ass. Cum was bubbling inside of me. I needed to release it or I'd go insane.

"I'm coming," I said, as an inferno streaked down my arms to my hands. "Fuck, come with me."

"Yes, yes, I am…oh, Darius." He'd yelled my name and it had turned into a strangled cry.

I unloaded my pleasure into him, my belly tense, and my breath held. It was a blissful, almost painful release, it was so powerful. On and on my orgasm rolled through me, my cock pulsing in his ass. Sparks shot from my fingers, bouncing off his skin and the bench, and onto the stone floor before fizzling out.

Rhys finally stilled, dropping his forehead to the bench.

I remained deep inside him, dragged in a breath, then leaned forward so my chest was on his back.

"Hey," I managed, kissing the base of his neck. "You okay?"

"How could I not be?" he said, his breaths ragged. "The man I'm in love with just fucked the Hell out of me."

I laughed, a sudden burst of noise. His choice of words had amused me.

"You sure you've never done that before?" he asked.

"No." I kissed below his ear. "And for the record, I'm glad my first time was with you."

"Me too." He sighed. "You can do that all night if you want."

"The fucking or kissing your neck?"

He chuckled. "Both."

"I'd love to, but—"

"You have the small matter of saving our souls, I know."

"And I think that takes priority...for now." I gave his skin a nip, enjoying it between my teeth.

He groaned and squeezed my softening cock with his asshole. "But we can have another five minutes like this...right?"

Chapter Eighteen

Lloyd

I'd found a spot by the door, in the shadows, that was perfect for observing who was coming and going from the dungeon. I'd seen it busier, but still, there was quite a lot of sexual activity going on, and spectators.

Glancing at the room Rhys and Darius had gone into, I couldn't help a shard of longing. Not that I begrudged Rhys his time with our cambion. I would have simply enjoyed being the vampire he was mated to in the eyes of The Order.

Right now I could imagine what they were up to. Rhys only ever bottomed, so he'd be offering his ass to Darius to sample. And I had no doubts our sexy savior would be thoroughly enjoying every ride into that ass. He might be inexperienced, but the guy had enough sexual energy to rival any lightning bolt. I had a feeling now we'd introduced him to the pleasure his body could give and receive, he'd be making up for lost time.

For a moment I watched a human male enjoying his female vampire's pussy, feasting on it as though her taste was a drug he craved. Then I spotted the door to Darius's and Rhys's room open.

Oscar, who'd been standing outside, unfolded his arms. His expression didn't change as he followed them toward me.

Rhys appeared relaxed and wore a wide grin.

Darius was holding his hand,. His cheeks were flushed with his beautiful blood and he had a swagger to his walk, as though pleased with himself.

I couldn't hide a smile—he was damn cute when he'd just come.

"Hey," Rhys said, as he walked past me. "All good out here?"

"You turned a few heads, as we'd hoped." I nodded at the large oak doorway. "Come on, time to go."

Heading up the stone steps, I was aware of George falling into place behind us. I led the way through the corridors to the reception area.

Samree was still at the desk, filing her nails. "Hey, guys." She cast an eye over us all. "Did it go well with Master Concorde? Was he pleased with your offer of the Siberian property?"

"Very," George said.

"Enjoy the equinox celebrations," I added, keen to change the subject.

She huffed. "I'd enjoy them more, Lloyd, if it were the autumn equinox. Spring and summer really don't agree with my skin."

"Mine neither," I said.

Oscar paused and wrote in the guestbook, signing Darius out.

"Have fun," Samree directed at Rhys. "With your new mate."

"News from the dungeon travels fast," I muttered to George.

"Yeah, let's get out of here," he replied.

We stepped into the daylight and I pulled up my hoody, pausing then to wait as Oscar and Rhys donned their shades and George tipped his cap lower, casting a shadow over his eyes.

"Where are we going now?" Darius asked.

"I was thinking we should get back to the Tower," I said, glancing at George. "What do you think?"

"Yes, good idea." He nodded.

"Let's get inside this time," Oscar said. "Take a look around."

I stepped up to Darius and touched the back of my knuckles to his cheek. "Is that okay with you?" I studied his eyes. The last thing I wanted was him to be scared or concerned with the plan. But instinct was telling me that was where we needed to be. If the key to Master Concorde's salvation was in a temple in Kathmandu, then it was reasonable to think ours could be in an ancient building in London.

"Of course." He smiled at me, his gorgeous eyes flashing with emotion and determination. "We need to do this, and the sooner, the better." He looked over my shoulder at George and Oscar. "I can't imagine not being with you, any of you. I want to know it's always going to be that way."

I leaned forward and swiped my lips over his. "We've got a few hurdles yet, but we'll make it happen."

"Lloyd," Rhys said sharply. "For crying out loud, anyone could see."

"Shit, sorry." I glanced around. Luckily there was no one about.

"He's supposed to be only mine." Rhys stood closer to Darius, pressing their upper arms together.

"Yeah, I know." I frowned. "But he isn't, not really."

"He has to be here."

"To protect him," I said. "Though keep in mind, Rhys, we're sharing, that was always the plan and—"

"Hey," Darius said. "There's enough of me to go around…as long as you don't get too thirsty."

He smiled and my frustration evaporated. This man was more than enough for us. He was everything we'd ever wanted.

Everything I've ever wanted.

"Come on." Oscar glanced at the sky. "I don't want to be out in the midday sun if we don't have to be."

Half an hour later we were walking into the grounds of the Tower of London like a group of regular tourists.

Except we weren't.

On the highest ramparts, visitors strolled around, taking shots of the bridge, the river and the skyline. On the neat lawn ravens pecked, and a family had stopped for a rest and to enjoy the fine weather.

I took the lead and directed us through an archway, dodging humans of all nationalities as we went. What I really wanted to do was get into the bowels of the place. Find out where Master Benedict might have been kept before his unsavory end.

"Why are there statues of animals?" Darius asked, pointing at a pair of metal monkeys sitting on a wall.

"Exotic animals were a status symbol," George said. "Over the years many were given to royalty and they were housed here. Apparently a polar bear used to fish in the Thames."

"No way." Rhys laughed.

"Yes way." George smiled.

We passed a sign for the Jewel House, a crowd easing by it.

"Popular in there, isn't it?" Oscar said, his deep voice quiet. He always tried to play it cool in crowds. His size and brooding demeanor brought enough attention without adding a booming voice to it.

"The Crown Jewels," George said. "Under armed guard."

"Wouldn't stop us if we wanted them," Rhys said with a chuckle.

"And steal from Queen Elizabeth the Second, who allows The Order to reside in her commonwealth." George raised his eyebrows at him. "That wouldn't do us any favors."

"I know." Rhys threw a wink at Darius. "Just want our guy here to know we'll get anything his heart desires."

"I don't think a crown would suit me." Darius smiled, then swung his gaze to the left. "What's down there, do you think?"

I followed his line of sight. "Let's go and see."

The crowds thinned and our footsteps on the cobbled pathway became audible. The high stone walls loomed all around us and we went through yet another archway, its heavy iron portcullis peeking from the innards as if waiting to drop.

I glanced at the patch of sky above us. The place had a strange, creepy atmosphere. For a moment I wondered if that was something to do with the demon heading our way again, but the blue above me, and the stillness of a pile of lilac blossom in the corner was reassuring.

"What is this place?" Rhys asked, looking upward at the high walls and small windows.

"Torture Tower," George said.

"How'd you know so much?" Rhys frowned.

George chuckled and pointed to a sign.

Torture at the Tower.

"Ah, okay." Rhys bumped Darius's shoulder with his as Darius giggled.

"I feel sorry for old Master Benedict being stuck here," Oscar said. "There's no way out, not if silver is involved."

"Why silver?" Darius asked.

"I told you it causes pain," Rhys said. "Often good, erotic, fun pain. But in the past, humans have used it—"

"And shifters," I added.

"Yeah, you're right, Lloyd, and shifters," Rhys went on. "To contain and control us. They know we can't fight it. It's as though it saps our strength as well as causing us a great deal of pain."

Darius nodded. "So do you think they knew Benedict was a vampire?"

"I think we can presume so," George said. "It's why he was killed the way he was."

Darius was quiet, then, "So where do you think the cells are, where he might have been kept?"

I came to a halt. The others stopped around me. There were members of staff dotted about who clearly would only allow access to certain places.

George pulled out his iPhone and tapped the screen. "Let's go this way."

I fell into line behind him, Darius and Rhys at my side, Oscar behind us.

Rounding a corner, out of the sunlight and into the shade, it became clear we were alone and away from the masses.

George stopped by a small oak door with wrought iron furniture, the hinges shaped like spears.

The moment he bunched his shoulder and gritted his teeth, I knew we were going through it.

He shoved at it, one hard blow ripping it from its hinges. The old wood and metal had been there for centuries, keeping the innards of the tower secure from intruders, but it hadn't stood a chance against a determined vampire.

"Quick," he directed at Darius, "get in."

Darius rushed forward, and I couldn't help admire his bravery and his absolute commitment to helping us.

I love him so much.

Quickly, I went in after him. There was no way we could let him out of our sights in here. We were trespassing now, and the Tower of London didn't have a reputation for being lenient on offenders.

"This way." George nodded to the left. "I can't hear anyone down there, but hurry."

I set my palm in the small of Darius's back. "Don't be nervous," I said. "We're here with you."

"I know, Lloyd, thank you."

We took a left through the shadows. It was musty and damp, definitely not a place the public were generally allowed.

We passed a heavy metal door, then the floor dipped as though the stone underfoot had been worn down by boot-fall over the centuries. Around another corner stood a row of barred cells.

I came to a halt, Darius on one side of me, Oscar on the other.

"Wow, look at this." Rhys stepped up to one and held the bars. "Pretty grim, huh."

"Yeah," I said. The cell nearest me had mold growing up the damp wall. There was no natural light, and a hole in the floor was releasing a nasty stench.

"I know modern prisons aren't great," Darius said. "But they're better than this."

"Not that some people deserve it," Oscar muttered.

I looked at the corridor behind us. If Master Benedict had been kept in this section of the tower it wouldn't have been one of these cells. They couldn't have held a vampire. Iron bars were no obstacle. He'd have had no difficulty escaping.

"There must be more cells," George said.

I guessed his train of thought was going down the same route as mine.

"What's this?" Darius stepped forward. "There's a cell at the end, it looks different."

I followed him.

He was right. The cell at the end, much smaller than the others, was different. It had sunlight pouring into it from a mossy grate, and different color bars.

Darius gripped them and peered in. "It's tiny."

I did the same, my shoulder brushing his. But the moment I did I knew it had been a mistake. I yelped as burning pain shot from my palms, up my arms, and across my shoulders. My skull seemed to squeeze my brain and my chest crushed in on itself. I struggled to stay standing as I released the bars and staggered backward.

Oscar caught me. "What's up?"

"Fuck!" I rubbed my hands together. "Those bars are made of silver."

"They are?" George bent to study them. "Damn, that's clever." He straightened and turned to me with a grin. "It also tells us this was the cell reserved for vampires, or suspected vampires."

"Bloody Hell," Darius said. "I wonder if it's open."

He gave the door a tug, and I was grateful for his immunity to silver. It didn't move. He yanked it again, his t-shirt straining over his shoulders. This time the metal let out a creak and the base of the door scraped over the gritty floor until the gap was three feet wide.

"Cool," Rhys said, slipping through it.

"Yeah, thanks, babe." Oscar squeezed Darius's shoulder as he walked past.

"I hope we find something." George turned to me.

"Me too." I knew what he was saying. If we didn't, we were all out of places to look. This was the only thing that made sense, and it did seem as if Master Benedict had led us here.

I stepped in behind Darius, hoping George was keeping his keen ears alert to anyone approaching.

Oscar and Rhys were peering at the walls. They were easy to see owing to the light coming in. This had no doubt been designed to cause maximum discomfort to the vampire prisoner who hated sunshine.

I slid my fingers over the gritty stonework. The old surfaces were gnarly and dented. I suppressed a shudder as I imagined the awful experience my fellow vampires must have endured in this small cell.

"Hey, what's this?" Rhys said. "Come and see."

"What is it?" I rushed to him, as did the others.

"There's something scratched into the stone."

I peered closer. He was right. The markings on this stone, at eye level, were different to the random dinks and imperfections of the others.

"It's a circle," Darius said, stating the obvious and running the tip of his finger over it. "But for some reason it's been halved. This side is deeper than the other, as if it's been scratched at."

"Darker too," Oscar said, glancing at the light streaming in. "It's in the shade at the moment."

I nibbled on my bottom lip and rested my hand on Darius's shoulder. I was sure this was an important find. I didn't know why, perhaps it was instinct or a connection to the ancient vampire I, like my fellow vampires, revered so much. It was his wisdom and teachings that helped us function in a world of humans.

"And below it are four more smaller circles, but they're not hollowed out."

"No, they're like rings," George said.

"Do you think this is a sign from Master Benedict?" Oscar asked.

"We know he was incarcerated here," I said. "And this is clearly the only cell which could hold a vampire."

"In this section," Oscar said.

"Do you think they'd have gone to the trouble to make two cells with silver bars?" George asked. "All that silver must have been expensive."

Oscar shrugged and resumed studying the stone.

"What's this?" I pointed to another notched out shape to the left of the circles. It was two parallel vertical lines with another over the top, like a doorway with the lintel over-hanging.

George pulled out his iPhone. "I'll take a photograph. We need to get going."

"We do?" Darius asked.

"Yes." He snapped a shot. "Someone is coming."

"Fuck, quick." I reached for Darius's hand. "You can't be here. We need to go."

Chapter Nineteen

Darius

We exited the Tower of London and onto the street without capturing the attention of any members of staff. I was glad to be out of the gloomy dungeon, but my stomach was rumbling.

"Now where?" Rhys asked. "Back to the apartment to think this through?"

"Or to The Order to see Master Concorde again," Lloyd said. "Perhaps he'll be able to help with those images and what they mean."

"No," George said. "Let's try to figure it out ourselves first, before we ask him or go back to The Order."

"Yeah." Oscar gave me a quick hug across my shoulders. "I'd rather not have our guy under scrutiny again so soon. We've got away with it once today."

"And besides, he'll be busy with the equinox festival," Lloyd said, seeming to be thinking aloud.

"So back to the apartment." Rhys nodded. "Okay. Let's go."

"Er, hang on." I held up my hand. "One issue with that."

"What?" A flash of concern went over Lloyd's face and I saw it in the others' too.

"There's no food there, and in case you've forgotten, I'm human, or at least half human, and I need to eat."

Lloyd's handsome features relaxed then creased again. "Fuck, sorry. And yes, you do need to eat." He reached for my hand and breezed his lips over my knuckles. "Sorry for forgetting that."

"No problem." I smiled, enjoying both his and Oscar's closeness. *What would it be like to be with them both, naked, fucking?*

A shiver of desire went through me. They were both so damn gorgeous and passionate; it could only be good if we all leaped into bed together.

"There's a pizza place over there—will that work for you?" Rhys asked, pointing over the road at the red and green façade on *Pizza Right Now*.

"Perfect." I could almost taste the tomato, oregano, and the ham and pineapple topping I'd order.

"Just don't order garlic, okay," Oscar said.

"Why?" I asked.

"It will make your blood taste of it." Oscar shuddered. "Not nice."

"I'll remember that, but I'm not a fan of garlic anyway."

"See, he's perfect for us." Lloyd grinned.

We wandered in and took a seat at the back, away from the bright sunshine streaming through the big front window. I placed an order, and as we waited for the food to arrive George opened the photo of the image in the cell. "What does it mean?"

I took it and studied it. The big circle was sectioned down the middle so it looked light and dark, and the four rings beneath it were all of equal size but not halved the way the big one was. "These rings have a dot in the middle, after the first two," I said, zooming in. "As if they're punctuated, two and two."

"Oh yeah," Lloyd said, leaning close to me. "You're right."

I enjoyed his weight on my arm. "What does it mean?"

Rhys ran his hand over his hair as if checking the style was still neat. "No idea."

I frowned and stared at the close up image again. "What if…?"

"What?" George asked. "Tell us."

Oscar stopped stacking small cardboard drink mats on top of the salt and pepper pots. "Tell us."

"What if this is the Earth." I pointed to the big circle. "And it's representing night and day."

"Half is night and half is day." George nodded.

"And what is it…" I paused as thoughts collided in my brain. Was it really so simple?

"And what is it…?" Lloyd repeated, staring into my eyes.

"And what is it today?" I finished.

"I don't follow." Rhys folded his arms and sat back. His dimples had disappeared.

"Today is the spring equinox," I said, tapping the screen. "Half day and half night. This image represents the date. Today's date."

"Fuck!" Oscar set his hands hard on the table, toppling the small structure he'd created out of the condiments and mat.

"I think you might be right." There was excitement in George's voice. "In fact *I'm sure* you are."

"Okay." Lloyd sounded a little more hesitant. "But if that's the case, what's this?" He gestured to the smaller circles.

"The time." The knowledge came to me as I'd spoken the words.

"Zero, zero, zero, zero?" Oscar said.

"Yeah, with this mark in the middle, it's simply saying midnight."

"Praise be to Master Benedict." George tugged off his cap, scraped his hand through his hair and slapped the hat back into place. "That's exactly what he's telling us."

Lloyd shook his head, a slow smile spreading on his face. "I think that's right, we've solved half of it. We know when to drink from Darius."

"Shh." Rhys frowned as a waiter approached carrying four huge pizzas. "Lloyd."

Lloyd glanced at the waiter then curled his hand around his tumbler of water and bowed his head. His hoody was still up and his face more or less hidden.

When the food was set down, I reached for a slice of pizza, then as soon as I'd munched it and my stomach had stopped growling, I said, "Now we just need to find out *where*."

"At the Tower?" Rhys suggested. "Everything else has been there."

"I don't think so." George was poking at a bit of pizza on a plate but his attention was on the phone. "This part of the image is the where, but he hasn't given us much to go on."

"No." Oscar frowned and resumed stacking the mats on top of the salt and pepper pots. "It's just three lines. Not exactly much to go on."

"I guess it was hard scratching into stone, likely he used his finger," Rhys said.

"Ouch." I grimaced.

"Tough skin." Lloyd winked at me.

I reached for another slice of pizza, sipping on my cola as I did so. Hanging around with guys who didn't eat wasn't easy. I'd have to make sure I didn't lose weight, not least because I was expending more energy with them.

I glanced at Rhys. He was looking my way. I smiled, remembering the fun we'd had in the dungeon. The man was hot and so fucking reactive to what I'd done to him.

A snake of lust went through me. I'd happily do that all over again, here, now, in the pizza restaurant and to Hell with who saw us expressing our love and lust for each other.

I tore my attention from Rhys, and bit into my pizza, enjoying the sweet, doughy flavors.

Oscar had resumed his stacking. I stared at it, chewing as I did so. What did it remind me of?

I swallowed and bit into my food again. He'd balanced a small cardboard drinks mat on top of the two pots, as if he'd made a doorway.

A doorway.

Like the scratching Benedict had left us.

Except it wasn't a doorway. It was a structure.

And in real life it wasn't made of plastic, glass and cardboard—it was made of stone, just like the canvas Benedict had used; the stone wall of the cell.

"Bloody Hell," I muttered as the hugeness of it dawned on me. Like a dimmer switch going from dark to full beam I knew exactly what it was, or rather where we had to go for the men I loved to be saved from damnation.

"You okay?" George asked, resting his hand on my leg beneath the table and studying my face.

I swallowed. "More than okay."

They all turned to me.

"I know the *where* in the what, when and where."

"You do?" Rhys said.

George nodded, his expression serious. "The *what* is that we must drink your blood, my love."

"And the *when* is at midnight on the equinox," Lloyd added. "Tonight."

"And the where." I paused and pointed at Oscar's structure. "Is Stonehenge."

"What?" Rhys sat forward. "Stonehenge. How do you know?"

"It looks like that," I said. "And Stonehenge is not a new building, or anything in the natural world. Like the Kathmandu temple, it's an ancient but manmade structure."

"And it was definitely around when Master Benedict was." George rubbed his chin. "And not far from London...in vampire terms at least."

"Stonehenge," Oscar repeated, looking from me to his small and simple creation. "Yeah, it could be. It's a series of stones, set like this. Two upright ones holding another large horizontal one. And he's accompanied it with circles, the only other shape in the message."

"And the stones are set in a circle," I said.

"So let me get this straight." Rhys sat forward with his hands on the table. "If we get our asses to Stonehenge, tonight, and all drink from Darius at midnight, that's it, we're saved."

"If the fable is to be believed," George said. He sat back and folded his arms. "Though thanks be to Benedict if we've figured it out correctly."

"How will we know?" Lloyd said.

"I don't know, but we've got to try." George put his phone away. "And as soon as Darius has had his fill of pizza, we'll head to Wiltshire. If Oscar's quick we'll all be there before nightfall."

"This is all well and good," I said, grabbing more pizza, since I didn't know when I'd eat again. "As long as you all only…" I paused and glanced around at the other tables, then leaned in. "Only drink a little bit from me," I said quietly, "I don't have an endless supply of blood, you know."

"Just a taste each is all it will take." George rested his hand over mine. "Don't worry, we'd never do anything to risk or hurt you, Darius."

"Which reminds me." Oscar held up his hand and clicked his fingers.

A waiter appeared, eyeing him nervously. "Yes, sir."

"A mug of hot water," Oscar said gruffly.

"Certainly, sir." He backed away.

"What's that for?" I asked.

"Tea," they all said at once.

"Tea?" I couldn't suppress a laugh. "I've got cola."

Oscar pulled a small teabag on a string from his pocket. "We should have given you this already. It's an old herbal remedy designed to rejuvenate humans mated with vampires. It means you'll quickly make more blood, and our small feeds won't affect you."

"And it's even more important when you have so many mates," George said.

I recalled the vampires at The Order offering their human female Bea a drink of tea. She'd seemed keen to have it. "I'm normally a coffee kind of a guy but I'll try it."

Oscar and I arrived in Wiltshire as the sun slipped from the horizon.

Oscar pulled the bike into a darkening layby in a lane half a mile away from the Stonehenge Visitor Center. My other vampires were already there, waiting. They'd run the ninety-mile journey, traveling at speed, and not looking any different for it.

I dismounted, took my helmet off, then stretched my arms over my head and leaned backward. My spine ached, so did my hips, from sitting hunched for two and a half hours. Not that I didn't enjoy clinging to Oscar's big sexy body. I did, a lot.

"You okay, babe?" he asked, rubbing his hand up and down the center of my spine.

"Mmm, yeah, I will be in a minute."

I glanced around at the shadowy outline of the hills. The stars were out in the east and beginning to creep their way over the sky.

"We've got a few hours to get to the actual stones." Rhys said. "Do you need to sleep or eat first, Darius?"

"No, I'm good. That pizza filled me up." I rubbed my belly. "And I'll be okay till bedtime for sleep." I frowned. "Wherever it is we'll sleep."

"I've booked a hotel nearby," George said. "I figured you didn't get a full night's sleep last night so you'd be too tired to go back to London." He bit on his bottom lip, holding in a smile.

I didn't bother to disguise mine. My first night with George had been incredible. I couldn't keep the smile up, though, and it dropped quickly.

"What is it?" Oscar asked.

"I guess the thought of going to sleep and the dreams worsening and becoming more threatening doesn't appeal." I shuddered at the memoires of the twisting, twirling demon and his sinister grating voice. "Do you think he's here, my father?"

"Why would you think that?" Lloyd asked, glancing at the clear sky.

"I just..." I couldn't put it into words. It was very beautiful in the heart of the English countryside, but thoughts of the demon seemed to be battling for attention in my mind as we'd closed the miles to Stonehenge.

"It's natural to be concerned," George said, resting his hand on my arm. "But we'll protect you, no matter what form he comes in. If he does at all."

"Yeah, hopefully we'll get this done without disturbance and be able to destroy your father afterward." Lloyd paused. "Sorry, that sounded awful. I meant the demon. Because you're obviously nothing like him and—"

"It's okay," I said. "And I've called him my father too, but the truth is, never having had one, the word has little meaning to me." I turned to George. "Which reminds me, why did Master Concorde say you were his son? Are you related?"

"No." George shook his head. "Not in the conventional sense, anyway." He pointed to a gate. "I think we should start walking, it's a couple of miles north east of here."

"Oh, okay." I wondered why George hadn't elaborated.

I've still got so much to learn about these vampires of mine.

Oscar climbed over the gate. It creaked under his weight. Rhys and Lloyd jumped it in one swift move.

George climbed over it, the way I did, though I knew he could have done it much easier.

"I remember," Oscar said, as we fell into a line, "when we were on the plane, babe, and talking about artwork."

"Yeah," I replied. "You told me about The Raft of the Medusa."

He nodded. "I knew then that you had the protection of your mother, of a good, kind and pure bloodline from her and her ancestors."

"How's that?"

"Well, I told you about the wretched souls on the raft, and how they'd begun to eat each other in their desperation."

I continued to stomp ahead through the spring grass. "I remember, Oscar. It's a grizzly tale."

"Yeah, it is. But like the artist, and the light on the horizon, you had hope for the men."

"I hadn't even seen the painting."

"You didn't need to," Oscar said. "Because you told me you believed the body is a vehicle, a transport through life, but it's up here we really need to care for." He tapped the side of his head. "The mind, the soul."

"I do believe that."

"And in that moment I knew you'd help us, our wretched souls."

"I don't think you're wretched. Different, yes, but not wretched."

"At the moment we kind of are," Lloyd said. "Our future is this strange existence on Earth or eternal Hell."

"Life here is okay, isn't it?"

"Yeah, especially now I'm...*we're* with you," Lloyd said. "But it's always there, hanging over us. A stake through the heart, beheading, and then that's it, toasted for eternity." He shuddered.

"That's not going to happen." A shard of determination went through me. "I'm going to make sure of it, tonight. Soon." I glanced at my watch. "Very soon."

Rhys gave me a sideways glance accompanied by a smile.

"And," Oscar went on.

"What?" The air was becoming damp now night had fallen, and had brought with it the scent of the countryside; earth, pollen, dew.

"And you wouldn't hurt a fly," Oscar said.

"I'm no saint." I laughed.

"No," Oscar said. "But in your apartment that time, you made the effort to let a bug out of your window. Not many people would do that."

I shrugged. "Live and let live."

"Hear, hear." Lloyd stepped closer and slung his arm over my shoulder. "An excellent philosophy, Darius."

I slipped my arm around his waist and fell into step with him. Our footsteps swished as we walked across the meadow and our hips touched occasionally.

Soon the others had gone slightly ahead, making their way onto an official track through the burial mounds of which there were hundreds scattered in the fields leading to the monument.

"Can I ask you something, Lloyd?"

"Sure."

"Why did Master Concorde call George his son?"

"Ah, that."

"Yeah."

"He turned him."

"Turned him." I remembered Oscar using the same phrase. "You mean Master Concorde turned George into a vampire?"

"Yes, and having done that he took on the responsibility for the new vampire's actions." Lloyd paused. "You see, when a human is first drained dry and turned, they're very thirsty. Greedy for blood. It's when they're at their most dangerous. After a few years they calm down."

"A few years?"

"Which is a blink for our sort."

"I guess." I was quiet, then, "So why did he turn him?"

Lloyd looked ahead at George. "It was a long time ago."

"I figured that."

"Sixteen ninety-one." Lloyd paused. "George was traveling from Edinburgh to London when his carriage was set upon by masked highwaymen. They held the passengers, three women and George, at gunpoint as they ransacked the luggage and yanked the women's jewelry from their throats and fingers. From what he's told me, he stayed pretty calm when it was material goods being taken, but when one of the men dragged a young female into the woods, he put up a fight, a useless fight considering how outnumbered he was."

"Fuck. What happened?"

"Master Concorde happened to be passing. George vaguely remembers him putting an end to the highwaymen, and setting the women back in the carriage, but George was nearly dead, he'd lost so much blood from a gunshot to his abdomen."

"And then what?"

"Master Concorde had a choice. Let George die. Feed from him, then let him die. Or drink him completely dry and turn him."

"So why did he choose the latter?"

Lloyd glanced at me and smiled though his face was shrouded in darkness with his hood in place.

"Because he saw a good soul. George had given his life trying to protect others. Master Concorde believed his soul deserved another chance, no matter what that chance was."

"Wow." It was hard to believe, but I did believe it all. George was exactly the type of man to risk himself for others. "I think you're all good souls, Lloyd."

"I'm glad you think so." He held me closer. "I do love you, you know. Even though it seems fast, it's not, we've always been destined for this, to be together."

"I know. I can feel it." I banged my chest. "Here."

Chapter Twenty

Darius

As midnight drew nearer, I became restless, checking my watch and scanning the huge stones set in a large circle. They were majestic, bigger than I'd expected. Moonlight sparkled in the moist grass, making it look as if the stones were set on a bed of diamonds.

Would it go to plan? Could I save these men with my blood? Was my father watching on, even now?

We'd easily traversed the perimeter fence around the monument. George had disabled a CCTV camera by hacking into the system. I'd watched him in amazement, thinking of all the times he'd passed through in his long life, the things he'd learned and seen. I fell a little more for him, and longed to have some quiet alone time to discover his memories and ask about his past.

Then I'd looked at Oscar, checking out the shadows beneath the stones, his big bulk moving with grace and small droplets of dew glistening around his biker boots as he'd strode through the grass. He, too, had my heart. It was cliché to say he had a rough exterior but was soft inside, because there was so much more depth to him. I was greedy for time with him, too. Not least because I wanted to find out if I could handle getting fucked by his big cock.

I shifted from one foot to the other and clenched my buttocks. Just thinking of sex made me horny, despite the serious situation.

Rhys was leaning back against a stone with his hands in his pockets and staring at the ancient woodland to the east. I adored his easy smile, his dimples and the way his carefully styled hair flopped forward, giving the impression of boyhood despite his many years on this Earth. He was fun to be with, sexy as fuck as well. He was a man who'd already moved into my heart.

Lloyd had stayed close to me, smoking not one, but three cigarettes while we'd waited for midnight. I'd enjoyed the tangy scent of the tobacco as it had swirled upward then melted into the night. When I'd shivered, despite it not really being truly cold, he'd hugged me close and kissed my cheek.

'I can't wait to taste you.'

I shivered again, remembering the intensity in his words. I wanted Lloyd to taste me. I wanted him to kiss me all over, fuck me, give me an orgasm. I hadn't had the pleasure of getting naked with Lloyd, yet I felt so close to him. Perhaps when this was over we'd share a bed, tonight, and make each other come, over and over.

"It's time." George stepped up to me, holding his pocket watch. "If you're in agreement, Darius."

"Of course I am." I unzipped my jacket then shrugged it off. "How could you doubt it?"

"It's polite to ask," George said, slipping his watch away then taking my jacket.

"How do you want me?" I ran my fingertips around the collar of my t-shirt.

"Now there's an offer." Oscar raised his eyebrows and swiped his tongue over his bottom lip.

"Definitely minus the t-shirt," Rhys said, stripping off his own. It had *Rio Grande* and a small Stetson embroidered on it. He dropped it on top of my jacket, which George had laid on the ground.

I admired Rhys's chest for a moment, then Oscar smoothed his wide palm over mine and distracted me. "We'll be careful. I promise."

"I know you will." I stared into his eyes. "I trust you."

"You *must* be special." Oscar laughed. "To trust four vampires."

"You need me."

"Yeah, we do." Lloyd was behind me. He slipped his arms around my waist and pulled my back to his cool chest. He'd removed his hoody and t-shirt and his skin on mine sent a swirl of desire through me. "We really need you, in so many ways, and for all of time. Nothing bad will ever happen to you."

"We love you," George said, breezing his lips over my mouth. "You're the one we've been searching for, and now we've found you, you've made us very happy."

"So happy," Rhys said, kneeling in front of me and taking my hand. He turned it, so my wrist was exposed and just an inch from his mouth.

My vampires cocooned me, surrounded me. I felt safe and protected, needed and desired.

Have I ever been happier?

I worried about myself sometimes. My blood was about to be drunk and I was happy?

"No fear, just pleasure," George murmured as he kissed over my cheek to my neck.

Lloyd was also kissing my neck, his chilled lips leaving a trail of sensation that went down my spine to my asshole.

I moaned, tipped my head back, and closed my eyes.

A sharpness entered my right wrist—Rhys sinking his fangs in first. Instantly my asshole tightened further and my cock twitched.

"Ah, yeah," I gasped, locking my elbow and relishing the soft suction he'd created.

Another two sets of fangs pierced my flesh. George at my jugular, Oscar on the ball of my shoulder.

I jolted as blood rushed to my cock, filling it fast. Their saliva was a potent aphrodisiac, and having so much of it at once...

I groaned, and with my free hand I clutched Lloyd's forearm which was wrapped around my waist. "Oh fuck," I managed as a fourth set of fangs stabbed into the opposite side of my neck—Lloyd.

Bright lights swirled in my vision. My pulse thudded in my ears. My heartbeat sped up and my knees weakened. Rather than them taking from me, it felt more like they were feeding *me* something.

Desire.

Passion.

Lust.

I whimpered, glad of the support their arms and bodies were giving me. My cock was at full mast now, pressing against my jeans. It hurt, it was so bloated. I was sure I'd have zipper marks.

My veins heated and tingled around their mouths. Adrenaline shot through my system. I trembled, and my stomach and ass quivered as my temperature went up, scorching over my shoulders and to my biceps.

"My cock," I gasped. "Fuck." Damn, it hurt. I needed to free it from its confines. The sensation was like nothing I'd ever felt before. The craving so powerful I wondered if I'd survive it.

Still they sucked, drinking before, during, and after the strokes of midnight. My skin was alive, heat shooting down my arms and fizzing in my fingertips. But sparks didn't release. They stayed there, boiling and churning, adding to the desperation bubbling inside me.

Lloyd was the first to stop feeding. "That was worth the wait," he whispered against my ear.

I couldn't answer. My brain was fudged. All I could think of was my swollen cock and finding release. My hands were on fire, but my cock more so.

George pulled back, his fangs still on show. Two small drips of blood sat on the ends as he smiled at me.

"George," I managed, then glanced at my groin. I groaned when I spotted the thick wedge of flesh. "I need..."

"Shh." He kissed me, feeding me my own bloody flavor.

I swiped my tongue into his mouth. I was breathless and hot. My body didn't feel like mine any more. They owned it. I was theirs and they were mine.

George broke the kiss and studied my face. "You okay?"

I opened my mouth but no words came out. I was frantic, too frantic to articulate.

Oscar pulled back, wiping his hand over his lips. He glanced at the sky, then me. He frowned. "Babe?"

I was shaking as I pushed at Lloyd's arm around my waist. "I need..."

"What? What do you need?" Lloyd whispered as he released me.

Rhys raised his head and stared up at me. A trickle of blood rolled off his chin onto the grass.

"Jeez, your saliva. Fuck!" I dragged at the top button on my jeans. "I need...I need to fuck. Someone fucking fuck me." I shoved at them, dragging my boxers with the tangle of material.

Finding release, claiming an orgasm was all I could think of. Need had possessed me.

They were all quiet for a split second, then Lloyd spoke. "I'm up for the job." He pressed the center of my back, forcing me to bend forward.

Eagerly I got to my hands and knees, glad of the cool earth on my hot flesh and the night air washing over my now naked ass. "Hurry."

"Bloody Hell, he really needs it," Rhys said, moving to my side. He wrapped his hand around my shaft and squeezed. "He's rock hard."

I yelled out in pleasure. Finally. Stimulation.

"You got lube?" Oscar said.

"Yeah," Lloyd replied. He gripped my buttocks and separated them.

I knew I was a sight, begging for it, offered up for it, but I was past caring. I needed one of my men to sort me out...fast.

"Damn, you're hot like this." George ran his hand over my damp hair, removing the strands stuck to my forehead. "So in need of us."

My asshole was invaded, not by fingers but by cock. Lloyd's cock.

I squeezed my eyes closed and groaned. This was only the second time I'd been fucked and there was no preamble, no prep.

I was glad of the lube as he continued to push forward, his wide cock head parting my quivering sphincter. I held my breath as it stretched to the point a nip of pain caused me to cry out.

"Relax," Rhys said, stroking my cock from root to tip in long, firm movements.

Relax.

I couldn't, and didn't even try to. Instead I bucked backward, taking more of Lloyd's cock.

He moaned my name and gripped my hips harder. He seemed to give up control and sank deep, plunging into me until his belly slapped against my ass cheeks. "Ah fuck, yeah!"

"Benedict give me strength," Oscar moaned, running his hand up my back to the nape of my neck. "I've got such a fucking hard on watching this."

"Oscar!" I whimpered. "Please, more. Give me more."

Lloyd pulled back, then shoved into me again, riding over my prostate.

I grunted as pleasure spun through my system and my balls contracted.

Rhys was masturbating me, his excited breaths washing over my torso. When he reached the tip of my cock he twisted his hand a little, stimulating my glans and making me dizzy with pleasure.

"Here, take this." A big hand gripped my hair and pulled my face up. I opened my eyes. Oscar was in front of me, on his knees, holding his cock.

His huge, thick cock.

"Open your mouth, babe," he said.

I did as he'd asked, and as Lloyd and Rhys worked me, Oscar sank his enormous shaft into my mouth.

My jaw ached it had to stretch so much, and he quickly reached my throat. I resisted the urge to gag even though Lloyd was shunting me onto Oscar's cock with each thrust of his hips.

I was spiraling toward an orgasm—one so big, so consuming it scared me. My pulse was deafening, my asshole was taking Lloyd's dick in fast, wild strokes, and my mouth was full. Blistering heat shot down my arms, heating my palms and sizzling against the cold, damp grass.

"Come," Rhys said. "We want to see you come. You're spectacular like this, Darius. You were made for us, made for fucking."

His sexy words tipped me over the edge. For a few blissful seconds I held the intense pressure hostage in my cock and ass, then with relief I released it.

Ecstasy consumed me. I didn't know where my body stopped and my vampires' bodies began. My ass spasmed around Lloyd's cock, and my dick spurted, coating Rhys's hand. I swallowed rapidly as Oscar came in time with me.

"Yeah, he's coming. *I'm* coming," Lloyd shouted. "It's here."

He flooded my insides with cool cum, adding to my bliss. I would have cried out, told them how awesome it was, but my mouth was stuffed with cock.

On and on my climax claimed me. It was like nothing I'd experienced before. Several thick shots of semen shot from me, until my contracted belly hurt with each subsequent spurt. My fingertips burned and I was sure sparks were flying from them and seeping into the ground.

"Fuck, that was amazing." Lloyd slowed and ran his hands from my hips to my buttocks. "*You're* amazing, Darius."

Oscar pulled from my mouth, but I still couldn't speak. I was panting, gasping for breath. My vision was fogged, and my ears buzzed. Pleasure was still rippling through my cock as Rhys held it.

'Hey." Rhys kissed my cheek. "Take a few deep breaths, eh?"

I inhaled; short, sharp snatches of air.

"That's it," he said.

Oscar stroked my hair, and Lloyd was still buried deep.

Gradually my trembling body came back under my control, though the heat in my chest, shoulders and arms remained. "I'm okay."

"Babe, you're more than okay—you're perfect," Oscar said.

"I'm pulling out." Lloyd withdrew.

I was aware of every millimetre of his cock leaving my body. When his glans popped out, my asshole clenched tight.

"Wow, I didn't...expect that." I fell onto my stomach on the grass, then immediately flipped over onto my back.

For a second I focused on clouds slipping over the stars, then both Rhys and Lloyd's faces appeared.

Rhys grinned and smoothed his hand down my belly and stroked over my cock again, which was softening as it lay on my pubic hair.

"Was I too rough?" Lloyd frowned. "I'm sorry if I was."

"No, you gave me just what I needed."

His brow softened. "That's what I always want to do for you."

"Only a few scorch marks," Oscar said, stamping on a smouldering patch of earth to my side. "Nothing to concern ourselves with."

I rolled my shoulders, then flexed and unflexed my fingers. It was as though they were still bubbling with heat and sparks.

"Get up," George suddenly commanded.

Lloyd and Rhys snapped their attention to him.

I closed my eyes and sighed. I needed to rest. My work was done, I'd fed my vampires according to the fable, and I'd been thoroughly fucked as my reward.

"Someone is coming," George said.

Chapter Twenty-One

Darius

"What?" I spun to my side and stared in the direction George was pointing.

"It's okay," he said. "Human footsteps, and still a way off. But get up, get dressed."

"Security?" Oscar tucked himself away and straightened his leather jacket.

"Possibly." George shrugged. "But realistically it could be anyone. This place wasn't exactly hard to get into and with security down as well."

"True." Lloyd reached for my hand and helped me to standing.

Rhys already had his t-shirt back on, and he passed me mine. "Here."

"Thanks." My asshole was tender as I refastened my jeans, though it wasn't an unpleasant sensation.

"Over there," Oscar said, stepping close to me, his shoulder brushing mine. "See?"

"Yeah," Lloyd said, flanking me and folding his arms.

"Should we hide?" I asked.

"No," George said. "We'll talk our way out of it if necessary, and if we can't..."

"You'll what?" I asked.

"We have ways." Rhys smoothed his hand over his hair. "The same methods we'd have employed if spotted in the Tower."

I swallowed; the taste of Oscar was still on my tongue.

Out of the shadows, a lone male figure appeared. He was striding toward us, his paces long, and with what looked to be a large camera swinging from a strap around his neck.

"Do you know him?" Lloyd asked me.

"No, why would I?" I said. "Do you?"

The vampires were silent so I took that as a no. I rubbed the two small bite marks on my wrist as I watched him approach. The holes were hot, as were my arms and hands. It was as if they were still full of fire.

"Military?" Rhys said. "What do you reckon?"

"Mmm." Lloyd moved nearer to me. "A soldier who likes to take night time photographs. Strange, right?"

"Stranger things happen," I said.

The moonlight had spread over the man now. He was tall, with short, dark hair, and stubble peppered his jawline. He wore camo combats and a tight, black t-shirt. Tattoos spread over both his forearms, and a set of dog tags hung from his neck.

"Hey," he called, holding up his hand. "Didn't expect to see other folk out here so late." He had a faint Scottish accent.

George glanced over his shoulder at Lloyd.

"Find out more," Lloyd said to him.

George nodded, then, "Neither did we," he called. "Expect to see anyone that is."

The man drew to a halt just ten feet from us. He was handsome, his features angled, his mouth wide and pliant and set in a friendly smile. "I'm taking a few wee shots for a competition. Thought the stones would look good at night. It's a thousand quid prize."

"I take it you didn't ask permission," George said. "To be here."

He chuckled. "Do you think they'd have said aye?" His smile dropped. "Shit, you're not Security for this place, are you?"

"No," George said. "Doing the same as you, enjoying the stones in the moonlight."

He smiled again and studied each of us in turn. His attention landed on me and his eyes narrowed as though he recognized me from some advertising campaign or other.

I rubbed my hands together, wishing the heat would settle. My fingertips felt as though needles were being stabbed into them. If the stranger hadn't appeared I'd have discharged some sparks to make my hands more comfortable.

"Beautiful," the stranger said, still looking at me. "Absolutely beautiful."

"I thought you were here for the stones," Lloyd said, his voice even lower than usual. "Taking photographs."

"Er, aye, you're right, we don't want them going anywhere, do we?" The man held up his camera and appeared to take a few shots of the large stone behind us.

I swallowed and glanced at the trees to my right. A light wind ruffled over the canopy.

"What's your name?" George asked.

He hesitated, then, "Lieutenant Patrick Sinclair."

"You're serving?"

"Aye, on leave at the moment."

"And still in uniform?" Oscar muttered.

"Yeah, that's odd," Lloyd replied quietly. His shoulders tensed.

I bit on my bottom lip as a sense of unease grew.

"Do you mind," Patrick said, "if I get a few more shots while there's moonlight?"

"Go ahead. We don't own Stonehenge." George stepped to one side.

"Cheers, mate." He began to click away, edging closer to me, Oscar and Lloyd.

After a minute a cloud slid over the moon. The wind picked up and the leaves on the trees created a ripple in the distance.

"So what are your names?" Patrick lowered his camera. His attention was on me again.

I moved from one foot to the other, my shoulders skimming both Oscar's and Lloyd's.

"I'm George." George stepped closer to Patrick, glancing at the sky, then at the new person in our midst.

"Nice to meet you." Patrick nodded at George, then turned to Rhys.

"This is Rhys," George said, gesturing. "And Lloyd, Darius and Oscar."

"Darius." Patrick's eyes flashed as he looked at me again, his gaze seeming to scan my body from head to toe and back up. "Unusual name."

"I guess."

Is he gay? Does he know who I am from my job?

"It's a pleasure to make your acquaintance, Darius," Patrick said, stepping forward with his hand outstretched.

I felt very singled out by him as he approached, his wide shoulders tense, his boots stomping on the ground, and his gaze locked on mine.

As he drew nearer, I held out my hand.

My fingers tingled. I struggled to contain sparks. His eyes were mesmerizing, so dark and penetrating, and his eyebrows were pulled low, shrouding them in shadows. I felt as though I could fall into him, or him fall into me. He was sucking me closer. My mind, my thoughts, they were tumbling forward. His face was all I could see. He was all that I wanted to be...

Our hands were so close now, preparing to shake. I trembled. My spine seemed to weaken, as if it had turned to dust. I let out a gasp knowing electricity was about to shoot through me and it would hurt.

It would hurt a lot.

"No!" Oscar crashed his arm down on Patrick's, sending him reeling and his camera bouncing into the air then crashing back down on his chest.

"What the—?" Patrick clasped his arm and hunched over. He glared at Oscar. "Why'd you do that? It hurt."

"It's him!" Oscar stepped in front of me, one arm behind himself, holding my body close to his back. "It's the demon."

"Demon?" Patrick said. "What are you talking about?" He frowned and turned to George. "Why'd he call me a demon? I was only being friendly."

I clutched Oscar's shoulders, glad of the support, and locked my knees.

Lloyd set his arm about my waist to steady me, as if instinctively knowing Patrick's closeness had done something weird to my body.

"Demon?" George clenched his fists and rounded his shoulders. He glanced at Oscar, then me.

"Yes," I croaked. "I think it is. I think it's him."

A sudden roar of thunder peeled over the sky and a brilliant flash of lightning lit the stones for several glowing, white-hot seconds.

"You really think so?" Lloyd asked me.

I peered around Oscar's bulk. "Yeah, I do." The strange sensation of thoughts being suctioned from my mind had faded now Patrick had removed his attention from me and stepped back. I was no longer fearful of the surge of electric I'd known touching his hand would produce.

"Get him," Rhys shouted, then moved so fast I could only see the blur of his outline.

"No! Stop!" George yelled, grabbing Rhys and hauling him backward. "It's a staked crossbow."

I gasped.

Patrick was standing tall now, and in his hand he held not a camera, but what looked like an old-fashioned wooden pistol with decorative metalwork. The top of the barrel was open, showing the bullets, and as George had said, it had a crossbow look to it.

"Aye, that's right, stop," Patrick sneered, his features changing from handsome to snarling. No longer stooped, he held the stance of a man preparing to fight. Not only that, the tilt of his chin showed he was expecting to win.

"You!" Lloyd said, fury in his tone. "You *dare* to come here."

"If you're asking if I dare to claim what's mine, then aye, I do." He armed the crossbow. The mechanism made a harsh clicking sound. "And you will not be able to stop me."

"We will destroy you," Oscar said. "Your time is up, demon. That piece of shit will not stop us."

"I don't think so." Patrick moved the gun so it pointed in the direction of Rhys and George who were now closest to him. "And actually, I think it will. You vampires can crawl back from most things, but you can't survive this."

Nausea washed over me. The sight of the gun pointing at men I loved was sickening.

"In fact," Patrick said, derision in his voice, "it's the opposite. It's *your* time, heathen vampires. Your time to burn in Hell for all eternity."

"We drank from the cambion in accordance to the fable." George placed his hands on his hips and puffed up his chest. "There will no Hell for us. Death, yes, but not Hell."

Patrick frowned. "Fable?"

"Yes, Darius is the key to our salvation," George went on. "As you well know from your encounters with Master Benedict."

Patrick laughed, but it held no humor. "Ha, that old soul, what does he know?"

"He knows me," I said, "and you know it."

Patrick turned to me. "How would I know it?"

"My dreams. You've been tormenting me for years in my dreams. And Benedict has been there too, guiding me, protecting me. Letting me know that I can help these men whose only crime is to be a vampire."

He raised his eyebrows. "You remember them? The dreams?"

"Of course. And thank goodness I do so I could secure these men's souls. I suppose we should all thank you for creating me."

"I created you for *me*!" he snarled, spittle collecting at the corners of his mouth. "Me! You're mine. Your perfect, immortal body is mine."

"You will not hurt him and you will not have him," Lloyd shouted. "Do not underestimate our love for him, or the power of it."

"Ha, your power is weak. I can break down your walls. Another moment at the riverside last night and I would have shown you that." Patrick faced me but kept the crossbow aimed at Rhys. "They're using you for their own ends. Can't you see, son? Let me in and I'll do justice to our underworld."

"It's not *my* underworld," I said. "*This* is my world, *this* is where I live. My mother is here. She's my family, not you." It was strange to think this young soldier believed himself to be my father, but of course the poor boy had been possessed.

"Where you *have* lived, under the guardianship of the female I chose to bear and raise you," Patrick said. "Because now it's time to say goodbye to these bloodsuckers. They're not your destiny. Greater things await us."

I clenched my fists. My hands were on fire. My chest was tight and heat was raging through me. These men *were* my destiny. Our souls were already connected—at least it felt that way.

"Prepare for pain," Patrick said to Rhys, taking a step forward and closing the gap between the gun and Rhys's chest. "At least I'm led to believe a stake bullet with a silver tip fired to the heart of your sort is painful. I wouldn't know." He laughed, an evil sound that echoed around the age-old stones. "Pain is no concern of mine."

Stake bullet, silver tip. Through the heart.

"No!" I gasped. I may have protected my vampires from burning in Hell for all of time, but they'd still leave me if staked through the heart. And I couldn't bear the thought of any of them not being at my side. A piece of me would go with them. And I couldn't imagine a future without Rhys and his quick smile and sexy swagger. My eyes stung at the thought of anything happening to him.

"Fuck," Lloyd muttered.

"I'm taking him down." Oscar stepped forward.

But as he did so, forcing my hands to drop from his shoulders, sparks left the tips of my fingers. They glistened as they fell to the ground through the darkness.

"Darius." Lloyd cupped my elbow. "There's so many."

"I know." And there were. Rather than the usual dripping, the sparks were falling in a cascade and it was getting bigger, stronger, almost like a flame thrower.

For a moment I stared at this new power leaving me, wondering where it had come from. My intense orgasm? The love in my heart? But then I stared at the gun directed at one of the men I was in love with.

Wooden.

I stepped to the side, so I had a direct line to it. I aimed both of my hands at the crossbow and shot sparks through the air. They arced in one seamless, beautiful stream of fire, tearing blistering heat and pain from my arms.

I grimaced and held in a groan.

Lloyd slipped behind me and held me up. "I've got you."

Oscar dodged out the way of the fiery air.

The flames were licking over the crossbow. Patrick was hanging on to it with both hands and grimacing. "You...you would do this to me, your creator?"

A sudden whizzing sound sliced through the air. A stake bullet with a silver tip.

"Shit!" Rhys ducked to the side, pushing George with him.

In my peripheral vision I saw they'd tumbled to the ground. But only for a second, then they were up and closing in on Patrick.

He shot again, a stake landing as fast as a bullet might into the soft earth. He then spun, toward me. The crossbow was on fire now. So were his hands. Flames were licking up his forearms, highlighting his tattoos, and catching in his t-shirt.

"I did this for us," he yelled at me.

A huge crack behind me told me another stake had been released. It had hit one of the ancient stones.

"Fuck." Lloyd tugged me to the right. "That was too close for comfort."

Oscar went to the left. His fists clenched.

Patrick let out a wail. The scent of burning flesh filled the air. The crossbow was burning as bright as a star now, as were his arms. His pants too were on fire, flames eating at the camouflage material. He reminded me of Guy Fawkes atop a bonfire.

I cried out too. The strain of producing so much fire was draining every sap of energy I had. But I had to keep going.

"Get him!" Oscar lunged at the burning man.

Rhys and George were a split second behind him.

Patrick was knocked to the ground.

All three vampires were over him. They seemed to go into a frenzy, their bodies jerking, writhing, and bucking.

A bolt of lightning streaked from left to right over the sky, zigzagging in time with a furious roar of thunder that rattled my teeth and vibrated through my feet. A squally gust of wind pressed against me and I staggered as it knocked my arc of fire off course.

"Enough," Lloyd said against my ear. "Enough. You've destroyed the crossbow."

"And him?"

"The others are doing that."

I lowered my hands, slumping against Lloyd.

"I've got you."

I gave up responsibility for remaining upright and allowed Lloyd to hold me as I watched the scene before me.

The demon's legs were smoldering. George was over him as if drinking his blood, Rhys was stepping back, wiping his hand over his mouth. Oscar had Patrick's arms pinned above his head—a head that was at a strange angle to his neck.

A huge spot of water landed on my cheek, then another and another. The sudden storm had brought rain with it.

Patrick's legs jerked, then stilled, feet falling outward as though all tension, all life had gone from them.

George unfolded and stood. "You okay?" He clasped Rhys's shoulder.

"Yeah, better now that bastard is dead."

Dead.

I gulped as rain streaked down my cheeks. I'd just witnessed a murder. No, more than that. *I'd* helped murder someone.

I held my breath as I stared at Patrick's burned body. It was still smoking, hissing as the raindrops landed on him. He was charred, his clothing melted onto his flesh. A sob grew in my chest. It grew so big it burst upward, a strangled gasp that hurt my throat.

"Darius." Lloyd spun me around and pulled me close. "It's okay."

"It's...it's my fault."

"No, you protected yourself and us."

"But..." I broke from him and staggered forward, unable to stop staring at the young soldier's body. "That's not the demon, that's an innocent man." I pointed at George. "You promised me no one would get hurt, no one who wasn't evil."

"I told you not to promise that, George." Oscar stood and placed his hands on his hips. He stared at the body. "Fuck."

"Damn it." George straightened his cap. "Rhys, you do it." He pointed at Patrick.

"Do what?" Rhys glanced at George and then me.

"Yes, if it can be done," I said. "Do it."

Vampire.

"It can be." Lloyd nodded. "If we don't delay."

"You want *me* to do it?" Rhys directed at George.

"It's high time you performed your first turn."

Rhys stared at the soldier. "You think I can?"

"We've got your back," Oscar said. "And our man here doesn't want blood on his hands. We have to respect that."

"Yes," I said, stepping forward and grasping Rhys's hand. "Do it. This soldier, the *real* Patrick, was a victim of a demon's evil plan. We have to atone for that."

"And we will," George said. "Rhys, hurry, this is a very short window. You need to drain him dry."

Rhys pulled in a deep breath, then nodded. "Okay."

He crouched down, set his mouth over the oddly angled neck of the corpse, then began to drink. As he did so a shiver went down his back and he kind of swayed in time with his feeding.

Lloyd was breathing heavily and watching with wide eyes as though the spectacle excited him. Oscar's lips were parted, fangs still visible. George had his head tilted, looking pretty chilled, all things considered. He pulled out his pocket watch and checked the time, then slipped it away.

My heart was pounding. This seemed to be a very time sensitive situation—between death and being drained dry.

"What's going to happen?" I asked Lloyd, a tremble in my voice.

"You'll see."

"Will he be okay?"

He hesitated, then, "Yeah, after a while."

"What do you mean after a—" I halted as Rhys stood. He stared down at the lifeless body with his arms hanging at his sides and his fangs dripping blood.

"It hasn't worked," I said, frantic that I was going to have to live with the death of this poor soldier for the rest of my never-ending life. Panic washed through me. I couldn't stand the guilt.

"Hang on, be patient." Lloyd grasped my hand. "Watch."

Each second was like an hour, but eventually Patrick's feet twitched, then he pulled in a huge gasping breath.

Oscar, Rhys and George stepped closer to him, surrounding him.

I swallowed, and my eyes pricked with tentative hope. Had Rhys turned him?

Patrick's torso bucked up, then back to the ground as though he'd been electrocuted. Then his head lifted and his neck seemed to slot back into place.

In an instant, a flash, he was on his feet, naked, his clothes ribbons of charred fabric and dust around his feet.

His skin was perfect. Unmarked. Not burned or scarred. His cock hung flaccid from a patch of dark pubic hair.

He opened his eyes and glared at me. They were huge and glinting with madness. He lunged forward.

Oscar grabbed his right arm, Rhys his left. They yanked him backward.

George and Lloyd put themselves between him and me.

"What's going on?" I asked, fearful something had gone wrong.

"New vampires," George said, "have an uncontrollable thirst."

"Blood. Human blood!" Patrick shouted, his lips curling back to reveal sparkling white fangs as he stared at me. He battled with Oscar and Rhys, trying to break free, but they kept a tight hold on him.

"Shit," I said, alarm gripping me. "How can this work? He's so...wild."

"It will," George said. "He'll calm down, and he'll learn."

"He'll be able to control the thirst," Lloyd said. "Eventually."

"Ah, good." As long as he could eventually, time wasn't an issue.

"Give me, I need it," Patrick yelled. "Now!"

"No." George stood before him. "Not until you can be trusted."

Patrick's mad eyes seemed to stare through George. "Give me man."

"No." George set his hand on his shoulder.

He battled harder, twisting and turning. "There is human. I want."

Oscar and Rhys were having to adjust their stances to keep him held firm and away from me. It was clear he was much stronger than a human now.

"It's okay," I said, stepping past Lloyd and toward Patrick.

"Careful," Lloyd said. "It's you he wants."

"Yeah." Rhys frowned. "And if he hurts you, I'll stake his heart myself and feed it to ravens."

"It's okay." I walked up to Patrick, not breaking eye contact and my shoulders set back.

He was staring straight at me. As if I was all that existed.

"Darius," George said quietly. "Watch him. He's unpredictable."

"I've got this," I said, tilting my chin and taking in Patrick's wild but beautiful features.

Suddenly he stilled his battle with Oscar and Rhys. Though he was breathing hard and his fangs visible, I sensed him calming.

"Hey, Patrick," I said to him, my voice soft and a gentle smile tugging my lips. "Welcome to my vampire harem."

Need More? (Yes, there's more...)

Thank you for reading HIS VAMPIRE HAREM. Loved it? Of course you did. And you can keep on reading by getting your copy of HIS VAMPIRE HAREM BOOK 2 and find out how Darius and his vampires handle Patrick!

About Lily Harlem

Based in the UK Lily Harlem is an award-winning, USA Today bestselling author of sexy romance. She's a complete floozy when it comes to genres and pairings writing from heterosexual kink, to gay paranormal and everything in-between. She's also very partial to a happily ever after.

One thing you can be sure of, whatever book you pick up by Ms Harlem, is it will be wildly romantic and deliciously sexy. Enjoy!

Printed in Great Britain
by Amazon